THE THIRTEENTH APOSTLE

ORDER OF THADDEUS • BOOK 2

J. A. BOUMA

EmmausWay Press

An Imprint of THEOKLESIA

PO Box 1180 • Grand Rapids, MI 49501

www.emmauswaypress.com

PROLOGUE

JERUSALEM. AD 123.

"Over here!"

Lucius swung his torch in the direction of his man's gravely grunt, the pale, burnt orange casting long, inky shadows and lighting the way through the ancient field of last repose. He hurried over to the man, his leather open-toed sandals kicking up a low-lying cloud of red dust from the dry ground that lived up to its name.

Blood Field.

Nestled in the heart of the valley of Hinnom on the southern edge of Jerusalem, the plot had served as a source of red clay for the sacred pottery of ancient Israel's cultic class, earning it the name Potter's Field. Later, it served as a final resting place for the unclean and strangers of the land. But it was its unsavory history that led to its current moniker, serving both as a site of pagan practice, where kings of Judah had sacrificed their children to the forbidden god Moloch, as well as a run-off site for the blood of the sacrifices made to Yahweh in the former Temple.

Yet it was a third reason that drew him to the site in the dead of night, the one that certain religious fanatics had given for why it indeed was an unclean place of death and destruction, blood and betrayal.

The tall, pale man with long, greasy black hair and angular features shuffled over to his servant, who was hunched over a small mound of dirt and sod. His stomach lurched with joy at the sight, hope surging and a smile curling at the prospect of finally discovering the sacred, hidden relic of his people's venerated martyr.

"Step aside, Vibius," he said brushing past the man. He reached inside his heavy linen cloak and carefully retrieved a folded piece of parchment from the inner lining. "Hold this," he commanded his servant as he passed his torch to the short, stocky, dark-skinned man.

A midnight Mediterranean breeze picked up pace through the field of unmarked graves, waving the strong, haunting arms of the surrounding sycamore trees and threatening to extinguish the pair's only source of light. Vibius quickly shielded the flickering flame with his wide frame as his master cursed under his breath. The obstacles erected by Lady Fate had been dark and daunting over the years. It seemed she had one more trick up her sleeve, summoning Gaeus, goddess of Earth, for assistance.

Lucius glanced around the abandoned field and held his breath as the breeze continued its assault. Not a soul in sight. The wind began to retreat, and he caught his breath in relief. When he did, he recoiled at the fetid stench of something rotting, left behind by the retreating breeze. The prey of some feral animal or even a body left exposed in a too-shallow grave.

"Curse the gods," Vibius moaned. "What's that horrid stench?"

Lucius ignored the man. He breathed through his mouth as he carefully unfolded the sagging, worn parchment stained with decades of concentration from countless fellow brethren puzzling over its contents. The map that led him to the mound of dirt before which he stood.

"Bring that torch over here," he commanded.

His servant lumbered over and held the source of orange glow high so his master could read.

Lucius squinted at the caramel-colored paper, then glanced up and around at his surroundings.

This is it. Has to be...

Satisfied, he motioned toward his servant. "This is the place. Dig."

The man handed the torch to his master, then waddled forward and swung his iron shovel toward the mound.

"Careful!" Lucius instructed.

The portly man nodded, then carefully leaned into the tool, its blade easing into the hardened earth a few inches at a time. Then it gave, and he withdrew a load and tossed it aside. He repeated the process, heaving one load of hardened red soil after another until the small mound had disappeared. A sunken depression in the Field of Blood began to emerge.

A rustling behind the two caught Lucius' attention. He spun around toward the sound, torch high and extended. His breath picked up, keeping pace with his thumping heart as he swept the light around the area. They had purposefully sought the final resting place of their martyr in the dead of night for this very reason, to avoid anyone who might stumble upon their interest in robbing the grave of an outcast.

Suddenly, the light caught two beady eyes several yards away in a cluster of olive trees. The orbs stood still, then all at once vanished in the same rustle that first drew their attention.

Lucius closed his eyes and sighed audibly. He spun around and held forth the torch. "Get—"

"You there! Halt, in the name of the law!"

Lucius froze. His servant sank inside the earthen sarcophagus, crouching low to hide from the unexpected visitor.

"Turn around, you," the man growled, the unmistakable metal clang of armor belonging to the *Vigiles Urbani*. The Roman watchmen of the city.

Lucius slowly turned to face the prefect guard and stepped back slightly to shield Vibius from sight. Sure enough, the man wore the prefect breastplate and helmet. His hand was gripping the hilt of a menacing iron sword that clung to his right hip. Lucius stood a head-and-a-half taller than the man, which gave him an advantage he would surely need.

"Sodden grave robber, are ye? Come to rummage through the final belongings of the deceased, are ye?"

A tremor took hold of Lucius' right arm, sending the flame weaving in the darkness.

"Hellooo!" The guard knocked his hand against his helmet, sending a dreadful clang echoing across the darkened field. "I asked you a question. What business do ye have here at this late hour?"

Lucius opened his mouth to answer, then quickly shut it. He narrowed his eyes, then steeled his resolve. He knew what he had to do.

In one quick motion, he twisted his right forearm to the left and lifted his elbow at a sharp angle, thrusting downward and shoving the flaming torch into the opening of the guard's helmet, setting his face aflame.

The man reacted as Lucius expected: he instinctively grabbed for the object of fire and fury. When he did, Lucius retracted the torch so that the man grabbed hold of the flaming head, singing both hands.

The nighttime air flooded with the sound of screams and the pungent stench of burnt hair and flesh. The prefect guard tried to recover, but Lucius immediately kicked him in the chest, sending him scrambling back onto the hardened red earth. He pounced on the guard, withdrew his sword, and thrust it with both hands dead center between the vacant orbs that had been set ablaze.

All at once the Field of Blood was quiet, calm, serene.

Lucius was heaving throat-fulls of air as he struggled to stand, the surge of adrenaline giving way to a shaky after-effect of withdrawal. He righted himself, then staggered forward toward the hole in the ground where his servant was cowering, head buried between his legs and arms clenched above.

Lucius picked up the shovel and tossed it into the hole. It landed next to the man with a muffled thud. He jerked and screamed with fright. His master cursed him and kicked a cloud of red dirt at him in anger.

"Shut up! You want the whole bloody praetorium to be roused to vengeance? Now get back to work. Let's finish this."

Vibius sat shaking, unmoving.

"Now!" Lucius hissed.

The man jumped at the shovel and quickly returned to the task at hand, slinging small loads of red and brown dirt overboard in rapid successions. Lucius crouched lower to monitor the man's progress. His servant made quick work of the grave. Within minutes, Vibius had removed several more layers. They were getting close. Just a matter of time before....

Then Lucius saw it.

"Stop! No further."

He jumped into the hole and grabbed the shovel from his servant, throwing it up top and shoving the man aside. He thrust the torch at his man, who fumbled to take it, nearly sending it to the ground.

The man climbed out of the open grave and held the light over his master as he knelt in the red earth. Lucius was searching the ground and carefully peeling back a layer of soil with his palm. Then another. He grabbed at something and carefully tugged at it. He gave another tug, then another before it gave.

It was a pouch, tan and leathery. The kind used to stow a few days' wage.

Lucius brought the pouch up to the light for careful inspection, then let loose a broad grin of satisfaction.

Vibius joined him, a greedy grin splayed across his own face. "Payday!"

Lucius' face fell, his eyes narrowed. Then he opened the bag and tilted it toward his hand. Out slid four coins, gleaming and silvery in the light. One end of his mouth curled upward again. He set them in the dirt above the hole, then tilted the bag again. Out dropped three more.

A quarter of the way there. Come on. Be the one.

He set those coins up top, as well, then emptied the rest of the pouch into his large palm. Three, five, eight. Then empty.

Can't be...

"That's all?" Vibius complained. "Fifteen lousy silver coins?"

Panic gripped Lucius. He turned the bag inside out, but there was nothing more. He threw the coins on the ground above.

But then he remembered the ancient myth: "And they took the thirty pieces of silver, the value of Him who was priced, whom they of the children of Israel priced, and they gave them for the potter's field, as the Lord directed me."

An unmarked grave pledged for a forgotten stranger would have fetched just over two weeks wages. Fifteen pieces of silver. Leaving fifteen left over.

For a total of thirty pieces of silver.

Lucius smiled and mumbled, "They must have given up the rest of the blood money when they buried him..."

He quickly knelt back down to the ground and started carefully spreading more of the red dirt aside with his palm. Vibius stood over him holding the torch, his face wrinkling with curiosity.

"Master, probably best we leave. We found what we'd come for, haven't we?"

Lucius stopped digging and sat staring at the ground. "Yes, we have," he whispered.

There it was, the skull of an adult male.

He continued digging, picking up his pace, unearthing within the potter's Blood Field the bones of a man whose neck bones had been cracked. All consistent with the myth perpetuated by those wretched, jealous fools. Retrieving a large leather satchel with a drawstring tie, he started carefully removing the bones from the grave and placing them inside.

Vibius gasped and shifted nervously from side to side, but said nothing.

Within minutes, Lucius had retrieved all of the bones. He set the bag on the ground above, then climbed out of the hole.

"You just gonna leave the silver, then?" his servant said with surprise. "Isn't that why we bloody well came?"

Lucius turned around. "You take them. I have what I came for."

Vibius grinned greedily. The man pushed the torch into the ground, then crouched to retrieve the silver coins.

Lucius turned to leave, then thought twice and carefully set down the leather satchel. He picked up the shovel, but hesitated. He stood over his servant, his back turned to him as he searched the dirt for the precious silver. With one swift movement, the tall man smacked Vibius with a powerful blow, smashing in his skull and sending him flat against the earth.

He breathed heavily, then looked around the vacant field. No one, nothing. Good. He kicked the man into the hole, then made quick work shoveling the red soil back into the death vault that once held the martyr's bones. After he was finished, he flung the iron tool far into a patch of bushes beyond and retrieved the fifteen silver coins, placing them inside the leather purse and stuffing it inside his cloak.

He picked up the leather satchel of bones and slung it over his right shoulder, then turned toward the City of Zion. He smirked, then set off in the other direction, walking out into the darkened night.

The thirteenth apostle rises again.

CHAPTER 1

CHICAGO, USA. PRESENT DAY.

For once in his life, Silas Grey was on time. Perhaps a first for the good professor. Never too late to form a new habit, he always told his students. But let's be real: he knew it wouldn't take.

It wasn't like he had any excuses for being late, anyway, what with the semester wrapped up, papers and final exams graded, and summer break underway. Life had slowed to a crawl, which called for a celebration. But while his colleagues jetted off to faraway places in Europe and South America searching of the three blessed Rs—rest, relaxation, and research—Silas had another 'R' in mind.

Religion.

But unlike some of his other trips traipsing through far-off lands searching the sands of Egypt or hillsides of Israel or catacombs of Rome, this one was strictly personal. He needed to recharge the spiritual batteries after an intense few months of professional trial and tribulation. He also needed to sort out a few things personally. What better way to kill both birds than by venerating the memory of one of his spiritual ancestors?

The Uber pulled to a stop in front of the sacred building two minutes before the app said it would. He thanked the pleasant college student as he exited, a kid sporting floppy, blond hair and board shorts who was trying too hard to grow a mustache. Like the rest of academia, he was on summer break. The guy reminded him of one of his favorite students, Jordan Peeler.

He smiled thinking about him, wondering how he was getting on reading Dietrich Bonhoeffer's *The Cost of Discipleship*, the next in a series of books on Christianity he had recommended him for his exploration of the faith. The highlight of his role as professor of religious studies and Christian history at Princeton University was helping his students engage the big questions of life and walking with them through their spiritual journey—whether they converted to Christianity or not. Jordan was one of his more eager students, challenging Silas's assumptions about the faith as much as he challenged his. He thanked God every day for the life he lived as a professor.

As the Uber driver sped off, he offered him a tip on the app: $50 seemed right. Probably a week of beer money, but whatever. He prayed he used it wisely.

Before he put his phone to silence and entered the church, he had one more thing to do. He texted his assistant, Miles, to check in on his cat, Barnabas. He had picked up the beautiful, slate-gray Persian while serving with the Rangers during the early days of Operation Iraqi Freedom. The skin-and-bones feline had wandered into camp looking for a handout. He had always been a dog lover, but the pathetic sight and the cat's single clipped ear, which told all the story he needed, tugged on his heart. He knew he was breaking protocol, the U.S. Central Command having created an order called GO-1A just before 9/11 outlawing companion animals. But he was nearly done with his tour, and it seemed like the right thing to do. And when things went south that fateful day on the road to Mosul, Barnabas lived up to his name: son of comfort. Now he was fat and happy, and he needed to make sure Miles kept him that way.

He typed out this message: *All well with Barnabas? Remember:* 2 *scoops a day.*

Five seconds later he received a reply: *Yes! I know! Enjoy your VACATION!*

Silas smiled. He could almost hear the man huffing through the messaging app. What he wouldn't do without his faithful teaching assistant. He and his administrative assistant, Millie, kept his life sorted and head on straight. He was grateful for the chance to decompress, and happy Barnabas was being looked after.

He texted back: *THANKS! I owe you :)* He stowed the phone and ran up the concrete steps to enjoy the special afternoon Mass service.

Opening the solid oak double doors to the red-bricked St. Pius V Catholic Church flooded Silas's senses with a heavy dose of spicy incense and childhood nostalgia. All through his childhood, his military father dragged Silas and his twin brother Sebastian to St. James Catholic Church in the heart of Falls Church, Virginia. Though a widower, their mother having died during childbirth, he made sure the boys looked their tip-top best for Mass and paid attention to Father Rafferty's homilies.

He never planned on a vocation in religion. That was supposed to have been his brother, but he lost the faith over two decades ago. Yet, there he was, one of Princeton University's few remaining professors of the dying profession educating America's upcoming generation in religious studies. Increasingly, he felt like he had made the biggest mistake of his life, spending nearly a decade training to shepherd young adults through their spiritual journey and give the Church a fighting chance by validating the faith through research and other academic projects. Which is what brought him to the Dominican Shrine of St. Jude Thaddeus at the church.

A murmur of gathering voices echoed through the high-vaulted, cream-colored, brightly lit nave of the shrine dedicated to one of Jesus' twelve apostles. Jude Thaddeus had asked the Savior, "Lord, how is it that You will manifest Yourself to us, and not to the world?" In response, Jesus promised to reveal himself to anyone who loved him and kept his word. Later, he wrote a letter to churches in Asia Minor and died a martyr's death along with another of the Twelve, Simon the Zealot. Small relics bearing the memory of his witness to the faith had been distributed around the world, the largest of which, Thaddeus' forearm encased in a silver reliquary, eventually made its way to the Dominican parish off South Ashland on Chicago's north side. These relics had been brought together for the first time and were on display for the months leading up to St. Jude Thaddeus' feast day on October 28.

Silas had come that Sunday morning to reflect upon the legacy of Thaddeus after completing a harrowing mission a few months prior for a religious order Thaddeus founded. Known as the Order of Thaddeus, its members had contended for and defended the Christian faith in the face of the ebb-and-flow of hostility the Church faced for nearly twenty centuries—from threats both within and without. And Silas had stumbled upon them when he was nearly blown to smithereens while trying to scientifically prove the validity of the Church's most sacred relic, the Shroud of Turin.

It didn't turn out the way he had expected, dashing both professional and personal hopes, but he did get a job offer out of it. The Order's Master, Rowen Radcliffe, had invited him to join not only the religious order, but the fight for the faith itself. Silas had declined Radcliffe's advances, but now that the semester was over, he wondered if he owed him giving it a second thought. After all, he and his team did save his life. As well as the Church's prized relic containing the most significant memory of the faith: the resurrection of Jesus Christ.

Silas glimpsed the sacred object of silver gleaming from the front and approached it before the start of the service. Growing up he had serious reservations about venerating such objects of the faith, much to the chagrin of his thoroughly Catholic father. And when he grew in his faith later as a Protestant, he thought such acts were idolatrous. But then he read the perspective of a famed New Testament scholar, N. T. Wright, who suggests relics can be explained in terms of God's grace working in and through the physical life of the person, even after death, their bodies becoming regarded as a special place where God's love and presence are made known, to both the faithful and those seeking faith. He figured if that Anglican could accept such practices, then so could he, which led to a rich academic career in studying such religious artifacts.

As he approached the collection of Thaddeus's memory markers, his heart started to race with affection, his breathing keeping pace. There it was, a pillar of silver with a hand affixed to the top reaching heavenward. In the middle was an oblong cutaway, and inside, behind thick crystal embedded in red velvet, were unmistakable human bones.

A shiver ran down Silas' spine as he took in the sight of the relic bearing the memory of the apostle's witness to the love and presence of God. He smiled at the thought of that arm offering Jesus Christ himself the bread he broke at the last supper, and penning the letter to the churches in Asia Minor that had been the foundation of his professional life and personal faith.

A hearty laugh at the back of the nave interrupted his pious contemplation, one that was similar to another he had heard countless times from a not-too-distant memory.

Silas cocked his head and furrowed his brow as he searched for the perpetrator. He walked back toward the rear of the sacred space, stopping short in shock.

No, way. Can't be...

The tall man with a mop of black, curly hair above broad shoulders spotted him. There was a look of confusion mixed with wide-eyed surprise. He immediately broke away from his party and made his way toward Silas.

Silas turned around and groaned, acting as if he didn't see the man. His mind tried to come up with a plan of escape, but then he turned back around. Forcing a smile, he walked toward the man, meeting his old war buddy in the middle of the center aisle. They had gone through hell and back together. They had been best friends and spiritual allies in the deserts of Iraq and Afghanistan serving Uncle Sam and Her Majesty's military. And they hadn't seen each other in a decade, by his own fault.

Silas swallowed hard as they approached each other from across the nave, his gut twisting with anticipation wondering how he would respond.

CHAPTER 2

"Silas Grey?" the man boomed in perfectly polished British English. "My land, as I live and breathe!" He was wearing a wide grin and welcoming eyes. Not what Silas expected.

The sound of his voice made Silas think of Celeste Bourne, former MI6 who joined the Order of Thaddeus as head of a specialized unit protecting the Church and faith. He wondered how she was doing and had a curious longing to see her.

"Eli Denton. What's it been, a decade?"

The two embraced, Denton's imposing frame giving too much love for Silas's liking. He gently pushed back, probably too soon for old war buddies, but he had his reasons.

"I see you've let your hair grow," Silas said.

"And I see the American military still has a stranglehold on yours!"

Silas instinctively brushed his hand over his close-cropped, black hair. He smiled and nodded. "What do they say? You can take the boy out of the Army, but you can't take the Army out of the boy."

Denton laughed. "Once a Ranger, always a Ranger."

Silas smirked. "Something like that. But I see you've moved on to bigger and better things beyond Her Majesty's armed forces. I've followed your work over the years. An impressive output."

Truth be told, he had watched with an envious eye as his former friend from his tours in Iraq and Afghanistan post-9/11 completed a PhD in early Christian studies from rival Yale while Silas studied at Harvard, going on to earn a coveted teaching spot at Cambridge in their School of Divinity and publishing widely and broadly on the subject. Though Silas often struggled to keep the envy at bay, at least he could appreciate Denton's hard work and professional pluck. What broke the camel's back was when the man scooped a once-in-a-lifetime opportunity to get in on a translation effort of a newly discovered, early Christian manuscript, which was later dubbed the Gospel of Judas. Silas severed all ties and didn't look back, never hearing from him again.

Until now.

"Yes, well," Denton replied, "you know what they say: publish or perish."

Silas smiled and said nothing. He steeled himself, his brain screaming for relief from one of his little, blue pills he kept in the middle of his desk to quell his anxiety in such times, a holdover from the damage from the war. He would have to settle for a quick prayer instead.

"So what brings you to the shrine?" he offered. "I thought you had abandoned the faith, relegating it to the tales of children and old women, as I recall you saying in an interview."

Silas chided himself for gaining an ounce of pleasure in pointing out what was widely known in his professional, academic circles. Denton may have been an expert on all things associated with Jesus and his early movement, he just wasn't a follower, a believer.

Denton smirked. "That I am not. But since I am in the States on holiday for the summer, and given my interest in early Christianity, I couldn't miss an opportunity to get a rare glimpse of the relics of one of Jesus' twelve apostles."

Silas said nothing, wanting to exit the conversation and regain his privacy before Mass began. He checked his watch, an old, beat-up Seiko his father had given him. Nearly time to start. Good.

"Say, old chap," Denton started, clearing his throat, "I've been meaning to reconnect to chat with you about a little project I've been working on. And, as Fate would have it, here you are."

Denton chuckled, Silas echoed nervously. "Project...What do you mean?" he asked.

"Well, the thing is—"

He was cut off by the sound of a pipe organ summoning the faithful to worship. Denton stopped and smiled. "Perhaps we can have a chat after the service. Shall we sit?"

Denton motioned toward a vacant spot near the aisle a few rows from the front. Silas took a breath and cringed inside, but smiled. "Sure. Why not?"

Denton slid inside the wooden bench that had held generations of worshipers over the decades, folding his frame next to a petite, older woman with a flowery dress and string of pearls. Silas took a seat next to him and bowed his head, confessing his hardened heart toward his former friend and asking the Lord to bless his time of contemplation and celebration.

The parish priest rose to greet the assembled. "Greetings, in the name of the Father, and of the Son, and of the Holy Spirit." Though no longer Catholic, Silas crossed himself out of habit. Curiously, so did Denton. "We are gathered here today to honor the memory of one of Jesus' twelve apostles, Saint Jude, also known as Thaddeus. Perhaps, not the most well-known of the twelve, Thaddeus was an important one. For not only was he one of two blood-relatives of Jesus, making him a vital, enduring link to our Savior. He also gave the Church an enduring challenge that stands as important this day as the day he gave it."

He paused and picked up a thick Bible that looked as well-worn as the man holding it up to his face to read. "'Beloved,' the apostle wrote, 'while eagerly preparing to write to you about the salvation we share, I find it necessary to write and appeal to you to contend for the faith that was once for all entrusted to the saints.'"

The man paused again and looked out at his flock. "What could be more important than writing concerning our common salvation? Yet, there was a topic of far greater import for the churches in Asia Minor that Thaddeus wanted to address. And that was the urgent task of earnestly contending for the once-for-all faith given to the saints."

Silas glanced at Denton, who was sitting blank-faced, seemingly uninterested in what the man of God had to say. Which wasn't always the case.

He recalled the two first met at one of Silas's most pivotal life-defining moments: the on-base, evangelistic chapel service put on by the military chaplain. Together, the two had chosen to devote their lives in faith to Jesus Christ. Though Silas had grown up in the Church, it wasn't until his experiences in Iraq and that heart-warming service that he took his faith seriously. Call it a foxhole conversion, but what he saw and what he experienced led him to seek greater meaning in his life. He realized Jesus was whom he had been waiting for his whole life. So had Denton.

The two instantly bonded over the experience. They attended Bible study together on base through the joint operations in the area, growing in their knowledge of the faith. And when one of their joint missions went to hell, killing their friends and comrades in arms, they wept and suffered together. After their mutual times were up with Uncle Sam and Her Majesty, the two parted with a bond stronger than merely a band of brothers; they were brothers in the faith.

But over the years, as they pursued their separate studies and separate lives, and as a root of jealousy burrowed deep in Silas's heart, the two grew apart. Jealousy and envy had always been one of his fatal flaws. It had ruined relationships in the past, got him into trouble with his Ranger superiors a time or seven, and it often fueled his professional drive instead of a commitment to his faith. And then he had heard and read about Denton's "de-conversion," as he put it, because of his academic work. Discovering this falling away had grieved Silas. Perhaps he would have a chance to talk with him about it, because his own work had had the exact opposite effect: it deepened and confirmed his faith. And Silas longed to instill the same faith in his students.

Something the priest said grabbed Silas's wandering mind: *sepio*.

"Latin for 'earnestly contend' or 'struggle for as in a great battle,'" the priest said. "that was the language Saint Thaddeus used to speak of our own modern responsibilities, as well. It was a responsibility that our apostle ultimately gave his life to in martyrdom."

Silas smiled weakly. Not only at the homiletical point, but also at the personal memory attached to that word. SEPIO was an arm of the Order charged with protecting and preserving the faith. Radcliffe had insisted he was a perfect match for the project and urged him to put his military and academic skills to work in service of the Church by joining SEPIO as an operative.

He had been flattered, but demurred. He said it was because of his work at Princeton and dedication to his students, but it was deeper than that. The truth was he was scared. Scared of jettisoning a promising career and the comforts of an impending tenure. Scared of forgoing the accolades he had started to accumulate from his research. Scared of losing to his professor brother. Scared of getting back into the kind of action that he left a decade ago, which claimed not only his best friend, but also his soul. The demons hatched from that experience still waged a daily war against him, and he wanted no part of it.

And yet he couldn't shake the chance to be on the front lines of doing what the priest reminded him that Thaddeus exhorted: contending for and defending Christianity. It was as if the priest anticipated the dissonance, for he closed his homily with a thought-provoking set of questions.

"So how about you? How are you contending earnestly for the faith? To what lengths are you willing to struggle for this faith as in a great battle? May we heed the words and warning of our beloved apostle. May we follow him in the same footsteps of martyrdom, giving of our lives for the message and mission of Jesus. And may we contend earnestly for the faith which was once delivered to the saints."

At once the gathered congregation said "Amen." Silas joined, Denton scoffed softly.

A song began playing on the organ as the priest prepared the host for Mass, the bread that was believed to be the body of Christ, broken and sacrificed for the sins of the world. He raised it toward the heavens in thanksgiving. Then he raised the chalice, bearing the memory of the shed blood of Christ.

In an instant, fire and fury exploded from the back of the nave, sending a volley of concrete and bodies toward the front.

The lights cut out, darkening the sacred space, but the late morning sun was streaming into the back, dancing eerily across the dust and debris and dark smoke.

Women screamed, men shouted in protest, parents called for their children, bodies hit the floor—both for protection and in death.

Silas Grey and Eli Denton, two former military grunts, were activated. Their training clicked into autopilot, and the two ran toward the danger to provide triage for the injured and assess the clear act of terror.

"Who the bloody hell did you Americans piss off this time, Grey?" Denton said as he and Silas cleared fallen concrete off an elderly woman who was bleeding from the head.

Silas checked for a pulse. It was weak, but it was there. An older man crawled over to her, shaking and crying. Her husband, he presumed. He told him not to move her, but wait for help to arrive. Because he would be surprised if the Rangers themselves didn't descend on the place after the recent terror in Orlando and Las Vegas.

A secondary explosion sent everyone for cover again, which started a fire among a cluster of overturned wooden pews. Denton jumped to his feet and pulled two people from near the emerging furnace. It wasn't apparent whether they were alive or not. But at least they were out of harm's way.

Silas caught glimpse of a red cylinder from the former foyer that now lay in ruins. He ran for it, yanked it off the wall, and hustled back to the fire that had jumped to a nearby wall. When he reached the inferno, something caught his attention from the front.

Three dark shapes had emerged, converging around a spot on the floor. One of them knelt next to what looked like an oblong shape. Burnt-orange and yellow light glinted off the object, and a glimpse of polished silver let Silas know all he needed to know about what it was.

The forearm relic of Saint Thaddeus.

All at once it disappeared. No more glinting reflection, no more burnt orange and silver. No more nothing.

"What the bloody hell are you waiting for?" Denton yelled. "The fire's not going to put itself out!"

"Look!" Silas yelled back and pointed to the front.

Denton turned as the trio darted across the high-altar area and shoved through a door off to the side.

"What the..."

Silas didn't wait for his question. He knew what just happened.

The relics of Saint Jude Thaddeus had just been stolen. After being attacked by a terrorist's bomb.

And Silas had a good idea who was behind it.

CHAPTER 3

Silas threw aside the fire extinguisher. "Come on!" he yelled motioning toward the front.

He ran toward a wooden door made to blend into the wood-panel walls on the left that the hostiles exited through, ignoring Denton's call to wait. He pushed through it without hesitation, coming into a small entrance area with an exit that had just clicked shut. He shoved through the door, which deposited him onto a small alley adjacent to 19th Street.

He padded toward the ordinarily quiet street lined with trees and parked cars in front of neat city row houses, ready for a fight, but cautious to stumble into one unprepared. He reached it and looked both ways trying to assess the situation.

In the distance, he heard sirens screaming toward the terrorism chaos. The bright, sunny morning sky had turned sour, transformed into a raging inferno of thick, black smoke and menacing fire. The west entrance to the street was blocked by large chunks of debris from the toppled bell tower. A few cars had been overturned and flung from the blast. A few bodies lay just outside the maw of death ripped open in the side of the sacred space.

An explosion from the front of the church made Silas instinctively duck for cover and shield his head with his hands, sending his mind reeling and thirsting for a pill of relief. Since that fateful roadside bomb in Mosul took out his best friend Colton over a decade ago, Silas had struggled with anxiety and getting a grip during stressful situations.

This one ranked up there with the best of them.

His on-again-off-again battle with PTSD in the years since his service had gotten under control with medicine, diet, and exercise, but there were moments he felt he was about to burst. He almost did during a critical mission with the Order a few months ago, costing him a man on the team. Celeste would have denied the truth of that statement, but he still felt he and his struggles were responsible. It was one of the reasons Silas declined Radcliffe's offer to join SEPIO, which would surely have put him in more than his fair share of panic-inducing situations.

Get it together, Grey!

He closed his eyes and took a deep breath, catching a whiff of the burning building up wind. Shaking his head, he searched the surrounding area. He spotted one of the hostiles running north dead-ahead down an alley on the backside of what looked like a U. S. Postal Service building. He heard the echoing of footfalls to his right as two more ran east down 19th Street.

Silas hesitated which way to pursue. Then Denton burst through the exit, making his job easier.

He motioned toward his old friend and pointed down the alley running north. "You go north, down that service road, and run down the bastard. I'll go east to take down the other two."

"You're serious?"

Silas started off down the middle of the street, then turned around. "Of course! Just like old times."

"Sodding..." he heard Denton grumble before taking off down the side street.

Silas tapped into his Ranger training to climb out of the haze of the moment and push himself forward. The two black-clad hostiles had almost a two-block lead on him. Thankfully, he had kept up with a strict regimen of running and weight training through grad school and during his life at Princeton, leaving him in better shape than when he left the Army.

The two men ahead reached a cross street and ignored a stop sign at a one-way intersection, but then stopped short before getting run over by a white-paneled delivery truck. The lead man didn't stop quick enough, thudding off the side and stumbling to the ground. The other man nearly tripped over his friend.

Just the providential interference Silas needed.

He ran faster, the delay giving him enough time to reach the dazed hostiles. Five yards away, he caught sight of a black bag.

He aimed for that.

Bending low, Silas head-butted the back of the assailant, sending him bending at an odd angle and stumbling forward to the middle of the street. The man lost hold of the black bag. It clanged a couple of yards to the opposite curb.

A car honked and swerved in anger, narrowly missing the man's head. But it ran over the black bag with a thud.

Silas cursed the desecration. He ran over to it and picked it up. It was heavy. Felt like there were multiple objects inside, too.

Great. Just busted a holy relic of one of the Twelve into pieces!

He crossed himself, then went to check its contents. A hand grabbed his shoulder and spun him around. The other man had recovered and offered Silas a powerful right hook into the left side of his face.

Silas stumbled backward, his foot catching the curb awkwardly. He landed hard on a short, red fire hydrant and fell backward, losing the bag.

The man quickly recovered it and went to join his partner, who had taken off east again along 19th Street.

But Silas wouldn't let him. He scrambled up and lunged for the bag. The man held a firm grip, launching a game of tug-of-war. An angry, sagging pick-up truck carrying far too much honked at them as they wrestled over the black sack. They went a few rounds before the bag's zipper gave and opened the rest of the way, spilling its contents all over the road.

It was nothing but some work tools, a mess of wiring, and two blocks of pale clay, C4 from the looks of it. Probably leftovers from the morning fireworks.

But no silver reliquary of Thaddeus' forearm. Which meant the guy who jetted past the post office must have been the carrier.

He hoped Denton was having better luck. He may not have had the relic, but he'd be damned if the two men got away.

Silas let go of the bag, reversing the momentum of the hostile and sending him flat on his butt. He launched for the man, but he kicked Silas off. As he scrambled away, Silas recovered and caught his leg. He yanked on it hard, bringing the man back to the pavement, then climbed up on his back, putting him in a stranglehold.

That's when he saw it, on the back of his neck peeking up behind the collar just below the edge of the ski mask. A simple stick tattoo of two intersecting black lines making what could be mistaken as a Roman cross, but its ends were bent at odd angles at all four corners. Silas knew better, he had seen this before.

It was a phoenix, the legendary bird of the ancients rising from the ashes to new life. And the calling card of an even more ancient threat.

Nous.

Silas scowled and recovered from his distraction, but not before hearing the unmistakable chambering of a round with his name on it.

The other Nous agent had returned, pointing a Beretta at his head.

Silas's personal weapon of choice. Ironic.

The man said nothing. Didn't have to, the gun did all the talking. Silas loosened his grip and sat back, jaw clenched, eyes narrowed. The man's partner scrambled away.

"You'll never get away with this," Silas growled. "I know who you are."

Again, nothing.

Suddenly, a black passenger van blew through the stop sign and screeched to a halt. Its side door slid open. Inside was another man, face masked in black, cradling another black bag. The third Nous agent, Silas presumed, and carrying the apostle relic. Up front sat two more. The two others quickly climbed into the van, the one backing into it with his Beretta trained on Silas.

Then at once, the door slid shut, and the van raced south past Silas out of view.

Silas cursed, then stood. He winced from the pain in his face from the blow. He moved his jaw and felt his swelling cheek. It wasn't broken, he would live. Across the street, he saw a few onlookers huddled and talking in hushed tones. He ignored them and began walking back toward the church.

In the distance, he could see several emergency vehicles huddled protectively around the red-brick cathedral, two spouts of water streaming into its front. Help had arrived. And Denton was jogging toward him, his shirt ripped and blood smeared down the front of his face. He slowed and threw his head back panting.

"What happened?" Silas grilled Denton. "How could you let him get away? He had the relic!"

"Gee, thanks, mate. Appreciate the concern for my torn clothes and bloody face!"

Silas said nothing, putting his hands behind his head and pacing the street. What a mess.

"Had the bugger, right in my grip, but he bloody well got away, that's what happened!"

Silas turned to walk away. "I see that."

"And not before clocking me in the kisser, I might add."

"I'm sure you'll live," Silas mumbled as he kept walking.

"Where are you going?" Denton called after him.

He called back, "To make a phone call. Got some friends who are going to want to hear about this."

CHAPTER 4

Silas stepped over a large chunk of wall that had been part of the bell tower and splashed through a stream of black, sooty fire-hydrant water running out from the large cavity on the church's west facade. He wanted to get far away from ground zero of America's latest terrorism site as quickly as possible and avoid any entanglements with law enforcement. The people he wanted to call would want to take the lead on this one, and the last thing he needed was to get wrapped up in some agency's investigation.

He used the wide girth of a fire engine to slip out of 19th Street undetected and into a crowd of onlookers near the entrance to the post office behind a line of yellow crime-scene tape. Denton did the same. They both stood silently with hands in their pockets while they carefully surveyed the area.

"So, mate," Denton said in hushed tones, "mind giving me the four-one-one on what the bloody hell is going on here? You seem to be privy to some divine insight."

Silas said nothing, instead slowly looking away to avoid eye contact with a man sporting an ATF vest a few yards away. He stood on his tiptoes as if he was craning for a better look of the excitement to appear like a rubbernecker.

"Not here," he mumbled. He motioned with his head to leave and turned to walk across the street. Denton waited a beat, then followed as he walked toward a narrow, over-grown slice of land squeezed between a beige-brick row house with a white iron gate that meant business and a red-brick row house sporting a yellow sign that read RECICLARTE. Whatever that meant.

Silas looked over his left shoulder, then to the right as he opened a rusted gate that guarded the urban jungle. It creaked softly as he opened it. He slipped past it and walked toward a large bush a story tall, leaning against the beige house and hiding a pale house that looked long abandoned. It would offer them the privacy they needed to make their phone call.

Denton followed, glancing back to make sure they hadn't been followed. Two guys trespassing on what was probably crack-house property was the least of the neighborhood's concerns. He reached the safety of the foliage as Silas was taking out his phone.

"Hold up a beat, would you?" Denton said. "You said you knew some blokes who would want to know about our party. What are you talking about?"

Silas swiped his phone to life and searched for Rowan Radcliffe's contact information. Denton huffed and grabbed the phone away.

"Hey, what the—"

"What's going on, Silas? Who are these people you're referring to? And who was that we were running down?"

Silas made for his phone, but Denton held it above his head. He could jump for it, but Denton was a full head above him. It would be a losing battle. He huffed heavily and put his hands on his hips, then folded his arms, and leaned back angrily against the wall.

"If you must know, the Order of Thaddeus."

Denton furrowed his brow in confusion, then glanced back at the church, as if making a connection with the shrine named after the apostle. "What's that you say? Some sort of religious order, I presume."

Silas nodded. "Probably the oldest of the Christian communities, founded by the apostle Jude Thaddeus himself."

Denton smirked. "Never heard of them. And that's saying something."

Silas smirked himself at the arrogance. "I hadn't either until a few months ago, but apparently they've worked below the radar for nearly twenty-one centuries guarding and preserving the memory of the once-for-all-faith—"

"Delivered to the saints," Denton interrupted. "Yes, I know of the exhortation from the good apostle's letter. But what on earth does a bunch of celibate, cloistered, dogmatic Catholic old men have to do with what just happened at that church?"

Silas's eyes narrowed at the insult to his friends. "First of all, it's not a Catholic order, but an ecumenical one, or at least not anymore. And there are good, dedicated men and women trying their damnedest to save the faith."

Denton threw his hands up. "Oh, sorry, my bad."

"Secondly, the Order has been locked in an ever-increasing fight with an ancient threat to the Church." Silas pointed toward 19th Street. "The markings of which I just saw on one of those terrorists that nearly blew us up, stole the apostle relic, and sped away to God knows where!"

Denton folded his arms and smiled, still holding onto Silas's phone. "Ancient threat to the Church? You're not getting all Dan Brown on me, are you?"

Silas huffed, then shoved off the beige brick wall and grabbed his phone. "I don't have time for this BS." He turned his back to his former friend and dialed Radcliffe, then turned back toward him as it rang. "Nous, by the way."

Denton's eyes widened slightly before narrowing. "What was that?"

"Nous. The ancient nemesis of both the Order and the Church. The man I wrestled to the ground was a Nous agent."

"Nous...I see. Divine, mystical knowledge. The all-knowing god-man, of the Gnostic variety?"

Silas nodded. "Exactly."

The other end of the receiver came to life. "Hello? Who is this?"

Silas smiled at the gentle British voice at the other end of the line. He pictured the old man in his black cassock, hair silver and coifed. He was surprised that hearing it made him miss the man and the rest of the Order.

He put the phone on speaker. Holding it between him and Denton, he said, "Rowan, it's Silas. Sorry for giving you a start. I know this is a private, secured number."

"Professor Silas Grey?" Radcliffe said in surprise.

Silas chuckled. "The one and only."

"My lad, it is good to hear your voice! I must confess, after your unceremonious rejection of my offer of employ I never thought I'd catch sound of your voice again. Perhaps you've reconsidered?"

He smiled and shook his head. "Unfortunately, no. That's not why I've called." The light tone of Radcliffe's voice made him think the Order Master was still in the dark about the morning's events. Which wasn't surprising, considering it was still so fresh.

"Oh, that is disappointing. But I have to imagine a man of your stature is far too busy to call up an old man for an afternoon chit-chat. What's going on, Silas?"

He looked at Denton and cleared his throat. "There's been an attack, at St. Pius V in Chicago. Terrorists blew the whole entrance and nearly half the nave off."

Radcliffe gasped. "Good Lord. How horrifying! But I haven't received word of this act of terror."

"Just happened. An hour or so ago."

"Then how are you aware of this act of evil and not I?"

"Because I was worshiping there when it all went down. My friend..." Silas stopped short and looked at Denton again. "My friend, Eli Denton, and I were attending a ceremony of dedication together when the bombs went off. He's here with me on speaker."

"Dear me. Surely you're alright."

"We're fine. Just sorry SEPIO wasn't around to come to my rescue like last time." His mind jumped to three months ago when he was presenting a paper at Georgetown University when a more powerful terrorist blast took out all of his colleagues and close friend Father Arnold. Had it not been for the Order extracting him from the wreckage, he would have been a goner. That event was the spark that launched a much greater conspiracy. He wondered if the theft of the apostle Thaddeus' relic was similarly part of something more significant.

"Listen, we're calling because there's a bigger issue here than a terrorist attack on a Christian church."

"Really? What's that?"

"A relic of one of the twelve apostles was stolen by a small team of operatives who infiltrated the sanctuary shortly after the blast."

"What?" Radcliffe exclaimed.

"And, here's the thing: I'm positive Nous was behind it."

"My God..." Radcliffe audibly exhaled, then took a large breath for stability. "Which apostle?"

"Jude Thaddeus' forearm. It was encased in a silver reliquary. I'm guessing they also swiped a few other lesser relics that were on display for the ceremonious reunion."

"What a shame... And it does have all the hallmarks of a Nous operation. Explosions and theft and all. But you seem so certain. How so?"

Silas nodded. "Positive. I ran down two of the Nousati and got into it with one of them. At one point I caught the tell-tale markings on the back of his neck. The intersecting black lines forming a phoenix."

"Tell-tale is right. The ancient scourge of the Church and Order nemesis rearing its ugly head, yet again." Radcliffe huffed, then went silent.

Silas glanced at Denton, who had been quietly listening with furrowed brow with head down and hand resting over his mouth. He seemed to be taking the revelations in strides.

"But why now?" Radcliffe asked. "And why Jude's relic?"

Silas shook his head. "I've been wondering that myself since it all went down."

"Because Jude Thaddeus isn't an obvious choice if you're going to steal an apostle relic. After all, he has been largely overshadowed by his darker-named-twin Judas."

Silas noticed Denton gave a slight startle at the mention of the betrayer of Jesus, known as Judas Iscariot. It was subtle, but it was telling. He watched him as Radcliffe continued, explaining how the Church had distinguished the better apostle from the betrayer one by referring to him as Jude, instead of the more common Greek Judas, a Hellenized form of the Hebrew Judah. Silas recalled seeing such guarded reactions from Denton back in Iraq during joint-mission debriefs, particularly before the fated mission that led to his buddy Colton getting blown up.

"What do you make of it?" Radcliffe asked, interrupting his thoughts. "What's your gut on this, given your extensive military background?"

Silas shook his head again. "Maybe Nous is sending a message."

"What do you mean, a message?"

"Well, look what the Order just put them through. SEPIO disrupted a massive conspiracy to destroy the Shroud of Turin and the tomb of Jesus at the Church of the Holy Sepulcher, as well as the surviving, scientific evidence to support the foundational belief of the Christian faith, the resurrection of Jesus

Christ. What better way to strike back at the Order than by targeting and then taking out the relic of their founding father?"

Radcliffe grunted. "Good point."

Silas went silent and glanced at Denton again, this time making eye contact. He averted Silas, then looked at him again before blinking rapidly and shrugging his shoulders.

"But, Silas," Radcliffe resumed, "doesn't this seem small potatoes for Nous? Except for devotees of Jude, why would anyone care if his apostle relic was stolen? Now Paul's or Peter's, that would be a different story, that would make headlines. But the man overshadowed by Judas Iscariot?"

There was that look again. A flinch, a flicker. Denton was hiding something.

"Excuse me, Radcliffe," Silas interrupted, "I think my friend has something to add.

Denton snapped his head up, brows raised and eyes wide. Silas whispered gruffly, "I know you've got information about this. I don't know what, but I see it. You reacted to the name of Judas."

The man scoffed. "Stuff and nonsense!"

"Don't deny it! They were the same signs back in Mosul when you held back the intel that could have saved our asses from getting blown to hell by that IED."

Denton's features melted at the mention of the incident. He licked his lips, then tilted his head back and sighed.

Radcliffe said, "Silas, are you still there? What is going on?"

"Yeah, we're still here." Silas clenched his jaw and nodded to his former wartime buddy.

Denton hesitated, then said, "I may know what this is about."

CHAPTER 5

Silas leaned back against the peeling, beige wall and took a break. He didn't expect that response. How could Denton know anything about what just went down? What was his old friend hiding?

"Excuse me, Silas?" Radcliffe interjected.

"Yeah," Silas said staring at Denton.

"May I ask, who is your friend?"

"Sorry. Like I said earlier, Eli Denton. We served alongside each other in Iraq during the invasion after 9/11. He with Her Majesty's Army and I with Uncle Sam's Rangers. Then..." Silas trailed off and looked at the ground. "Then we went our separate ways. He finished his service before I did and left for America to get a Ph.D. in religious studies at Yale. Then went off to become a professor of early Christianity at Cambridge. That about cover it?" he asked Denton. The man folded his arms and nodded.

"Eli Denton..." Radcliffe said. "Now that you mention it the name does ring a bell. Though, from what I've seen, more a Dan Brown with a Ph.D. than anything else."

Denton unfolded his arms and stiffened, his mouth opening and brow furrowing at the indignity. Silas chuckled. Go, Radcliffe!

Silas said, “Well, he has certainly found fellowship with those who seem to relish in alternative versions of the Christian story.”

“Alternative *perspectives*," Denton corrected, "than the dominant ones that won the day from those in power."

“I beg to differ, young man,” Radcliffe interjected.

“Hold up,” Silas interrupted. “As much as I’d love to get into a verbal brawl over the merits of postmodern interpretation of early church history...” He looked at Denton. “You said you thought you knew what this was all about. That it was somehow related to you. Explain.”

Denton took a deep breath, shifting his weight to one leg and folding his arms again. “Perhaps…” he said hesitantly.

Silas sighed. “Come on, get to it.”

“I don't know who this…these Nous fellows are or what this terrorist organization is or whatever, but I feel like I may have been the target or at least the reason for the bombing and theft.”

Silas furrowed his brow and shook his head in confusion. “Why you? Why would Nous target an agnostic professor from Cambridge who just happened to be in a shrine dedicated to an apostle and bearing his relic?”

“Because this agnostic professor from Cambridge is about to embark on a project to bring new verification to a lost gospel discovered by the disciple bearing the apostle’s namesake, whose relic was just swiped.”

It took Silas a moment to catch on, but then his eyes widened with surprise. “The Gospel of Judas…”

Denton nodded. “That would be the one.”

“Excuse me, young man,” Radcliffe said. “By the way, Silas, I’ve brought Celeste on the line.”

Silas’s breath caught in his throat, and he found his mouth curling upwards in delight. Celeste Bourne, former MI6 and director of operations for SEPIO. And the reason he was still alive. He wondered how she was doing, wished he could see her in person.

"Hey—Hey, Celeste," Silas stammered.

"Hey, yourself. How are you fairing? Radcliffe filled me in on your latest adventure. Trouble sure does seem to have a way of finding you."

He chuckled. "I'd prefer it leave me alone for a while. At least for another semester." He cursed himself for his lame attempt at humor. He looked to Denton and said, "Anyway, you were explaining why Nous would have targeted you, something to do with that fake manuscript discovered a decade ago."

Denton frowned. "It isn't at all fake. And you jolly well know it is one of the greatest archaeological discoveries in our mutual field of study."

Silas did. Not since the Dead Sea Scrolls and the many manuscripts recovered in the Nag Hammadi cache has the field of early Christian studies been as ignited by the manuscript fragments of the Gospel of Judas and three other early, second-century manuscripts discovered a few decades ago. What made this find especially unique was that the early Church Father Irenaeus, bishop of Lyon, referred to the book in his famous *Against Heresies* tract combating false teaching within the early Church, giving historical credence to its existence early in the life of the Church. The subsequent publication of the evidence shedding more light on early Christianity was indeed cause for celebration.

It was also cause for consternation, as the so-called "Gospel" challenged the traditional apostolic witness and core worldview of the established Church. It turned the entire narrative of the New Testament Gospels on its head, presenting Judas not as the great betrayer, but the great hero who had been ordered by Jesus himself to carry out his deed. Not since the Gospel of Thomas had there been such a challenge to the official dogma of accepted belief surrounding the person and work of Jesus of Nazareth. Of course, the religious conspiracy theorists—the Dan Brown's with PhDs, as Radcliffe had charged—insisted it was proof positive that the Church had suppressed and oppressed alternative views on Jesus and alternative stories told about his life by minority voices, requiring a complete rethinking of traditional Christian orthodoxy.

And Eli Denton had been on the front lines of it all, basking in the spotlight for his early translation work. While Silas was just beginning his studies.

"Besides," Denton continued, "you're just jealous I got to help translate the original while you were—"

"Jealous my ass! You know as well as I do how little shame you had in kissing every one of those professor's—"

"Boys!" Celeste interrupted, "Let's sheath the swords for now, shall we?"

Silas leaned back against the wall and glared at Denton. "Go on."

With a look of satisfaction, Denton continued. "Anyway, a year ago I was approached by the foundation that has assumed stewardship of Codex Tchacos, as it is known. They were trying to assemble players from the original team to have another go at recovering and translating the Gospel of Judas. Two of them didn't see the point and were no longer interested. Another two had sadly passed away, which left me from the original team. I was only a Ph.D. candidate at the time, but they recognized my unique skill set as one of the foremost Coptic translators in the world, as well as my work in early Christianity. So they brought me out to their facilities, let me see and handle the manuscript fragments again, and signed me on to the project."

Silas could feel the back of his neck growing warm with jealousy. He cursed himself for being so weak, and so petty at a time like this. But when would he get his break?

"The past few months I've been noodling over a strategy for freshly examining and restoring the gospel manuscript. That's when I stumbled over some emerging technology surrounding image restoration and a...a new colleague of mine who shares a similar interest in better understanding the literary milieu of the early Church. He's on the forefront of developing a fascinating computer algorithm that leverages deep-learning artificial intelligence to restore damaged art, restoring the images to near perfection."

Silas said, "And you think this...colleague can help with the gospel, how?"

"By filling in the lacunae, the gaps and missing pieces of the manuscript and restoring the fragments through artificial-intelligent, restorative learning, a process that pieces together the vague, incomprehensible information into the original Coptic. In theory, it would give us a wholly restored original Gospel of Judas, unlocking its secret revelations and revealing Jesus' true teachings that have been shrouded in mystery for millennia."

The line went silent, and Silas stood in silence, processing the implications. He had read an article in *Wired* magazine a few months ago about what machine learning was doing to restore images to their former glory. One artificial-intelligence algorithm had restored an entire picture of a bird from an original that had been pixilated and distorted. He thought the technology could have serious implications for his own line of work, restoring ancient manuscripts to better inform and validate the faith.

Yet here was someone who wanted to use such technology to possibly destroy it. Who knew what would emerge from the distorted fragments, possibly challenging and changing what the Church had believed about Jesus?

"Mr. Denton," Radcliffe said, "this is all fascinating, though I must confess to feeling a bit queasy over yet another attempt to undermine historic Christianity. Be that as it may, we've got a set of terrorists on the loose who have stolen a precious Christian relic that bears all the hallmarks of an ancient threat to the Church stretching back millennia. You launched into this conversation by stating that you had knowledge germane to the investigation. Can you share more?"

Denton nodded. "Right. Sorry. The way I see it, they must

have known my whereabouts and either tried to take me out, knowing what I was about to embark upon, or sought to send me a message by eliminating the relic bearing the namesake of the gospel."

Silas furrowed his brow and shook his head. "First of all, that doesn't make any sense. Why would Nous give one lick who you are or what you were doing, not to mention how would they have even known you were going to be there in the first place? And two, why were you there in the first place? An agnostic walks into a Catholic shrine for a ceremonial dedication to an ancient lesser-known apostle?"

"Does sound like the beginning of a bad joke, doesn't it?"

"Seriously, why were you there?"

"Well..." Denton paused, looking down and scratching the back of his neck. "I came to see you."

"Me?" Silas exclaimed. "For what purpose? And how did you know I would be in Chicago?"

Denton paused again and took a breath. "I'll be frank with you—"

"Yes, please be," Silas interrupted.

"I've been in contact with your brother."

Silas shoved off the wall and exclaimed, "My brother?"

"Now, calm down. I know there's been a sort of rift between the two of you, but I had to get a hold of you. And he told me where you'd be."

Silas was stunned. It was true. The two had grown apart over the years, which had been mostly his fault. He had tried to engage his brother Sebastian in matters of faith one too many times, alienating him instead of welcoming him with the truth. Their conversations had become infrequent, and after he nearly died helping Silas on a mission for the Order a few months ago having played the family card of obligation, they had barely spoken. The last time they did was after their mutual semesters had ended a few weeks ago. He remembers mentioning the road trip to the relic viewing.

But how infuriating that Denton had contacted Sebastian, and that he leveraged him to get to himself. He hadn't spoken to Denton in over a decade, and yet somehow the two of them knew each other?

Silas continued, "So you traveled all the way from Cambridge to Chicago because you wanted something from me?"

"No, not from you." He paused, then said, "I came to invite you along to be part of the new Gospel of Judas project."

He didn't see that coming. "You want me to help analyze the Gospel of Judas?"

"I need a second set of eyes, someone who is as much an expert in early Christianity and the Coptic language as I. But who is also far more invested in the Church and its traditional regime. Figured you were the perfect candidate."

"Gee, thanks. But I don't know what to say."

Someone cleared their throat over the speakerphone. That's right: Radcliffe and Celeste.

"Excuse me," Radcliffe started, "I don't mean to interrupt, but time is of the essence if we're going to get a jump on finding and securing the Church's apostle relic. Silas, what do you think about a second round for SEPIO? I know you said no to my invitation a few months ago, but you're our only lead, and the one best positioned to help the Order on this. What do you say?"

Silas sighed. If there was anyone who cared about the safety and security of the Church's relics it was him. After all, he was one of the world's foremost relicologists. But there was no way he could pass up the chance to get in on what he missed a decade ago: translating and verifying the greatest discovery of early Christianity, even if it was a load of rubbish. And it was summer, so he was certainly free for the next few weeks. Then there was tenure: it would be a slam dunk after this work.

But then he thought about Radcliffe and Celeste and the Order, how they were relying on him to help track down the stolen relic and get to the bottom of Nous. The military side of him sure was itching for another fight after what they pulled a few months ago. And now this? Nous had to be stopped, that was for sure.

He pressed both palms on his face and rubbed, then sighed trying to decide what he should do.

But he made up his mind.

"Sorry, Radcliffe, Celeste. But I'm going to sit this one out."

There were sighs from the other end of the line. Celeste responded, "We could really use your help, professor. Given you've already made contact with the Nous agents, and have direct experience and working knowledge of the terrorist plot."

For some reason, he regretted disappointing her the most. But his mind was made up. "No, you don't. And we don't even know if this extends beyond a simple one-off theft. Granted, it's a big deal they blew up a church to steal an apostle relic. But my money says it's payback for Paris and the Church of the Holy Sepulcher. A message to the Order to back off. You don't need me to handle that."

He looked at Denton and nodded. "I'm joining Denton. But feel free to keep me in the loop. You've got my number."

There was a pause, then Radcliffe responded, "I understand. We'll let you know when we resolve this matter. And do keep us in the loop, as well. Your little expedition should prove enlightening."

Silas said he would and said goodbye, then ended the call.

Denton smiled and slapped Silas on the back. "Fancy a trip to Rome, mate?"

Yes, please.

CHAPTER 6

ROME, ITALY.

The quiet hum of the LearJet 85's engines was lulling Silas to sleep as he reclined in the soft, tan leather chair. Add to that the dark-mahogany minibar stocked with hundred-dollar bottles of booze at the rear and the same wooden accents around the windows and baseboard, and he could get used to this kind of academic life.

At just under $21 million, the luxe jet was the latest in top-of-the-line air travel for the uber-rich. Or flush mystery groups footing the bill for two scholars in early Christian studies on their way to Rome. He would have to probe deeper into who exactly was behind this restarted research into the Gospel of Judas manuscripts. Because it sounded suspiciously like the kind of fronts that populated religious conspiracy action-adventure thrillers perched on the shelves of airport bookstores than the kind of academic, charitable organization that cared about obscure, second-century Coptic codex fragments.

But first, he was going to savor the soft feeling of privilege beneath his fingers while resting his hands on the leather-wrapped armrests, take another deep breath of filtered, ionized, private-jet air unsullied by a hundred grimy passengers, and take another swig of the twenty-year-old Glenfiddich sloshing around in the Waterford crystal tumbler before his ice melted.

As he brought the tumbler up to his mouth, the plane dipped, sending some of the caramel liquid over the sides. Silas held the glass steady as they hit another wave of turbulence, then took a sip and set down the glass before the next one rolled them. He licked the spilled scotch off his hand, then glanced over at Denton. He was completely checked out, his head rolling to the side as one final bump of air knocked them around.

Silas leaned back and closed his eyes, wondering what on earth he was doing traveling halfway around the world again to chase down the truth about a religious artifact that meant not a lick to him or his faith. Or, at least it was highly unlikely it did. But then he took a deep breath, enjoying the tart scent of supple leather and sighed, enjoying, even more, the tart feeling of a sturdy scotch. He knew why. It was the reason he did most things in his life, the ones that eventually got him into trouble, anyway. Those double-trouble deadly sins of pride and envy.

Resting in the jet recliner, he recalled the feeling that came over him when he read about the discovery of the lost manuscript revealed as the Gospel of Judas. There he was, his old British war buddy, Eli Denton. His name in lights in every major newspaper around the world and credited in the books on its history and content as the "promising young graduate student from Yale" and "emerging Coptic expert" who helped crack the revelations embedded in the manuscript. Silas's neck started burning just thinking about it, and what he would have given to have been a part of the investigation. It could have been him, since he had taken up learning the ancient language as a side project during his downtime on base, and had nearly gone to Yale himself to study. He put it off to re-enlist another two years in memory of his father who died in the Pentagon that fateful 9/11-day, a decision he still regretted as it put his ambitions behind schedule.

He took another mouthful of his scotch, downing it to watery leftovers. He had hated Denton for it all. Hated himself even more for allowing the embers of envy to burn bright and strong, and then manifest themselves in the ugliness of pride that ruined what could have been a good friendship. It was the reason he chose to study at Harvard instead of Yale. Could face neither the man and his accomplishments nor the facts of what he had done, letting the relationship wither and die. He hoped he was better than that man he left behind in Iraq, the one who had decided to take up his cross in faith and grown to follow Jesus as his Lord.

But he feared that man was still inside waiting to raise his ugly head again.

Another atmospheric jolt sent Silas reaching for his glass. He looked again at his new partner. Still out. He motioned to the blond flight attendant wearing a far-too-short skirt for another drink. She nodded and rose to that mahogany bar-of-privilege. A few minutes later, she handed him a half-tumbler full of caramel liquid. This time neat, no ice. He thanked her, then watched her walk back to her seat. A little too long, a little too longingly.

Make that the trifecta of deadly sins: envy, pride, and lust.

He shook his head and frowned at his moment of weakness, then gulped down another mouthful of the smoky liquid.

"Good morning, sunshine," Denton said in sleepy British. He yawned, then said, "Scotch for breakfast?"

Silas raised his glass. "Breakfast of champions." He took another sip and set it down. "Get any sleep?"

"Out like a lamp. You?"

He shook his head. "No. Too busy figuring out what the hell I've gotten myself into. And why I've jumped on your Gnostic-gospels train to help research and retranslate it."

Denton raised an eyebrow. "Why did you?"

Silas pivoted his recliner toward Denton and brought the seat into an upright position. "In 2006, when the *National Geographic* broke the news, and the translation came out, it had been a few years after I converted to the faith. Well, we converted. Sure, I grew up Catholic, but I never really was all that religious, never really believed, never had a strong faith. But then I took it more seriously, being utterly captivated by the Jesus I encountered in the four Gospels in the New Testament. Remember that Bible study we did together through the Book of Mark?"

Denton smiled and nodded. “Sure. Good times.”

“It was. For us both, from what I remember. You too seemed captivated by what you read about Jesus, what he said and did, how he treated the marginalized of his day and the kind of life he called us to. His ultimate sacrifice to put this world back together again. To put us and our lives back together again...”

Denton shifted in his seat, looking uncomfortable. “That was a long time ago.”

Silas nodded. “That it was. Anyway, I'm almost embarrassed to admit this, but when your little project was unveiled, I was—” he stopped short, searching for the right word. “Thrown off.”

Denton sat up straighter and tilted his head. “What do you mean? How so?”

“Now, this was before I had gone off to graduate school, but I had already been digging deeper into the Bible more than I had in my life, especially the four Gospels telling the story about Jesus' life and teachings, his death and resurrection. So much so that I was afraid I'd become one of those Bible thumpers."

Denton laughed. “You and me both.”

Silas rolled his eyes. “Anyway, so when there was word that another gospel had been found and then I learned that there were other so-called Gospels...well, my faith started faltering. What if I had been duped into a lie, some sort of religious hoax? What if the stories we have about Jesus were manufactured, or the memory of the apostles was wrong? Why only these four Gospels—Matthew, Mark, Luke, and John—and not the others? What if the Church used its power and influence to suppress other biographies about Jesus and his life? What then...?”

Silas stared out a window beyond Denton, considering his journey of faith. Denton remained silent, waiting for him to continue. "But then I started digging further, learning that those other so-called Gospels, the books that were supposedly delivering 'good news' as the word *gospel* means, couldn't be further from the truth. They were elitist and exclusive, offering 'salvation' if you can call it that, to a select, enlightened few. They were anti-Jewish. Not only were they completely disconnected from the Hebrew Scriptures and the thoroughly Jewish context of Jesus and his disciples. They also trashed the Old Testament, and the God found there, claiming he was a stupid, foolish, lesser deity. All these books are is a bunch of esoteric mumbo-jumbo that offer fortune-cookie wisdom sayings as the means of self-salvation through escape, rather than the actual rescue found in Jesus' payment on the cross for our sins."

He stopped, then laughed and said. "Sorry for the sermon."

"No problem. I rather enjoyed your soap-box moment. Reminded me of the Silas I knew back in Iraq."

"Well, I hope that means you'll appreciate the one on this trip, but I doubt it. Because the only reason I'm here is to legitimize the real memory of the apostles' witness to Jesus' life and show how the so-called Gospel of Judas is no gospel at all."

Denton laughed. "I wouldn't have expected anything less from you. Which is why I dragged you along. I want an objective counter-voice to weigh against whatever it is we discover. One firmly entrenched in religious conviction and the traditional dogma of the Church."

"That's comforting, especially for the sake of academic inquiry. Because we both know you're not all that objective yourself. Having walked away from the Church and Christianity, and all."

Denton took a breath and turned toward his window. "Tis true. But it doesn't make the findings of the Gospel of Judas any less significant for the Church and the claims of Christianity. At some point, the mounting counter-perspectives to the traditional narrative will force it to change and come to grips with the modern world."

"Is that why you're flying to Rome?" Silas asked. "To try and force that change? You think you can erase two thousand years of the received memory from the witness of the apostles and collective witness to the power of Jesus' story passed along from billions of believers?"

He turned back toward Silas. "Not change. But perhaps amend."

Silas scoffed. "Yeah, well. You're going to have to get past me first."

"I accept the challenge."

The captain came across the intercom and instructed his two passengers and flight attendant to prepare for landing.

Denton said, "I guess we'll have to postpone our verbal sparring for now. But, mate," he paused to buckle his seatbelt. "I'm not the enemy. No matter what you think. My reasons are pure. It's all in the interest of faith. Nothing more, nothing less."

Silas said nothing, offering only a weak smile and nodding. He turned toward his window to watch the approaching world below. He wasn't sure what to make of Denton and this new project of his. Only that he had an unsettled feeling about what he was about to step into, and how it might impact his faith and the memory of the apostolic witness.

After making one of the smoothest landings of his life, yet another reason to fly private, the two were met on the tarmac at Leonardo da Vinci Airport by a black Mercedes polished to perfection. The driver escorted them to the car and opened the rear passenger door for them. Denton slid in first, then Silas. They took off toward Rome before taking the A90 north around the ancient city.

In just over an hour, they arrived at a closed steel gate flanked on either side of the drive by aged, beige stone pillars with a row of tightly spaced, twelve-foot evergreen bushes extending upward in both directions. They performed their job well, masking presumably a similar beige, stone wall, but also the activity of the Aeon Foundation behind it. As the driver eased the Mercedes up the drive, the gate swung inward. In the distance, Silas saw a building that could only have been described as a spaceship. It reminded him of the new Apple campus, just smaller, probably a quarter of the size. He could see five floors, the sides made of pure bluish-tinted glass. Its gleaming, polished-metal roof was angled outwards with rows of solar panels. The impression it gave reflected the foundation's name: an eternal realm for mere mortals, come down from the heavens to impart its secret wisdom to the masses.

"Impressive, isn't it?" Denton said.

Before Silas could answer, the car angled to the right and quickly descended, the campus disappearing above.

Silas mumbled, "It's something, that's for sure."

After a continued descent through a dark, narrow passage illuminated by carefully spaced LED lights, the car came to a stop in front of a set of frosted glass doors at an underground carpark. The driver got out of the car, then opened the rear, driver-side door for Denton.

As he exited, then Silas, the frosted doors opened. Out stepped a man, tall, blond, and dressed in gray linen pants and a black turtleneck shirt. A small smile curled upward on the right side of his mouth.

Silas's mouth literally dropped, and eyes widened, then narrowed. "Sebastian?"

"Hello, big brother."

CHAPTER 7

T*his is not happening.*

The car drove off, turning around in a wide circle in the subterranean chamber. On impulse, he followed after it, angling back toward the LED-lit tunnel where they came and where the car was heading.

"Silas," Sebastian called after him. Denton did the same: "Come on, wait a minute." He caught up to Silas and grabbed his arm.

Silas spun around and yanked it back. "What the heck is going on here?" he roared, stepping backward ready to bolt again to the car to take him away. The car drove off, however, leaving him stranded.

Denton leaned back and put his palms up in surrender. "Now, calm down, mate."

"Calm down?" he said. Then louder: "Calm down? Are you kidding me? You drag me halfway across the world after conspiring with my brother to undermine the Christian faith, and you tell me to calm down?"

"Oh, grow up," Sebastian said, joining the fight.

Silas pointed a finger at his brother. "You stay out of this." He shifted the finger to Denton. "And why didn't you tell me he was involved?"

"Look," Denton said calmly. "I knew things were...strained between you two. And I figured you wouldn't jump on board with the plan if you knew Sebastian was involved."

"You're damn right!" Silas's voice echoed around the concrete carpark.

Sebastian folded his arms and huffed.

Denton put a hand on Silas's shoulder. "This one is on me, not your brother."

Silas glanced at his hand, and Denton retreated. "Explain."

Denton sighed. "Your brother and I met years ago whilst I was studying at Yale." He turned to Sebastian and said, "You were working on your second degree, correct? Computer science or something?"

Sebastian nodded. "It was a dual Ph.D. in physics and computer science. Finished in record time, might I add."

Silas rolled his eyes. Ever the braggart. But, then again, he should talk.

Denton continued, "We met during the second year of my program in religious studies. We've kept in touch on and off. And when I needed the touch of a computer scientist, I phoned for help."

Silas said, "And you didn't think to mention that back in Chicago?"

Denton shrugged. "You said it yourself: you wouldn't have come. And I need your help, Silas. I truly do. Between his AI-imaging algorithm and your credentials as an expert in early Christianity and Coptic, I'm hoping we can do some real good here uncovering the mysteries of arguably the most important find in Christian studies."

Silas sighed heavily and ran his hand over his close-cropped hair. He couldn't believe he had been conned like this.

"Just think, Sy," Sebastian said, "another opportunity for you to prove Christianity in the right, and me in the wrong."

The slight grin on Sebastian's face made Silas's neck start to burn with irritation. He folded his arms and said, "I see you've recovered from our last outing. And, what, no trademark bow tie to show off your superiority?"

Sebastian smirked. "I'm on the mend. And I didn't find one to fit the occasion."

He rolled his eyes, then walked passed him and Denton and through the frosted double doors. They swooshed open when he was in range. Greeting him was a soft, brown bamboo wall and a set of brushed-metal doors with an elevator pad. He punched the 'up' arrow button, instantly opening the doors. Sebastian and Denton joined him inside the all-glass carriage.

"Where to?" Silas asked.

Denton pressed the number '3.' They were instantly taken upward. Within seconds, they had surfaced from the carpark beneath to a sunlit, open space with high ceilings and filled with greenery and natural surfaces of wood and stone. People were busy at work, hunched over workstations. A few were examining some manuscripts or a codex from another era.

Silas approached the glass wall for a better view as the ascended through to the second floor, putting a hand on its surface. "What is this place?"

"The Aeon Foundation," Denton explained, "specializing in preserving and restoring lost, ancient texts of wisdom, and broadcasting its findings for all the world to enjoy. A few years ago, they acquired the codex collection containing the Gospel of Judas for safekeeping from Frieda Nussberger Tchacos, the original benefactor after whom the codex is named. With her blessing, they also provided the access and funding for our little project."

Silas continued staring out into the spaceship-looking building as they ascended, silently noting the strong Gnostic connotations of the word "aeon," signifying enlightened, divine beings from the eternal, spiritual realm that transcends the fallen, ignorant world of Earth. He thought he might need to keep his eyes open for the true nature of what was behind Denton's project. Now he knew he would have to dig deeper into what was really going on here.

They ascended to their final floor, which was dramatically different. The natural light and earth tones were replaced with harsh halogen and dark, charcoal slate and concrete. And the open space was replaced by a single, short hallway with a security desk guarding a set of brushed-metal doors with a security palm-reading panel. Cracking the façade of the foundation to the true intentions below looked like it was going to be harder than Silas thought.

"Here we go," Denton said, leading the way out of the elevator to the guard station.

"Ahh, Reginald, my favorite chief of security in all the world. Just the man I wanted to see."

The tall, burly man wearing a too-tight, black military flight suit and serious, pinched face did not return the enthusiasm.

"Good morning, Dr. Denton. Dr. Grey. I presume you'll be heading to Area 4."

"Right. Another day, another dollar, as they say."

The man wasn't amused. He grunted toward Silas. "And who is this?"

Denton motioned toward the new guy. "Dr. Silas Grey. Brother of Sebastian, here. Silas, meet Reginald Schmidt, head of security for the Aeon Foundation."

Silas extended his hand "Pleased to meet you." The man looked at it, then reluctantly shook it. His grip was like a vice, purposefully, relentlessly squeezing it for a few seconds. Silas offered the same grip in return before the two let go.

"He is assisting us with Project 13 and needs credentialing. All should be in order. Mr. Borg approved the addition to the team himself."

"Did he now..." The man tilted his head back and eyed Silas from behind a bulbous nose. Silas widened his stance and didn't break the gaze, firm and unmoving. A beat later, Schmidt snapped his head back down and began typing on a console at the station. A minute later, he handed Silas a red and white-striped badge, the kind more likely to be found at a high-clearance, military facility than a charitable, academic foundation.

He took it and looked it over. It was complete with his name and somehow a tiny picture of himself. One he definitely hadn't given Chief Reggie. He furrowed his brow and clipped it to his pocket. Looking into the foundation was definitely high on his list of priorities now.

The chief set a tablet the size of an iPad on the desk and asked Silas to place his palm on its surface. When he did, it glowed bright white, pulsed, then went green. Schmidt took it away and told Silas he now had access to Area 4 and the Project 13 room. Then there was a loud click, and the brushed-metal doors opened, revealing the continuation of the halogen-lit charcoal hallway. Denton led the way, followed by Sebastian.

There were no windows, and Silas noticed each door was commanded by a glass-panel security pad similar to the one he just touched. They passed two personnel in similar black flight suits as the chief, wearing the same stern expression. Security sure was tight for the kind of work of enlightenment Denton said was supposedly going on there.

They passed a door as it opened and out stepped a bald, bespeckled man wearing glasses and a white lab coat. Silas stole a glance into the room as they passed the open door. Lying on the table was a red-hued statue, a long beak extending into the air, and a looped, cross-like ankh resting at its side. The man looked at Silas and quickly closed the door.

If he wasn't mistaken, it looked like Thoth, the ancient Egyptian god of wisdom. He was thought to have inspired all sacred writings and was often worshiped and venerated by those seeking salvation through enlightenment. Interesting...

"Silas, keep up!" Sebastian said. "Over here."

He quickened his pace and walked through an opened door. Area 4, he presumed. He whistled as he walked into the space. "Nice digs."

The air was cool and crisp, totally humid-free and smelling like an afternoon storm from the ionized filtered air. Which made sense, because spread out around the large, dimly lit space were twenty-six pages of ancient paper sitting atop illuminated tables, all scrawled with faded, black ink and missing parts of parchment, some tiny holes, some sizable chunks. Off to the side were more lighted tables with tiny fragments arrayed in neat grids.

Codex Tchacos, containing the Gospel of Judas.

The third-century codex had originally been found in 1978 during an excavation along the banks of the Nile River 120 miles south of Cairo. Inside a cave were some baskets of Roman flasks, a number of human remains, and two limestone boxes. Inside one of those boxes were four different manuscripts: a mathematical treatise, a fragment copy of the Old Testament Book of Exodus, some fragments of Paul's letters from the New Testament, and a codex containing the Gospel of Judas and three other Coptic Gnostic texts previously known from the Nag Hammadi discovery from the 1940s. Remarkably, they had laid undisturbed and preserved in the dry desert chamber for over sixteen hundred years, waiting to be unleashed on the Church like a well-preserved Paleolithic virus.

Through a series of financial transactions and intrigue and heated negotiations between several different parties, it found its way into the hands of Frieda Nussberger Tchacos, a wealthy dealer in ancient art. She eventually persuaded a foundation to get involved in helping preserve it and then the *National Geographic* and a small team of scholars to translate and verify the manuscript's authenticity. Although not an immediate hit on the world stage, having been first introduced at the turn of the century through obscure academic conferences, once *National Geographic* showcased the find through a special television production and in print editions of the translation, the Gnostic Gospel was an instant international hit. Not only because it was the most significant, ancient religious find since the Dead Sea Scrolls and Nag Hammadi Gnostic Gospels during the '40s. But mostly because of the alternative story it told about Christianity's most infamous, nefarious character, Judas Iscariot.

Silas walked over to the first page of the Gospel of Judas, sandwiched between a plate of glass and brightly illuminated table. He instantly recognized the Coptic script and began to translate. It read: "*The secret account of the revelation that Jesus spoke in conversation with Judas Iscariot during a week three days before he celebrated Passover.*"

"Careful, Sy," Sebastian said leaning over Silas's right shoulder. "You might spontaneously combust from the heretical revelation."

Silas smirked. "Don't worry. I'm wearing my clove of garlic and crucifix."

Sebastian laughed and walked over to a workstation at the back of the room. "Come over here and meet Galileo. An algorithmic AI that intuitively restores damaged images to their rightful, original condition."

Silas followed. "Galileo?"

"You know, the Italian chap tried by the Inquisition, found, and I quote: 'vehemently suspect of heresy,' that one?"

"Cute."

"Figured it was an appropriate name for the AI meant to offer scientific inquiry into one of the Church's most suppressed accounts of Jesus' life."

Silas rolled his eyes. "So what's your play in all of this, baby brother? This isn't like you, caring about an obscure religious text, as heretical as it might be, as you say."

"What can I say? I'm a man of science. I like to help where I can serve the greater good of humanity by expanding the horizons of knowledge and enlightenment."

"But this isn't science, it's voodoo spirituality."

"Actually, it is science," Denton said, joining Silas as Sebastian worked. "Your brother, here, leveraged his computer science know-how to piece together the fragments of the dilapidated manuscript folios that were pulverized and broken up into a crumbling mess."

Silas folded his arms. "Sounds interesting. How does it work?"

"Want to do the honors, mate?"

Sebastian kept working away on his workstation, doing what Silas had no clue. He said, "I created an algorithm that applies automated texture synthesis in combination with perceptual-loss focusing on creating realistic textures from the surrounding and inferred patterns of the ground-zero image truth, generating a single image super-resolution."

Silas raised an eyebrow. "Is that all?"

Sebastian spun around in his chair and huffed in annoyance. "It basically infers an image from the damaged pictorial data using the surrounding information to generate a near-accurate image that's fully restored."

"In other words," Denton interjected, "Sebastian has given us a fully restored Gospel of Judas in its original state!"

Silas considered this. "Sounds sci-fi to me, something out of *Blade Runner*."

"It was. Until now," Sebastian said matter-of-factly. He returned to his workstation and typed a few commands, bringing up a muddy image of a muted, dark-wood window frame behind some sort of red structure. It was pixelated and garbled.

"What's this?" Silas asked, folding his arms.

"A little demonstration. Given your perennial skepticism and need-to-be-against attitude, I figured you would need some convincing before we got started." He hit a few more keystrokes, and a gray alert window with a green status bar appeared. The bar slowly filled to the right as the image transformed before Silas's eyes. Gradually, but surely, the window became clearer and the structure defined. If he wasn't mistaken, it looked like one of those old-school, English telephone boxes with the curved roof. He could even make out the grain of the wood that the high-definition camera had picked up. After the status bar grew to 100 percent, indicating the image had rendered, it closed. Silas was stunned at what he saw.

Clearly displayed were the letters *TELE*, the partial image of the full TELEPHONE signage on all English boxes. The original image, the muddled, grainy one, had only a muddy, putty-colored rectangular bar. And yet the AI algorithm had interpreted the underlying data and surrounding pixels to render the correctly restored letters of the original, distorted word.

Which meant this Gospel, this Gnostic Gospel, or whatever the heck it was, could be restored to its originality. Silas sighed, wondering what secrets the Gospel held that were waiting to be unlocked by Sebastian's AI algorithm. What story it would tell that might threaten the one he had believed and trusted.

Sebastian was looking at Silas, smiling with satisfaction. "Now are you convinced?"

Silas smirked. "I gotta admit I was skeptical. But...wow. That's incredible, how it restored the original text like that." He rubbed his chin and mumbled, "Can't argue with that kind of proof."

Sebastian smiled with satisfaction. "No, you can't."

Denton said, "Just imagine what your brother's technology will mean for manuscript restoration and research. For the Gospel of Judas and for discovering the underlying story behind the Jesus of early Christianity!"

Silas looked at him and nodded. "But what about the Gospel of Judas and its lacunae? All of the holes and missing pieces to the information of the codex? How do you render what isn't there?"

Denton said, "That's where it gets interesting. Several of the broken pieces had been preserved by Tchacos and the previous foundation which held guardianship over the Gospel of Judas. Since they had ended up in a crumbled mess over the years once they were removed from the dry, arid wilderness, they didn't know what to make of them." He smiled and slapped Sebastian back. "But my mate, here, arrayed them all piece by piece on those lighted tables and scanned them along with the codex folio pages, then let his algorithm do its magic. It has been working at interpreting the data for the past day now. If all goes according to plan, the computer will arrange the pieces for us in their proper order. Even fragments as tiny as a baby's pinkie nail!"

Sebastian added, "And then the AI algorithm will interpret the textual image data of the preserved pages to interpret the sections that were previously indecipherable, and fill in the blanks using deep-learning, algorithmic techniques for the missing pieces. Just like it did with the lettering on the British telephone box in the demo image."

Silas furrowed his brow and shook his head. "But how? Without the original textual data?"

Denton shrugged his shoulders. "Science, Silas."

"You should try it sometime," Sebastian added.

Silas rolled his eyes. "How much longer?"

A sound came from the computer. Silas noticed a green flashing from the monitor. He looked at Denton, then to his brother.

Sebastian rubbed his hands together and returned to facing the workstation. "Now. Showtime, folks."

CHAPTER 8

Silas and Denton both stepped closer to Sebastian's workstation and peered over his shoulder at his monitor to look at the results.

There it was, in living color. A row of images at various stages of rendering, a few showcasing the fully-restored folio pages of the Gospel of Judas, lacunae and all.

"It hasn't all been rendered yet. The images with the green borders indicate the ones that have been completed. We'll need the night for the rendering algorithm to complete its mission. But we're getting there."

"Brilliant," Denton whispered. "Just brilliant!" he exclaimed louder, slapping Sebastian on his back.

"I have to echo the Brit, Seba. Pretty brilliant stuff."

Sebastian turned around partially and smiled at his brother. "You know, I think that's the first time you've complimented me in our entire adult lives. I'll take it." Then he turned back toward the monitor.

Silas felt foolish and silently scolded himself for the truth of his brother's words. He had played the part of adversary for too long. Perhaps working together like this would change him into an advocate of his brother. *Help me love my brother as myself*, he silently prayed, echoing the words of Jesus.

Denton reached over Sebastian's shoulder and pointed at the monitor. "Bring up one of the images, that one there. I'm eager to get to work and sample the goods."

Sebastian obliged, bringing one of the twenty-six thumbnails to full screen.

Silas's phone rang, echoing around the enclosed space. He startled and brought it out. It was Radcliffe, calling for an update no doubt. "I should take this," he said.

Denton and Sebastian ignored him, engrossed in the image.

He walked away from the two for privacy, then brought the phone to life and answered. "Radcliffe, any news?"

"Celeste, actually. You never gave me your number, shame on you. So I had to borrow Radcliffe's mobile."

Silas smiled. It was good to hear her voice again. "Sorry about that. Hope you weren't offended."

"I was. Deeply so. I thought our relationship had progressed beyond the notes-under-the-desk stage."

Sebastian glanced up from his monitor, and made a phone motion with his hand and winked, mouthing "Celeste" and cocking his head in question. Silas stopped smiling and cleared his throat, realizing he was grinning like a schoolboy.

"Anyway," he mumbled turning away, "what's up, Celeste?"

"Haven't you seen the news?"

"No, I haven't. Denton and I arrived at the foundation headquarters outside Rome."

"Oh goodie. Any news on that front?"

"Not yet, but I should have something soon. My brother just completed some restoration work on the original Gospel of Judas manuscript pages, and we're about to get to work translating and analyzing the output."

"Your brother? Sebastian is there with you, in Rome?"

Silas chuckled. "Yeah. Long story." He turned around and

looked over at the two huddled around the monitor. Denton and Sebastian were both grinning with pleasure. Eager to join them he asked, "So, what's this news you called about?"

"Right. There's been another attack on the apostle relics."

"Really? Which one?"

Celeste answered, "James, in Rome."

"Brother of Jude?"

"Exactly."

"Another attack meant to send a message to the Order, you think?"

"We wondered about that since the two were related. But then Philip's relic was also swiped."

Denton looked up from the monitor and motioned for Silas to come join them. He nodded and held up a finger to let him know it would be one more moment.

Silas said, "But aren't Philip's and James' relics part of the same collection in Rome? What's the name of the Basilica...?"

Celeste answered, "You're right. The Basilica of the Holy Apostles."

"Well, there you go. Probably a two-for-one deal while setting sights on the original target, Jude Thaddeus. And, really, the Order."

"Maybe..."

Silas was getting impatient. His two companions were soaking up whatever it was they had discovered. Silas wanted in on the action. "But?" he said with an edge of impatience.

"But, why these three? Jude, Philip, and James the Lesser were pretty minor apostles. If you're trying to send a message, why them?"

He considered the question. She had a point. "I don't know, Celeste. But I've got to go."

"Right. Sorry to be a bother."

He smiled and shook his head. "You're no bother. Not at all.

Let me know if you find out anything more, and if there's anything I can do to help."

"You're quite welcome to join the hunt. Gapinski is growing restless with the dried-up leads and itching for a fight. We could use you."

Silas chuckled at the mention of the other SEPIO teammate who had joined him and Celeste on their last mission. "I'm sure he is. But the results are in, and I've got work to do here. I'll stay in touch with anything I find here. And good luck on your end."

The two said their goodbyes and Silas walked back over to the two still huddled around the monitor.

"Silas, mate, check this out." Denton pointed to the monitor at a section of a manuscript folio that had been restored, with the original of distortions and gaps sitting next to it. Silas carefully read the Coptic script the algorithm had revealed, translating it along the way:

There are three structures for sacrificing in Jerusalem. One opens to the west and is called the holy place; a second opens to the south and is called the holy of the holy; the third opens to the east and is called the holy of holies, where only the high priest can enter. The holy place is baptism; the holy of the holy is redemption; the holy of holies is the bridal chamber. The bridal chamber is within a realm superior to the realm we belong to, and you cannot find anything like it. At first the curtain concealed how God manages creation, but when the curtain is torn and what is inside appears, this building will be left deserted, or rather will be destroyed. Everyone who enters the bedchamber will kindle the light. Those who receive the light cannot be seen or grasped. Nothing can trouble such people even while they are living in this world. It is revealed to such a person alone, hidden not in darkness and night, but hidden in perfect day and holy light.

Silas took a breath and sighed. There was a familiar ring about this restored portion, one he couldn't quite place. Regardless, he immediately knew this was significant.

"Did you read what I read?"

He nodded and rubbed his chin. "Typical of Gnosticism, interpreting the Temple as a source of enlightenment."

"Right, but the text speaks as if the Temple is still standing as a source of enlightenment. It says the Temple will be left deserted and destroyed. *Will be*, as if the Temple is still standing!"

Silas said nothing, glancing at Denton, then back to the monitor of Coptic text.

"And if the Temple is still standing, that means the Gospel of Judas was written much, much earlier than anyone could have imagined!"

Silas shifted his position and brought his hand up to his chin to consider this.

Sebastian asked, "Why does that matter? Whether the Temple was still standing?"

Denton turned to Silas. "Want to do the honors?"

"One of the hallmarks of manuscript dating," Silas explained, "is using the data within the manuscript itself to determine a location within history. Experts on the New Testament, especially the Gospels, consider the destruction of the Jewish temple in AD 70 by the Roman army under the direction of Vespasian an important historical marker."

Denton added, "Many scholars believe a few of the New Testament Gospels were written sometime after AD 70 because they themselves seemed to presuppose its destruction. Matthew, Mark, and Luke all share a similar story of when Jesus and the disciples visited Jerusalem and marveled at the size and beauty of the Temple. Then Jesus remarked, 'These things which you see—the days will come in which not one stone shall be left upon another that shall not be thrown down.'"

Silas smirked. "Luke 21:6. Impressive."

Denton wore a smile of satisfaction. "Of course. I've memorized most of the New Testament. After all, early Christianity is my specialty."

He rolled his eyes. "Well, not all experts believe every New Testament Gospel was written after AD 70. Plenty argue Mark and probably Luke was written before it was destroyed. And the fact an ancient text doesn't mention its destruction doesn't prove it was written before AD 70. There is no reason the writer couldn't have been projecting a still-standing Temple back into the narrative after the fact."

"Oh, in the same way some of the New Testament Gospel writers could have projected a destroyed Temple as a prophetic utterance back into their own narrative account of Jesus?"

Silas opened his mouth to offer Denton a retort, but declined. He wasn't going to take the bait. Instead, he stepped closer to the monitor to re-read the Coptic. There it was, an alternative Gospel seemingly written as if the Temple were still standing. Most concerning. And yet... He couldn't place it, but there was a familiar ring to the account. Sounded similar to something he had heard or read before.

"So what are you thinking?" Denton asked, interrupting his concentration. "Just after Mark and Luke or around that time? Probably before Matthew and definitely before John."

Silas shook his head. "I don't know. But if I remember correctly, we know for sure it has to be after the book of Acts was written because the Jesus of the Gospel of Judas said someone else would replace him. An obvious reference to Matthias."

"True. But plenty have placed Luke's historical accounts in both his Gospel and the book of Acts before the Temple's destruction."

Silas had to concede that point. The idea that the Gospel of Judas was written during the same time as the real Gospels was ludicrous, especially before Matthew's and John's gospels. But he couldn't dispute the manuscript evidence, as preliminary as it was.

"Why don't we take a break for the day," Sebastian said. "I sure could use one for all the work I did getting ready for you two to arrive. And I could use a drink. Preferably something with alcohol."

Denton nodded. "I agree. Let's call it a night. Our accommodations are just down the hall. One of the many perks of working with the Aeon Foundation. They even offer room service and pay-per-view."

Sounded good. But dinner and a movie would have to wait. Silas had work to do.

CHAPTER 9

Tofu, vegetables, and rice were not high on Silas Grey's list of favorite foods. He was a meat-and-potatoes guy, all the way. But he was famished, not having eaten since the jet ride earlier in the day. So he didn't complain too loudly when a server had later brought up the tray of food after he had ordered dinner.

Denton had escorted him to his room down the hallway and around the corner from their research room. The three had been given rooms adjacent to one another; Silas at the end, Denton two doors down, and Sebastian between them. He had planned on scoping out the Aeon facilities, but once his feet hit the soft, beige rug overlying the pine floorboards of his room, his stomach had protested too loudly to let him leave. He ended up ordering room service. The pay-per-view would have to wait.

He stared out of the third-story, floor-to-ceiling window of his spacious suite as he enjoyed his "dinner" at a triangle bamboo table overlooking a park inside the inner sanctuary of the ring, a far cry from the dark, drab room that held the manuscript pages down the hall. A bubbling fountain in the corner surrounded by bamboo and watering a juniper bonsai tree added to the feng shui of the room, complete with geometrically sound furniture and solid-pastel textiles covering the bed and floor. He swallowed the last of the steamed zucchini and shoved a spoonful of rice into his mouth. It wasn't even buttered. Then he contemplated what to do with the tofu. He poked at the five cubes he had shoved to the side, then crossed himself and popped one in his mouth.

When in Rome...

The tan curd of mashed soybeans squeaked in his mouth as he chewed. Not bad, actually. Surprisingly salty, with a kick of something he couldn't place. He thought about phoning for the recipe, but he had more important things to do. Like, figure out who was behind the Aeon Foundation and what they were up to inside a spaceship in northern Rome.

Silas stood and wiped his mouth with a white, linen napkin thoughtfully placed on his tray, then walked to a glass door discretely at the right end of the floor-to-ceiling window. He slid it open and stepped out onto a small balcony overlooking the inner court. He closed his eyes and breathed deeply the still-warm air laced with sea salt and eucalyptus from the surrounding hillsides. He surveyed the interior of the facility, noting the dim light of several office suites from behind the tinted, curved glass of the building and acres of well-tended foliage beneath. To his right and left were privacy walls of frosted glass that shielded his prying eyes from the activity of other guests, including his brother. He imagined him right at home, having feasted on plates of sushi and glasses of Dom Perignon to his heart's content.

He left the balcony and walked to his nightstand, grabbing his red-and-white ID badge and exited his room. It was go time.

The stale corridor was a depressing difference from the sunny and serene room he just exited. Reminded him of the kinds of detention facilities he used to guard for the military in Iraq and Afghanistan than any of the research facilities he had worked in as an academic. He followed the dark passageway back toward the entrance to Area 4. As he walked, he wondered what the other Areas held. Given the vibes of the place, he didn't doubt there was an Area 51. He would have to keep his eyes open for anything that might help in discerning the depths of the foundation and its work.

He turned the corner and approached the door to their research room holding the Tchacos codex and Gospel of Judas. Beyond it further down the hall was the door out of Area 4 and back to the elevator. He continued onward, and the door at the end opened. Two men in black approached, both brandishing automatic weapons across their chests.

Suddenly, Silas felt exposed, and almost like he shouldn't be out wandering about the facility without permission. The two men continued walking toward him, seeming to slow their pace and eye him with skepticism.

He reached the research room and pressed his hand against the security panel, facing the door and glancing at the pair as they continued their approach. The door unlocked and he quickly went inside and closed it behind him.

The room was empty except for the glowing boxes housing the manuscript folio pages. He swallowed hard and took a deep breath, then pressed his ear against the door waiting for any sign of the guards' movements. He checked his watch. A few minutes ticked by since he had entered the room. Surely, they would have pursued him had they thought he offered a security threat. He looked around the room and swallowed again, then grabbed the handle to open the door.

He turned it slowly, then stopped and waited. Nothing. He slowly edged the door open, then opened it enough to stick his head out. The hallway was clear, and he heard no other sounds but the beating of his heart in his ears.

He took a deep breath and quickly walked back into the hallway, then down it and through the entrance. A single guard looked up from behind a magazine, his feet propped up on the station desk. Silas looked at him and nodded. The guard nodded back, then returned to his magazine. Perhaps he wasn't a prisoner after all.

The elevator stood open. He went inside and hit the button for the first floor. Might as well start at the beginning. The doors immediately closed and the glass carriage descended quickly to the first floor.

Silas walked out into a spacious area filled with the emerging, evening sunlight and still filled with people who were either busily working at stations located throughout the floor or scurrying off to work on something somewhere. He noticed the variety of people: young and old; men and women; Euro-American, African, and Asian. An interesting mix, all teaming up to unlock the mysteries of the universe and offer their revelations for the world.

As he continued walking down the center under a canopy of giant sycamores, he noticed something else: they all dressed alike. Apparently, there was a standard-issue uniform consisting of plain white-linen pants and smocks. Everyone was walking around in the same getup. And barefoot. He stopped near a bubbling fountain surrounded by hedges with bright, red flowers and sat on a bench to confirm his observations. Yep, every single person he saw dressed exactly alike.

He considered this interesting characteristic of the Aeon Foundation and heard a familiar voice stop on the other side of the fountain. Chief Reginald Schmidt. He was speaking with an older man who was dressed in the same white linen with gray hair that fell to his shoulders.

The man's back was turned to Silas, and the fountain's wide spray obscured the view anyway, but Silas hunched over and tried hiding his face behind the flowering bush while trying to catch snippets of the conversation.

Schmidt said to the man: "Denton brought him...Project 13... Borg approved it himself. Said ... to the project. But...eye on him."

The man replied: "Let's hope he...what we expect...whether the Gospel is what we are hoping ...."

Then Schmidt: "I have my doubts...strike me as cooperative... the Order to consider. And don't forget about SEPIO."

Then the man: "Leave that to me...be no bother at all. None."

The two men left, continuing on through the man-made forest erected in the spaceship-like facility. Silas thought about following them to gain more intel, but decided against it. What he heard was enough.

There was that name again, *Borg*. He remembered Denton had mentioned the name to help him gain entry past Chief Schmidt. And apparently this man Borg wanted him on Project 13, but presumably should be kept an eye on. He would have to ask Radcliffe about that name later. And speaking of the Order, why was it brought up as something to consider? Something else to follow up on later?

Silas stood and looked around, seeking direction for his next steps when a large glass opening at the back caught his attention. He walked toward it and noticed the entrance led into the interior of the circular building, to a courtyard. He could use some fresh air, so he walked toward it.

The door automatically opened on his approach. A warm, sweet-and-salty breeze caught him in the face as he stepped out into the expansive space, a welcomed relief from the cool, filtered air inside. The sun was beginning to set now, a gradient of burnt oranges and yellows changing to light blue and indigo filtering up from the horizon and into the cloudless sky. He walked further in, his boots softly crunching on a pebble path as he scanned the inner-side of the circular building. By now several more windows had alighted, different ones than those he had viewed from his balcony. He was struck by how many revealed dormitory dwellings such as his own, with what looked like families and couples and singles alike sitting down for dinner and enjoying the same evening on balconies. He assumed his Zen suite was a hotel room of sorts to accommodate researchers. But it looked like several of the people he had passed earlier lived in on-site facilities, perhaps all of them.

He continued walking, following the path around the circumference of the circle to the other side, passing rows of fruit trees arranged concentrically around the outdoor space. Blood oranges clung to overburdened trees, as well as olives, figs, and lemons. The path doubled back, taking him the way he came. He passed rows of grape vines, as well. Of course, he did, given they were in wine country. The path took him across the courtyard to a vegetable garden, with what looked like tomato vines and stalks of corn and heads of some leafy green. He kept walking, following the crunchy, stone path as it doubled back again to the other side.

He understood the layout of this part of the facility now: it was a labyrinth, an ancient, maze-like path used by various spiritual traditions to aid the walker in contemplating their journey and the path of life, including the Church. He had walked such paths during his graduate studies at one of the cathedrals in Boston. It had been an integral part of his spiritual disciplines, finding that it helped guide his times of prayer and contemplation.

As the path took him deeper into the center of the courtyard, he became more and more intrigued by the self-sustaining nature of what was beginning to feel more like a compound than a research facility. Why would they need to grow so much of their own food? Why house so many of its researchers? What was with all the coordinated clothing? That was probably creepiest of it, seeing the mass of long, white, linen smocks.

He finally reached the middle, finding a curious ring of some sort of flower patch inside. He turned in a circle, noticing the entire center was consumed by the white flowers. Curious, he stooped down to take a closer look, noticing several of the plants carried glossy, oval berries. Others bore white balls with black dots at the center, like clusters of eyeballs standing watch over the garden.

"Creepy..." he mumbled as he reached for one.

"I wouldn't do that if I were you."

Silas startled and stood up quickly, searching for the source. It was deep and carried an edge to it, one he recognized from earlier.

A bulky man stepped toward him from the path. It was Chief Schmidt.

"Out for an evening stroll, are we?" he asked, a thick German accent slicing through the night air.

"Actually, yes. I find it clears the mind after a long day of research." Silas stood still, then asked, "I'm sorry, but were you following me? Was I not supposed to be here?"

The man smiled. "Just taking an evening stroll myself. I find it clears the mind after a long day of security."

The two men stood across from each other, unmoving. Silas in the middle of a sea of white flowers and black-and-white berries, Schmidt on the path blocking his escape.

Silas smirked, then walked forward to push past the man. He suddenly put a hand on Silas's shoulder, preventing him from passing, the grip firm and threatening.

"You're a Christian, are you not?

Silas recoiled into the flower bed, clenching his jaw and narrowing his eyes at the man for the way he said *Christian*. "Excuse me?"

"A believer. A, what they call, follower of Jesus."

Silas was confused. Why was the man asking such questions?

"I believe that information is above your pay grade. Now, if you'll excuse me..." He trampled through the plants, crushing several clumps of the strange berries, returning to the stone path and walking away back toward the entrance.

Schmidt shouted, "Several people are curious about what you

find, Dr. Grey. Better not taint the results with your personal bias."

"Watch me..." he mumbled.

It took him a while, but he finally made his way back out of the labyrinth, never running into Schmidt again. He quickly made his way back to the elevator, and then headed straight for his room. When he arrived, he shut the door and promptly secured the deadbolt, just to be sure.

Unbelievable. He took off his boots and noticed the juice of the berries he found smeared on the sole. A few of them were even stuck inside the deep tracks.

"I wonder..."

He took his pinkie and dabbed it into a small amount of the liquid, then brought it up to his tongue. He hesitated at first, looked at it, then licked it.

Within seconds his tongue started to tingle. Some sort of toxin.

He promptly spat the residue on the floor, then again and ran for the kitchenette sink. He ran his mouth under the faucet, spitting again to try and remove any traces of the toxin.

His head began to spin slightly, and he felt the impulse to vomit. He crawled into his bed and laid under the sheets, regretting his decision as a wave of chills sent him into the fetal position. Not only to taste whatever was being cultivated in that garden, but also regretting taking part in Denton's and his brother's scheme.

Because whatever was going on here, he needed to get to the bottom of it.

CHAPTER 10

The next morning, Silas awoke with a start to rays of sunlight flooding through the curved glass in his room. He sat up and looked around, taking a moment to remember where he was, and what he was doing there.

Rome. Aeon Foundation. The Gospel of Judas.

He had overslept, making him late for the day of translating. He groaned and slid back under the covers. Why couldn't somebody else save the Church this time? But then he remembered the commitment he had made to Christ upon his conversion, the one the apostle Paul himself had made in the book of Acts before journeying to Jerusalem, after being warned by the Spirit of dangers to come: *'None of these things move me; nor do I count my life dear to myself, so that I may finish my race with joy, and the ministry which I received from the Lord Jesus, to testify to the gospel of the grace of God.'*

Live well and work hard, for the glory of God and the good of the world. That was Silas's motto.

Which meant getting out of bed in a mysterious, spaceship-like compound and translating a heretical "gospel" so that he could "contend earnestly for the faith which was once for all delivered to the saints," the second part of his life's mission.

No rest for the weary...

He relented, peeling off his covers and picking up the phone next to his bed to order room service again. When it came, he eagerly brought it to the bamboo table resting next to the window overlooking the courtyard below. It didn't smell half bad. But when he took off the metal cover, he was greeted with a tasteless stack of potato pancakes and even more tasteless tofu eggs. And no coffee.

After managing to force a few bites down, he showered and then headed back to the staging area for what he came to accomplish: the translation of the fully restored Gospel of Judas.

And the protection of the Church and faith.

Silas's footfalls echoed down the spartan hallway of slate and concrete, the LED lights casting shadows against the walls. When he turned the corner to the research room, he was surprised to see an addition: two guards were standing outside the doors. Two armed guards.

He hesitated on his approach, but straightened and headed for the door. They eyed him warily as he pressed his palm against the security panel. He eyed one of them as it pulsed a light blue hue, then the other before it changed to green. A click from the door indicated success. He opened it and went inside without saying a word to the guards.

"Good morning, big brother," Sebastian said as he swiveled from the table containing the Gospel of Judas manuscripts over to his workstation.

"What's with the goons standing guard?" Silas asked.

"Protection," Denton said looking up from one of the illuminated manuscripts.

"From what?"

He smiled. "You never know in these parts." He winked and walked over to a small kitchenette in the corner of the room. "Coffee?"

"Sure," Silas mumbled as he walked toward Sebastian.

Denton walked over with a mug full of strong brew and handed it to Silas. "Black, as I remember it."

He took it and nodded. "Thanks." He immediately took a mouthful. Nirvana.

Denton pulled up a chair next to Sebastian and sat. "I wondered if you were going to miss out on our little party. A late night out on the town?"

Silas smirked. He leaned over his brother's shoulder and took another swig. "Wouldn't miss it for the world. I assume we're ready to go?"

"Ready when you two are," Sebastian said. "Galileo finished rendering early this morning in the wee hours. Now it's your turn."

Fabulous.

Silas pulled over a chair for himself next to his brother as the thumbnails of the restored images appeared in order on the screen. A twinge of excitement was beginning to wind its way up his spine. The last time he was part of an archaeological discovery of this magnitude was when he found manuscripts stuffed in a set of jars on a dig at the historical site of Jericho, virtually proving the Ark of the Covenant's existence. Biblical history thrilled him. And he was back in the game with this opportunity, as mysterious as it was.

"Right," Denton said, clasping his hands together and grinning widely. "Let's get started, shall we?"

"*Vedi ora il potere della verità*," Sebastian said as he worked the keyboard.

Silas and Denton both looked at him in confusion.

Sebastian huffed. "So uncultured, you two."

"'*See now the power of truth*,'" Silas said, translating the Italian. He sat back with a satisfied grin.

Sebastian laughed and twisted in his chair to face him, "Alright, Einstein, but do you know from whom it came?"

Silas frowned and folded his arms. "Your hero Galileo Galilei, I presume."

"Precisely..." He brought up the first folio page onto the 40-inch flat-panel monitor. "Alright. Here we go."

Silas and Denton moved closer for a better view of the Coptic texts. Sebastian retrieved two large tablets resting in front of the keyboard and gave one to each of them. "Try these. I've mirrored the workstation on these devices. The monitor shows both the original and restoration side-by-side. But your tablet only shows the restored manuscript versions for your translating pleasure."

Silas took it and started scanning the first folio of the codex, the opening to the Gospel of Judas, which he had seen yesterday:

The secret account of the revelation that Jesus spoke in conversation with Judas Iscariot during a week three days before he celebrated Passover.

It was from the intact original, a typical Gnostic text that promised secret wisdom and never-before-revealed mysteries of the cosmos by none other than Jesus himself.

Denton said, "Obviously, this was part of the original manuscript. Nothing remarkably revelatory. Except for the fact it posits Jesus offering Judas secret revelation given only to him." He paused, then continued: "And not the twelve disciples."

Silas scoffed. "Whatever," he mumbled, continuing to translate the original that hadn't needed restoration. It spoke of Jesus performing miracles and great wonders for humanity's salvation; the fact that some walked in righteousness and others did not, leading Jesus to call the Twelve; more talk of Jesus revealing "the mysteries beyond the world" to them and "what would take place at the end of time."

The next part made him pause:

Often he did not appear to his disciples as himself, but he was found among them as a child.

Silas narrowed his eyes, and he breathed in deeply, then sighed. "Typically Gnostic," he mumbled again.

"What was that?" Sebastian asked.

He lifted his head as if starting to explain the nuances of Gnostic ideology regarding Jesus' bodily existence, but decided against it. "Nothing. Just more from the original."

"Ahh, yes," Denton said. "Shape-shifting Jesus."

"Shape-shifting Jesus?" Sebastian asked.

Silas laughed. "The Gnostic Gospels often depict Jesus as other-than-human or beyond human, because, according to them, everything about our material existence is dark and chaotic and evil, including the body. So this Judas Gospel portrays Jesus as a child and confusing his appearance. Again, typically Gnostic."

"Let's move it along," Denton said. "Next folio, please."

Silas continued translating the end of the first folio page as Sebastian brought up the next. It described a scene in which Jesus is having a conversation with his disciples while they celebrate the Eucharist. Then he laughs at them for what they are doing, *because it is through this that your god will be praised*, as it translates. In other words, they really don't know what they are doing. For by giving thanks of their material food, they are only praising *their* God—not the God of Jesus.

But wait...He looked up at the monitor, showing the side-by-side of the original and the restoration. There was a minor lacuna, a gap in the text highlighted in bold on the part that had been restored.

"Do you see it?" Denton asked.

Silas nodded.

---

*They said, "Master, you are **created from** the son of our god."*

The AI algorithm had restored *created from* to the original. Which flew in the face of the historic doctrine of the Church.

"*Created from* the son of our god," Denton said, the side of his mouth curling upward.

"Yes, I saw it. Thank you."

Sebastian sat back in his chair, folded his arms, and shook his head. "I don't understand. What's the problem?"

"The problem," Denton offered, "is that the official version of Jesus' person concocted by the Church says, 'We believe in one Lord, Jesus Christ, the only Son of God, eternally begotten of the Father, God from God, Light from Light, true God from true God, begotten, *not made*, of one Being with the Father.'"

"Meaning, *not* created from," Sebastian said, "as the Gospel of Judas claims."

Denton leaned back with a look of satisfaction. "Exactly."

Silas smirked. "If we are to believe this rendering—"

"Sy..." Sebastian said sitting up. "Be careful. No Luddites allowed in these parts."

Silas rolled his eyes, but continued pressing: "Seriously, if the AI has rendered the missing piece correctly, so what? It was obviously written as a counter-narrative to the revealed tradition of the apostles showing Jesus as pre-incarnate, uncreated God. Like John's *'In the beginning was the Word, and the Word was with God, and the Word was God.'*"

"Except we established yesterday that the Gospel of Judas was written before John's Gospel."

Silas shook his head. "We didn't establish anything. By a long shot."

"Well, the claim is entirely consistent with the way the Gospel of Judas portrays Jesus later, as a manifestation of Seth.

Would you be a good lad, Sebastian, and turn over to folio fifty-two?"

He nodded and flicked through images until he reached the codex page. "There we go."

"Look," Denton pointed. "More restored renderings, right before the Gospel makes claim to *'Seth, who is called Christ,'* from the original."

From his research of early Gnostic texts, Silas knew that Seth, the third son of Adam and Eve in the Old Testament, was viewed by the Gnostics as "another seed" who was assumed to be an exalted figure in the divine realm and a bearer of enlightenment. He quickly read and translated the rendering, the restored portions again appearing in bold:

The twelve rulers spoke with the twelve angels: 'Let each of you ***gain insight*** *and let them* ***understand that from*** *generations* ***past the incorruptible one, conceived by the Word, the living Jesus, with whom great Seth has been clothed is among those delivered by the*** *angels':*

The first is Seth, who is called Christ...

He didn't need to go any further.

"There he is. Jesus, Seth the Stranger, incarnated as the Christian savior who was *conceived.* Not begotten, as the Church powers dictated."

Silas shifted uncomfortably in his seat, still holding the tablet and not lifting his head to make eye contact with either Denton or Sebastian. The room was silent.

Denton broke the silence and said, "There's another folio I wanted to take a look at. One with a massive lacuna that I was curious what the AI algorithm would uncover. Sebastian, bring up folio fifty-four."

"Here we go..." Sebastian said, flipping a few images to the right.

There it was. The rendered restoration on the left, the original with a large piece missing on the right.

Silas's eyes immediately went to his tablet. He started translating.

"'*In him was eternal light,*'" Denton translated out loud, "'*and his eternal light of Enlightened Insight was the light for this generation.*'"

He stopped, setting the tablet on his lap and grinning widely. "Golly! Does that sound familiar or what?"

Silas sighed. It did. Eerily similar to the first chapter of the Gospel of John: '*In Him was life, and the life was the light of Men.*'

Denton continued, "And look how it continues, mirroring the same language of the apostle John."

Silas continued translating, the algorithm bold-facing the restored Coptic:

And the light of Insight of Enlightened Forethought has shone all *around* ***within their bondage of forgetfulness and ignorant*** *spirit that is within, which you have made to dwell in this flesh among the generations of angels. But God caused knowledge to be given upon Adam and those with him, so that the kings of chaos and the underworld might not lord it over them.*

"The Gospel of Judas makes one thing clear," Denton said interrupting Silas's concentration. "Jesus saves by revealing, not dying!"

Silas shot him a look.

"How so?" Sebastian asked.

"Just look. What Jesus brought humanity was the insight into our soul's origins and destinations. He brought enlightenment to free us from the bondage of ignorance. That's his greatest contribution to the world. Not this bloody ... well, bloody cross business!"

"Oh, come on..." Silas said, anger rising within as the implications of the renderings began to show themselves.

"Continue reading, if you don't believe me. I mean, golly! More from John's Gospel..."

Silas clenched his jaw and looked down at his tablet, continuing to translate the Coptic. Until he saw it, verse five from John chapter one making up the first line in the restoration.

His heart started racing, his palm started getting slick with sweat as he held the device and quickly kept interpreting the larger, bold-faced, restored ancient text, wondering what this would mean for the Church. For his faith.

For the light shines in the darkness and the darkness did not comprehend it.

I am the abundance of light, I am the remembrance of Fullness. I am the light dwelling in light, I am the remembrance of Forethought—"From where has my hope come as I dwell in the bondage of prison?" I said,

I am the Forethought of pure light,

I am the thought of the Virgin Spirit, who raises you to a place of honor

in my name, and he will **establish** *your star to rule over the thirteenth eternal realm.*

"No denying it, mate! Jesus is important because he brought us enlightenment to raise us up out of our ignorance." Denton set down his tablet on the table with a thud of satisfaction, then stretched out in his chair, arms behind his head and that wide smile again.

"Bah!" Silas said, setting down his tablet with equal force. "Clearly Judas—" he caught himself, then started again. "Whoever *wrote* the Gospel of Judas clearly swiped the language from John's Gospel and added it into the book to give it some sort of apostolic credibility."

Denton leaned in his chair and said earnestly, "Or was it the other way around? John swiped it from Judas?"

Silas scoffed.

"Seems clear as day to me, Sy," Sebastian said joining in. "The apostle John plagiarized from the apostle Judas.

Silas shot up off his chair and shouted, "That's ridiculous!"

"Is it?"

Denton said, "You know the Gnostics were big into the symbolism of light and Forethought as embodiments of enlightened wisdom that would save humanity. What's so hard to believe that the reason Jesus is so spectacularly important is that he came to open our minds to our true selves, to teach us a better way of living and live up to our greatest potential? To live our best life now. Why not?"

"Because that's not the apostolic witness!" Silas roared.

"I told you he would get like this," Sebastian said.

Silas looked to Sebastian, then to Denton. "Seriously, that is not what Matthew and Mark, Luke and John saw with their own eyes."

"Well, Luke didn't see it," Sebastian mumbled.

"Shut up!"

"Silas, mate, come on," Denton said.

"I apologize," he said turning to his brother. "My point is that the writers of the *Christian* Gospels are recounting how the long story of God's rescue for Israel and the world climaxed with the life, death, and resurrection of Jesus. He's not some Gandhi on steroids, come to smell the flowers and pet the animals and teach us all how to sing Kumbaya in harmony together! He was the son of God, come as the Suffering Servant who was *'wounded for our transgressions'* and *'bruised for our iniquities'* as the prophet Isaiah said. The one who was *'led as a lamb to the slaughter'* and who *'bore the sins of many'* on those blood-soaked boards of execution."

"Then why doesn't Judas include the crucifixion in his gospel if Jesus' death was so important?" Denton pressed. "If the cross is so vital, then why would one of Jesus' apostles not write about it? And why place all of the emphasis on the enlightenment he brought to humanity, rather than the supposed sins of humanity he bore?"

"Because it's a load of horse shit!"

Sebastian burst out laughing. "That settles the argument! Always love a good Silas cussing."

Silas closed his eyes and took a deep breath, cursing himself silently. He put his hands on his hips and dipped his head in shame. "I'm sorry for blowing up like that. You didn't deserve that. You both didn't. I was wrong. Please forgive me."

Silence enveloped the room.

After a minute, Silas pivoted toward the door, then said, "I need some air."

He opened it, left, and slammed the door on his way out.

CHAPTER 11

It just wasn't possible.

Silas was in a state of disbelief as the Italian countryside sped by under the weight of thickening, darkening clouds. He couldn't accept what he had read. It had to be some sort of elaborate hoax! But how? There it was in black and beige: an early manuscript contradicting the established apostolic witness, upon which the Church and the Christian faith was built. It all appeared legit. The demonstration certainly proved the tech genuine. And he would eventually be called on to authenticate the manuscript. What else could he do, but concede?

He sighed. This was a big mistake.

He cursed himself again for his outburst. Again, his flaws anger and pride taking the lead in his effort to defend his faith, where love and logic would be far more effective. And Christ-like.

The countryside slowly transformed over the past thirty minutes to small homes, and then to larger buildings, all bearing the faded look of time gone by. After the argument and the revelation, he needed a place to go process the implications of the restored manuscript and translation, clear his head, and re-center himself.

And he knew just the place to go.

The taxi made a sharp turn, swinging the car around in front of a tall, stone wall aged a golden brown with a wrought-iron gate that stood half open. He paid the man a wad of American dollar bills and exited the vehicle. The man gave him his card with a mobile number on it if he was in need of any more rides requiring large amounts of American cash. Not likely, but he nodded at the man and stuffed the card in his wallet.

He glanced around the neighborhood as he walked on the cobblestone road toward the gate, noting the trendy, modern eateries and clubs and multi-story apartments and hotels that surrounded the ancient church. Known as Chiesetta di Santa Maria in Cappella in the Trastevere district, a medieval warren of cobbled lanes near the banks of the Tiber River, the sacred space is an eleventh-century hospice church, that was recently heavily restored after being closed for several years from structural issues. During the renovations, something remarkable was discovered only several months ago: upon removal of a slab of marble near the medieval altar, a set of Roman-era clay pots were discovered. Inscriptions on the lids indicated inside were the bone fragments of not only three early popes—Cornelius, Callixtus, and Felix—but also of four early Christian martyrs. One pot, in particular, had caused quite a stir: it held bone relics of the one regarded by many to be the first Pope, with an inscription of Saint Peter himself.

After the remains were handed over to the Vatican for further study, the fragments underwent a detailed examination that included a DNA comparison between the newly-discovered bones and those of Peter's kept by the Vatican in internment. Rumors had swirled for centuries of the presence of an apostolic relic and early popes, stemming from a stone inscription within the church indicating its possession. One story told of Pope Urban II transferring the bones to the church that was closely linked with his ministry during a time of schism within the Church, believing it was a secure place to hide the relics bearing the memory of the earliest disciple of Christ. After the Vatican confirmed the serious possibility of their authenticity, they had been on display for veneration for the memory they bore of God's grace.

Silas was happy to discover the renewed life given to the small chapel compared to the decrepit state he found it in when he first visited a decade ago. He had discovered the off-the-beaten-path chapel while on pilgrimage circling the globe during a military leave. A few months after he had made a confession of faith at the ecumenical military service on base, he wanted to set out and tour the holy sites to give meaning to the faith he had grown up with, but left behind. Of course, Jerusalem was high on the list, as was Rome. While he visited St. Peter's Basilica, his tour guide recommended he visit the small chapel originally built in the late 11th century. He took him up on the advice and fell in love.

He walked through the small, cobblestone courtyard slick from an increasing morning drizzle overrun with a patchwork of green moss and approached the plain-spoken, brown, wooden doors. A Vespa and a few bicycles laid parked against the rough, gray-brown walls marked by a millennium of nasty weather, which meant he would be joined by a few faithful souls for the afternoon service, as well as any tourists who had happened by the modest church. Above the door was carved a portrait of the Madonna holding the Christ child, flanked on the side by two golden trees. He crossed himself and entered.

The door sighed as he opened it. He stepped inside, his senses being flooded with the sacred scent of spicy incense and musty age as a testament to the ten centuries of fellow believers who held court in the chapel, worshiping and petitioning and learning about their risen savior, Jesus Christ. The rectangular space inside was small and intimate, the way a church should be Silas reckoned. Rough-hewn boards creaked under his feet as he made his way inside the single-room nave supported by stone columns that had seen better days. The ceiling rose two stories, supported by wooden rafters and lined by eight tiny windows struggling to offer the sacred space enough light. Small, brass chandeliers between the stone columns and candelabras at the front did most of the heavy lifting, offering the worshipers the light to worship. A life-size statue of Mary stood atop a stone pillar at the front looking down at a small, stone altar with a golden cross and a set of candles, welcoming all who desired to taste and see that the Lord is good. And standing next to the altar was another stout pillar with a silvery reliquary housing the recently discovered bones of the apostle Peter himself.

A few of the two dozen or so heads turned as Silas took a seat in one of the wooden chairs near the back. An older woman with a tanned, tired face nestled within a lace shawl sitting in front of him offered a warm welcome. He smiled back and settled in for the service, then scanned the rest of the room. A young family, mother and father with a young son and baby daughter sat near him on the other side of the aisle; in front of them was a pair of young men, probably brothers; two couples sat in the row in front of them, one looked to be in their twenties, the other in their sixties; and back to his side of the aisle was another family of five with varying ages and a smattering of single men and women

A small man with a crown of silver-white hair hunched over a cane as he walked to a mahogany pulpit. He greeted the assembled faithful ones "in nomine Patris et Filii et Spiritus Sancti." *In the name of the Father and the Son and the Holy Spirit.* The small group replied "Amen" in unison. It was the only part of the service Silas understood, for the priest conducted it entirely in Latin.

He folded his arms and reclined in his chair, letting his mind wander and consider the implications of the Gospel of Judas and the day's revelations, if they could be believed. He understood why he was so unsettled by the revelations: it denied this memory, transformed the apostolic witness into a fable and raised up the account in Judas's Gospel offered as the true witness to Jesus' life and work. For centuries, the Church had understood that the climax of Jesus' life and essence of his work was his death on the cross for the sins of the world, and resurrection from the dead to put it back together again with new life. Yet what had been revealed in the Gospel of Judas denied this fundamental teaching of the faith. More than that: it called into question the faithful apostolic witness, the memory borne by the very bones encased in the modest silver urn up front.

After finishing his homily, the priest walked to the altar and began consecrating the bread and wine of the Eucharist to celebrate the memory of Jesus' death on the cross, his sacrifice as payment for the sins of the world. Silas watched the man as he raised the unleavened crackers and prayed. He did the same with the chalice of wine. He smiled at the memory of a verse from John: *"Those who eat my flesh and drink my blood have eternal life, and I will raise them up on the last day."* Amen.

The priest finished consecrating the elements and raised his arms for the modest congregation to stand and experience the body and blood of Christ themselves by walking toward the front at the altar to partake of the Eucharist. Most of the small group stood at the invitation and exited their rows, forming a small queue toward the front. The young family across the aisle didn't, neither did the brothers in front of them. Silas offered a hand to help his new, older friend navigate the aisle. She took it and offered a word of thanks in Italian. He imagined this was her personal church, having attended Mass and worshiped here since a little girl, not like him and the other tourists who only came to sample the spiritual goods like an amusement park. As he walked forward he smiled at the thought of hundreds, perhaps thousands of believers doing what he himself and the other faithful brothers and sisters in the faith were doing in that moment: bearing witness to the memory of Christ's crucifixion. Because as the apostle Paul taught, "For as often as you eat this bread and drink the cup, you proclaim the Lord's death until he comes."

When the older woman had finished receiving communion, Silas went to the altar, knelt before the priest, and cupped his hand, understanding that in that moment he was taking his turn among the cloud of witnesses, stretching back to the apostles, to keep the memory of Christ crucified alive.

As the priest handed him the wafer, he was flooded with resolve to preserve and contend for that memory.

He also heard the distinct sound of a weapon chambering a round. Then felt cold steel press into the back of his neck. A voice behind him ordered him to do something. It was in German, but he could guess from the tone.

Not again. This is getting annoying.

Silas put the wafer of Christ's body in his mouth, said a quick prayer of thanksgiving while chewing it, then swallowed and said another prayer for guidance and resolve. He put his hands behind his head and slowly stood. The priest had retreated behind the stone altar and was hunched over, averting his eyes from the invasion of his sacred space.

He turned around to face his attacker, who was standing a foot away with a gun aimed at his face. It was one of the men seated across the aisle, one of the brothers. The other man was standing at the back, having barricaded the door. Silas stood feet planted apart, staring down his attacker.

And that's when he saw it: the crooked nose and the tattoo. Like the man from Chicago who got away with Thaddeus' forearm.

Silas clenched his jaw and narrowed his eyes. "We meet again."

The man shook his head, seeming not to remember their encounter. He said in a thick, German accent, "Hand me that silver reliquary, and we will be on our way."

He glanced at the silver vessel to his right. *Over my dead body.*

In one swift movement, Silas leaned to the left. As he brought his right hand out from behind his head, the weapon exploded on cue, shattering the ancient stone behind him. He grabbed the gun by the neck and ripped it from the man's hands, then shoved the palm of his left hand into the man's crooked nose. He stumbled backward and landed hard on the wooden floor as a geyser of blood poured down the front of his face.

Silas quickly trained the weapon on the man, but he was outnumbered. And outmaneuvered.

As suddenly as Silas moved on his attacker, the second man moved for leverage of his own. "Drop it!" he shouted in the same German accent. Silas lifted his head to see the friendly woman who greeted him with a barrel of cold steel pressed against her temple.

He shouted again, "Do it now, or I swear to you I will blow off this woman's head!"

The woman screamed and whimpered incoherent Italian, her face twisting with fright beneath the lace shawl. The others had quickly flattened themselves against the ground, trying to find relief from the chaos and violence, joining the woman with a chorus of sobs and shouts for release.

"Silence," the man Silas had hit shouted. He stood holding his nose, then wiped his bloody hand on his pants. He pointed to Silas. "You. You were the fool who I fought in the street in Chicago."

"That would be the one," Silas said, still training the weapon at the man's face, returning the compliment from before.

"I will forgive you of your first and second indiscretion," he growled, "if you lower your weapon and hand me the silver reliquary."

"Not a chance, partner." He flexed his fingers and tightened his grip.

The man stepped forward. "You are outnumbered, and my

partner will not think twice to kill that woman, and continue down the line until either you or he is dead."

Silas glanced at the man in the back who was still holding the frightened older woman, arm around her neck and gun pressed at the temple. When he did, the man tightened his hold on the woman and lifted her tiny, plump frame off the ground. She writhed and moaned for air. Silas shouted and stepped forward waving the gun toward the man in the back. He only tightened his menacing stranglehold on the woman.

The military had taught him to execute with precision and plow forward with courage and determination. But it also taught him when to retreat, when he had been beaten.

This was one of those times.

"Fine," Silas growled. He backed up and inched toward the sacred relic, weapon still trained forward. He grabbed it and walked forward to hand it to the man. But he hesitated. "This ain't over," he growled still clenching the silver jar. "Not by a long shot."

The man's eyes narrowed, and one end of his mouth curled upward. "We'll see about that." He yanked the silver object, then turned and left, ignoring the gun still aimed at the back of his head. Then he burst through the front doors along with his fellow Nous agent.

Silas mumbled a curse at the loss, then looked around sharply remembering where he was. People started picking themselves off the wooden floor. A few of the women went to comfort the older lady. He turned around and saw the bullet that nearly struck his head slammed into Mother Mary and splintered off a chunk of the statue. He shook his head, then noticed the chalice had overturned on the floor, its wine soaking the floorboards. Resting next to it was a pale, wrinkled hand.

The priest!

He hustled to the man who was splayed out on the floor, his vestments a messy pile, and turning crimson. He knelt beside the man and checked for a pulse, but already knew the answer. Nothing. The bullet must have struck him after it struck the statue.

Silas cursed again, this time more loudly. And this time he didn't care if anyone heard or that he was in a church. The space had already been defiled by violence, cursing wouldn't change that.

And Nous would pay.

CHAPTER 12

Silas was enraged and breathing hard as he hustled down the Roman street, the distant sound of the gendarmerie police compelling him to keep moving. When the men left, he wasted no time following them, but they were gone, the whine of an engine in hot retreat ticking Silas off. He followed their lead, not wanting to get sidetracked by several hours of interviews and follow-up by the police.

The soft drizzle from earlier had given way to a biting wind and bitter rain. The drops slapped against Silas's face as he blindly navigated the streets of pale-gray, mismatched, uneven cobblestone. He hurried past a bar that was beginning to spring to life, in the direction of anywhere but the Basilica of Saint Mary Major. A seafood restaurant beckoned him inside to dry off and fill his belly with whatever it was that smelled of heaven, but he had to press onward.

What a royal screw up, Grey!

There was a day when he would have picked out the two men as potential danger in a heartbeat and prepared to do something about it. What's worse, there was a day when two terrorists would have been no match for Sergeant Grey, no matter how well-armed they were. Not only had he failed to assess the situation before it all went down. He had surrendered to their demands and caused the death of others.

I will always endeavor to uphold the prestige, honor, and high esprit de corps of the Rangers, went the Ranger Creed. But here's the kicker: *Surrender is not a Ranger word.*

Major fail all around.

He continued the self-flagellation as he walked with head down trying to negotiate his phone. The rain didn't help matters. It had happened again; another apostle relic had been stolen out from under him. And SEPIO needed to know, ASAP. Because clearly something big was going down!

He finally managed to dial Radcliffe. It rang and rang some more. Then went to voice mail.

He mumbled a curse as he ended the call, rainwater running down his face as he reached the end of the road near a retaining wall canopied by large, leafy trees along the Tiber. Lightning flickered across the river behind a set of nineteenth-century high rises. An echo of thunder sounded in the distance a few seconds later.

Silas stood under one of the trees for relief from the rain, looking to the right and to the left, gripping his phone as he decided which way to go. The sudden emergence of a jet-black Italian police car to the left sounding the alarm and raising its blue lights made his decision for him. He quickly pivoted to the right, head down, and started off along the river toward a bridge that would take him further away from the terrorism.

The sound of the Carabinieri faded as he turned to cross the River Tiber. He brought out his phone again, praying he would reach Radcliffe to give SEPIO the heads up.

His finger slipped as the rain continued. He huffed and used the underside of this shirt to dry the phone, then tried again. This time he was able to dial the number. He waited as it rang.

"Ahh, Silas, my boy. Finally come around to—"

"It's happened again!"

"What? What happened again?"

"Another terrorist attack. Another apostle relic."

"Hold on..."

Silas heard static and a loud bang, then a rustling. "Hello?"

Three successive beeps told him the call was lost. He cursed as he reached the other side of the river, growing cold and wishing for relief from the relentless rain. He saw an awning over a set of shops a block away and ran for it. His phone buzzed with an incoming call.

"Yeah."

"Sorry about that," Radcliffe said. "Celeste is here with me on speaker. Now, what were you saying?"

"I said, it's happened again. There was gunfire. A priest was shot. An older lady was taken hostage and nearly lost her life—"

"Slow down, Silas," Celeste said interrupting. "Where are you? What happened?"

"Santa Maria in Cappella, Rome. And Nous agents just swiped Peter's bones, that's what's happened!"

"What?" Radcliffe exclaimed. "But the bones of Saint Peter are interred in Saint Peter's Basilica in the Vatican!"

Silas reminded Radcliffe and Celeste of the recent discoveries during the renovations of Santa Maria. "Clearly, this takes the recent relic thefts to a whole new level."

"I'd say!" Radcliffe said.

Celeste added, "Especially since two more had been stolen in much the same way since we last talked. The apostles John and Matthew."

Silas said, "So Jude Thaddeus, James the Lesser and Philip, John and Matthew, and now Peter?"

"Right," she said. "Six relics. Some of the most important to the memory of the Christian faith."

"And six apostles..."

"That's true," Radcliffe said, sounding like he had a revelation. "Do you think that's the real design here?"

Silas shook his head, pacing now underneath the awning. "I don't know what I think. All I know is, this latest attack combined with the one in Chicago and the weirdness I've witnessed at the Aeon Foundation is making for a bad novel."

"Weirdness?" Celeste said. "What do you mean?"

He stopped and leaned against a shop wall. "I mean, it's like something Steven Spielberg scripted. The thing looks like a spaceship, the inside is some Burning Man nature festival, everyone's running around wearing the same white-linen frock costumes, and the inside of the courtyard looks like Whole Foods is paying them rent. It's almost like they're doomsday preppers getting ready for the apocalypse. That's the vibe I get anyway. Almost cultish. And get this: there are some weird berries being grown dead-center of the compound. Made my lips tingle and head go light."

"Always something," a voice grumbled on the other line.

Silas snapped his head up and smiled. "Is that you, Gapinski?"

"The one and only."

"Didn't know you were on the call. Nice to hear another friendly voice."

"Just walked in to see what all the fuss was about. Figured Silas Grey was somewhere to be found in it all."

Silas laughed. "You thought right."

"Excuse me, Silas," Radcliffe said. "Did you say ... cultish?"

"Yeah, I mean there's this cult-like vibe. But I was mostly kidding."

"Well, there may be something to that. Be a good lad and hold on a second..." He could hear shuffling. A few minutes of silence ticked by on the other end, then "Ahh, here it is" echoed over the speakerphone. More shuffling and what sounded like pages turning before Radcliffe came back on the line. "Are you familiar with the Cain cult of the second century?"

Silas tilted his head, narrowed his eyes, and furrowed his brow. "No...Can't say that I am."

"Take a listen." Radcliffe cleared his throat, then read: "'*Others again declare that Cain derived his being from the Power above. They declare that Judas the traitor was thoroughly acquainted with these things, and that he alone, knowing the truth as no others did, accomplished the mystery of the betrayal; by him all things, both earthly and heavenly, were thus thrown into confusion. They produce a fictitious history of this kind, which they style the Gospel of Judas.*'"

"Is that Irenaeus?" Silas asked.

"Precisely. Not only does it contain one of the only historical references to the Judas Gospel. It also connects the disciple with the sect of Cain."

"Cain?" Gapinski said. "As in the Cain-and-Abel, WWE head-to-head from Genesis?"

Radcliffe chuckled. "That would be the one."

"Excuse me, but what is this sect?" Celeste asked.

"The Cainites were a Gnostic cult who had understood themselves to be related to Cain, seeing themselves standing in a long line of those opposed to the god of the Jews, whom they believed to be a lesser god who had created this fallen world. Irenaeus staunchly opposed them because of the threat they posed to the Christian faith, as did other early Church fathers like Tertullian. And here he links them not only to Judas, but also the Gospel of Judas, having it in their possession and blaming them for its composition."

Silas considered this, then asked, "What does this have to do with the Aeon Foundation?"

"I'm not sure, really. But given their interest in the Judas Gospel and your mention of the cultishness of the place, I'd keep your eyes open and your wits about you if I were you."

Silas smiled. "Will do."

"Was there anything else?" Celeste asked.

"Yes, actually. I also overheard the head of security mention some interesting things in a conversation. Does the name *Borg* mean anything to you?"

Radcliffe said, "Borg? I'm not sure I've heard that name. What about you, Celeste?"

"Can't say that I have."

"Sounds like something I read in a Star Trek novel," Gapinski added.

Silas said, "Denton had mentioned it earlier when I first came to the compound. Used it to get me through security. Then this guy Chief Schmidt said the man had personally approved my being brought on board, something called Project 13."

"Interesting. Project 13, you say?" Radcliffe asked.

"Yes. Does it mean anything to you?"

Celeste answered, "We had received reports of some chatter surrounding the name from a few of our sources several weeks back. Never meant anything. Until now."

"I imagine it must relate to the Gospel of Judas somehow... and the Order."

"The Order?" Radcliffe asked. "How so?"

"Schmidt said something to the other man about having to consider the Order, and about SEPIO not being a bother. But, unfortunately, I couldn't hear the entire conversation."

"SEPIO?" Celeste said with surprise. "He said SEPIO?"

"Yes. Both the Order and SEPIO, by name."

Radcliffe hummed thoughtfully.

Celeste said, "That strikes me as most concerning. The Order is certainly engaged with the wider public. But SEPIO as an entity is not known widely outside our circles. I would advise you to proceed with caution, Silas."

He smiled at the concern. "Yes, dear."

"I'm serious! Given the five terrorist events that have taken place over the past few days, the increased chatter from our agents in the field, the combustible nature of the manuscript research with the Gospel of Judas, and now the makings of a possible link to a second-century cult ... there are plenty of red flags."

Radcliffe said, "Silas, I'm sending to your phone the coordinates of one of our safe houses in the city. And then I'm sending you Celeste and Matt Gapinski. Wait for them there and coordinate a response—"

"Sorry," he interrupted, "no can do. I'm knee-deep in the Gospel of Judas research, and something is seriously going on with that and the so-called foundation that's sponsored it." He caught them up on what they had uncovered and expressed some of his own reservations about the manuscript.

"Professor, I appreciate the urgency of the Gospel of Judas, but the relics containing the memory of the faith are at stake!"

Silas sighed. "And I understand the urgency of their protection and recovery. But something's going on at Aeon, and something bigger is going on with Denton and the Gospel of Judas manuscript."

"Come on, man," Gapinski added, "who knows what you might find at that compound? Could be some little green men growing in the basement or being autopsied, X-Files-style. You don't need that in your life."

Silas chuckled. "Thanks for the concern, Gapinski, but until I know more about what's really going on at the foundation and with the Gospel, you'll need to consider me a sideline participant."

Radcliffe huffed on the other end. Celeste continued the conversation: "Gapinski and I are still going to come your way."

"Fine," Silas said, renewing his pacing.

"Don't sound so excited, professor."

"Sorry. I think that's a good idea. And frankly, I may need your help with whatever is going on at the Aeon Foundation."

"We've got your back."

He smiled. "And I've got yours. I promise to meet up with you two soon and sort this relic mess out."

Radcliffe relented and wished Silas Godspeed as they hung up. Silas managed to flag down a taxi. He gave him the address, then handed him a wad of cash and told him to drive pronto. The man smiled and nodded, then threw the car into gear and sped off north and out of the city.

Time to get to the bottom of what was going on.

CHAPTER 13

The relentless rain and thick storm clouds had given way to blue skies and sunshine as Silas made his way out of Rome and back to the compound. After a swift, uneventful ride, the cabby stopped at the gate outside the Aeon Foundation and Silas got out. He threw a few extra twenty-dollar bills at the man, who gave several enthusiastic "Grazie!" replies to his generosity. He approached a security camera with his badge outstretched as the car sped away. The camera turned toward him and seemed to be considering whether or not he was legitimate. A few seconds ticked by and the gate began to swing inward.

He hustled up the long driveway, his boots crunching on the small pebbles as he approached a set of tall, curved-glass doors that served as the main entrance. Inside he could see the veritable forest he had walked through the night before. But as he approached the doors, it seemed like the inside was missing the hustle-and-bustle he had witnessed the day before.

The familiar security pad stood guard outside the massive, glass entryway. Just beyond was a guard station, where a large man sat staring at him through the glass wall. He pressed his hand against the pad and waited for it to allow his entrance as it pulsed from blue to green.

Except an angry red was returned along with an even angrier short buzz signaling his denial.

The large man inside snapped his head from Silas to his monitor, where he leaned forward and furrowed his brow in concentration.

Just great.

Silas huffed and wiped his hands on his jeans, then tried again.

Pulsing blue. Pulsing blue. Then angry red and song of denial.

This time the large man lifted himself out from his perch and sauntered over to the double doors. He pointed at Silas and motioned for him to join him at the door. They remained closed as the two approached each other through the thick glass.

"State your business," the man said, his command muffled and accented by gruff Italian.

Silas pressed his ID badge against the slightly curved, slightly blue surface. "I'm a credentialed researcher here on an urgent matter of great archaeological and scientific importance." He hoped the over-the-top description would act as a magical command of passage.

The man's twisted face cast doubts on the ploy. He leaned in close to inspect the badge. He made a face and shook his head. He said, "Then why you denied entrance?"

Silas huffed and waved his arms. "I don't know. Eli Denton is the supervising researcher." Then he remembered the name Denton had used, and Chief Schmidt had mentioned earlier: "And Borg personally arranged for my credentials."

The mention of the name seemed to shift the moment entirely. The man stood straighter, his face softened, his eyes widened slightly. He licked his lips and said, "Borg, you say?"

Silas nodded.

The face of consternation and irritation returned. "Wait here."

The man sauntered back over to his command post, then picked up the phone. Silas couldn't hear or make out what he was saying, but understood it to be rapid, angry Italian directed at some unfortunate soul. Then he slammed down the receiver and sank back down in his chair.

What the heck?

Silas put his hands on his hips, then folded his arms and began pacing in front of the entryway. A minute later he could see Denton jogging from the bay of elevators toward the security desk. He started speaking in rapid Italian himself, while the large security man waved his arms and talked back. He heard the name *Borg* again, as well as *Area 4* and *Project 13*. He was considering these words when Denton suddenly broke off from the conversation and walked toward the entrance. The doors *swooshed* open, and he motioned for Silas to follow him.

Denton put his finger to his lips, motioning for him not to say a word. He led them in silence toward the elevators. As they walked, Silas noted the striking difference from the day and night before: it wasn't just that it was missing the hustle-and-bustle; it was missing people, period.

What was even odder was what he saw as he looked through the double-doors of glass that stood opposite from the entrance into the courtyard.

It looked like harvest time.

Silas broke away from Denton and eased himself toward the entrance for a better view. He heard Denton curse and whisper loudly after him, but he ignored the call and kept moving toward the doors.

Much of the greenery and multi-colored fruits and vegetables were just gone. Trees had been stripped bare, the ground cleared of vegetation. The corn had been plucked, the wheat had been sliced down to the ground like a big combine had raked them bare. All that stood was the patch of mystery berries at the center of the courtyard. The rest had been harvested clean.

Silas felt his arm being yanked sideways. "Come on!" Denton growled in frustration.

"Where is everyone? It's like a ghost town here."

"Not another word..." Denton's eyes were wide, and they meant business. He pulled again on Silas's arm. This time he relented walking with him back to the elevators. The security man stood and eyed them suspiciously. Denton nodded toward him, Silas did not.

Brushed-metal doors opened, then closed behind them.

"Where the bloody hell have you been?" Denton growled as they ascended, getting in his face.

Surprised, Silas backed up slightly. "I took a stroll into the city."

"To do what?"

"To get out away from the crazy and think and pray about what the heck is going on here."

"What's that supposed to mean?"

"This. All of this," Silas said waving his arms. "The Gospel of Judas. The cultish spaceship compound. The lemmings downstairs dressed in white, wherever the heck they wandered off to. The doomsday garden in the center, what's left of it anyway. What the heck happened to the garden? And where the heck are all the white lemmings?"

The doors to the elevator opened. Denton went to leave, but this time Silas grabbed his arm and yanked him back inside.

"What the—"

"We need to talk," Silas growled as he closed the doors and hit the 'STOP' button.

"About what?"

"About this here foundation, Aeon. You've been pretty coy about the whole thing and given it seems the doomsday preppers seem to have gone into hiding, I think it's time you fill in the blanks for me."

Denton sighed, folded his arms, and leaned against the carriage wall. "What do you want to know?"

"For starters, who are these people?"

"I already told you, the Aeon Foundation."

"Got that. But like I said, fill in the blanks. You could start with how you got involved with them in the first place."

"They called me up out of the blue one day, said they had been following my work in early Christianity and wanted to fund a massive project that would restart work on one of the most significant archaeological finds of the twenty-first century. It was all hush-hush, but naturally I was intrigued. They flew me out and described the scope of the project, and I was hooked."

"But again, who is *they*?"

"Dunno. Some group that funds projects expanding the horizons of human potential and enlightenment, drawing on multidisciplinary fields of science and mysticism and philosophy, all to help humanity transcend the current state of things and move beyond into the immortal, eternal realm."

Sounded like the perfect sales pitch from someone a little more familiar than just an out-of-the-blue phone call. He kept probing for more.

"And, what, you just signed up, sight unseen?"

"Of course not!" he exclaimed. "I'll have you know, a very nice German gentleman by the name of Rudolf Bo—" He stopped short, as if his judgment had lapsed, revealing something he wasn't supposed to.

"Borg? Is that what you were going to say? Rudolph Borg? Because you used him as leverage with that Chief Schmidt fellow at the guard station just outside Area 4 when I arrived. And then it sounded like you did again downstairs."

His eyes shifted, and he cleared his throat. "Yes, well. Never mind. It isn't important. What's fact is that I thoroughly vetted the organization and found them completely on the up-and-up, and more than in line with my own interests and professional goals of serving humanity by bringing about a transcendent awakening through enlightenment."

Spoken like a true, modern New-Age prophet.

He continued: "They are particularly interested in resurrecting the ancient, early Christian manuscripts that tell an alternative story to the officially sanctioned one which was suppressed by the majority who reigned in power, thanks to Emperor Constantine."

Silas scoffed. "The alternative story told in the so-called Gnostic Gospels, you mean? The ones the majority of the Church rejected not because they won some sort of power play, but because the story they told was anti-Jewish; denied the fundamental story of the Old Testament, with all of its promises for God to rescue and restore the world; and denigrated the very good creation that God still cherishes—you mean that story?"

Denton folded his arms, narrowed his eyes, and threw back his head. "Look, I don't need this. I brought you on board out of the goodness of my heart because I thought my old military mate might take a fancy getting in on the ground level of breaking research into the faith he swears by, and the academic career he lives by. So, if you don't mind, we've got work to do." Denton slammed his hand against the 'STOP' button to re-open the doors. When they did, he rushed out and walked to the guard station, where he promptly put his palm on the security device. Within seconds it pulsed green, and the door opened.

"He's with me," he growled at the security guard, who grunted in approval. The two walked through, and the door shut securely behind them.

Denton stopped and sighed. "Look, I don't want to fight. Let's just get on with it. Truce?" He held out his hand.

Silas took it, smiled, and nodded.

Denton continued onward. "Well, at least you survived. Doesn't look like the ordeal messed you up too terribly."

Silas stopped short and furrowed his brow. "Wait a minute. What are you talking about?"

Denton stopped and turned around. "The city. The terrorist attack. Had to have been a dreadful ordeal."

He shook his head. "How did you know about that? I didn't mention it."

Silas thought he glimpsed a look of panic in the man's eyes, but it was a fleeting moment. "It's been all over the news. The hostages at the church, the relic theft, the murdered priest. Making for quite the cable-news moment, I reckon."

"Yeah, but I didn't say anything about being anywhere close to the church, let alone in the church."

"What is this, mate? Bloody twenty questions? I knew you loved Santa Maria from back in the day when you went on your pilgrimage during service. Figured if there was one place you'd go to think and pray, as you put it, that would be the place. Am I wrong?"

Silas considered this, then shook his head. "No, you're not."

"There you go." He turned, walking further down the hallway toward the research room. He stopped and engaged the security pad with his palm again, the door unlocked and he entered. "You coming or what?"

Silas said nothing, unnerved by Denton's knowledge of his whereabouts. He let it go, but he was going to have to keep a closer eye on his old mate.

Time to get back to work.

CHAPTER 14

The door shut behind him as Silas walked through the research room. Sebastian was clicking away on his keyboard, and Denton was rummaging through the cupboards in the kitchenette.

"Where did you run off to?" Sebastian asked without taking his eyes off his monitor.

"Out," he simply said.

"There. Got you," Denton said in victory.

Silas looked over to the kitchenette, finding his war buddy pouring something into two tumblers.

He walked over grinning, his mood transforming from the surly, belligerent man in the hallway to the fun-loving guy he knew in Iraq.

"I heard whispers of a bottle of 1972 Balvenie scotch leftover from the previous research party that occupied this room." He handed Silas a tumbler of the caramel liquid. "Neat if I remember, correct?"

Silas took it and nodded. "That you are."

"Where's my glass?" Sebastian complained.

"Sorry, drained the bottle. I took you for a wine snob, anyway. Not a scotch connoisseur like your brother, here."

He huffed and went back to his monitor.

Denton raised his glass. "Cheers to academic inquiry. Wherever it may lead."

Silas held his gaze, narrowing his eyes briefly as he tried to get a read on a look of mischievousness that had overtaken his face. He allowed the end of his mouth to curl upward, then nodded and clinked his glass.

"Indeed."

They each took a mouthful. Silas savored the heavy liquid, tasting of orange peel and oaky spice. Then he swallowed it, the long, sweet-and-spicy finish warming his belly as it hit his empty stomach.

Denton closed his eyes and sighed with pleasure. "Right. Let's get back to it, shall we?" He sat next to Sebastian who was bringing up an image.

"What's this?" Silas asked, taking his seat on the other side of his brother. Sebastian handed him and Denton their tablets, mirroring what he had brought up.

Denton said, "One of the things I have always found interesting since the early part I played in translating the Gospel of Judas is its depiction of the disciples and so-called historic Christian orthodoxy."

Silas frowned. "How so?"

He pointed to an image on the monitor. "I had Sebastian bring up one of the folios. Now, this isn't a restored rendering, but one of the intact originals. But look at what Jesus says to Judas."

Silas looked at the manuscript page and translated:

Step away from the others and I shall tell you the mysteries of the kingdom. It is possible for you to reach it, but you will grieve a great deal. For someone else will replace you, in order that the twelve may again come to completion with their god.

"Notice how Jesus separates Judas from the other twelve. And did you catch the clear, prescient reference to his replacing in the book of Acts?"

He did. He recalled the episode from the New Testament book, where the remaining eleven disciples chose Judas' replacement after he hung himself by casting lots between to proposed candidates: *Joseph called Barsabbas, who was also known as Justus, and Matthias. Then they prayed and said, "Lord, you know everyone's heart. Show us which one of these two you have chosen to take the place in this ministry and apostleship from which Judas turned aside to go to his own place." And they cast lots for them, and the lot fell on Matthias; and he was added to the eleven apostles.*

Denton said, "I think it is fascinating that the Gospel of Judas would portend his demise."

"Or, fascinating the author of the Gospel wrote it back into the posthumous piece of second-century writing," Silas retorted.

"Touché. The point is that Jesus sets Judas apart from the twelve. And then elsewhere, Jesus basically says that Judas stands outside the twelve, he transcends them. In folio forty-five, Judas has a vision of the twelve stoning and persecuting him. So he is harshly opposed by the others—"

"Obviously, given his betrayal," Silas interrupted. "It's nothing more than a reflection backwards on the historical events of his handing Jesus over to the high priests for crucifixion!"

Denton smiled. "Betrayal ... we'll go back to that. But keep in mind that elsewhere Jesus calls him the 'thirteenth spirit,' and then look, here. Sebastian, go to folio forty-six and forty-seven."

He did, and Silas translated silently from his tablet.

"You will become the thirteenth, and you will be cursed by the other generations—and you will come to rule over them. In the last days they will curse your ascent to the holy generation."

Thirteenth. Silas's mind jumped to what he had heard earlier from Schmidt, about Project 13. So that's it, then.

"There it is again. *You will become the thirteenth.* Judas is truly the thirteenth apostle because he stands outside the twelve, above and beyond them. Transcending them and their narrow ideology. He is portrayed as the one who truly understands Jesus, who he is and what he came to do." He instructed Sebastian to go to folio thirty-five. He did, and Denton read: "'*I know who you are and where you have come from. You are from the immortal realm of Barbelo. And I am not worthy to utter the name of the one who has sent you.*' There it is, his central confession."

"What's your point?"

Denton leaned forward toward Silas. "Judas is the only one of the twelve who truly knows Jesus. And earlier Jesus said that all the disciples had '*planted trees without fruit, in my name, in a shameful manner*' and '*The cattle you have seen brought for sacrifice are the many people you lead astray before that altar.*' He was interpreting a dream the Twelve had, and unlike Judas, he condemns them and all of the historic Church they led astray. It's all right there!"

Silas sat back and said nothing, his mind reeling from the revelation. He was also getting agitated. "This is all fascinating, but what does any of this have to do with Judas?"

He grinned and nodded to Sebastian. "Well, that brings us to another larger portion that was restored. Go ahead, bring it up. Again, the rendered restoration is in bold."

Sebastian scrolled over to a set of images, the original and the rendered restoration.

Silas took a breath and looked down at his tablet, wondering what he would find. He saw more of the restored Coptic in bold. He translated quickly:

Truly ***I tell you,*** *your* ***last days will*** *become* ***a beacon of hope***

> ***for all who would follow in your footsteps, sacrificing flesh for spirit, this mortal realm of corruption for the immortal realm above.***
>
> ***Remember,*** *grieve* ***not. For no one puts new wine into old wineskins; or else the new wine will burst the wineskins and be spilled, and the wineskins will be ruined. But new wine must be put into new wineskins, exchanging the flesh of Jesus for the spirit of Christ,*** *since he will be overthrown and destroyed.*

Denton said, "A beacon of hope or enlightenment, isn't that right? And Jesus urges his followers to take after Judas ... And did you catch the reference to the apostle Luke's Gospel? The bit about the old and new wineskins?"

Silas glanced up from the tablet and nodded at Denton. He smiled.

"Word-for-word translation, isn't it?"

Silas said nothing.

"Clearly Gnostic in its interpretation of shedding flesh for spirt. I find the bit about *exchanging the flesh of Jesus for the spirit of Christ* super fascinating, don't you?"

He ignored Denton and kept translating:

> *And then the image of the great generation of Adam will be exalted, for prior to heaven, earth, and the angels, that generation, which is from the eternal realms, exists. Look, you have been told everything. Lift up your eyes and look at the cloud and the light within it and the stars surrounding it. The star that leads the way is your star.*

Silas sighed and put down the tablet. He leaned back in his

chair to contemplate the revelation. Judas was portrayed as the ultimate human being, exalted above all, the one who has received full *gnosis*, full enlightenment from Jesus himself and serving as a guiding star from the rest of humanity who will be saved by transcending this life.

Denton continued. "'*The image of the great generation of Adam will be exalted*, Jesus says. Now, there's one more folio section to translate that I think will put the pieces in place. Go to folio fifty-eight, if you would." Sebastian did. Denton and Silas translated from their tablets in silence, the restored Coptic highlighted in bold.

Judas lifted up his eyes and saw the luminous cloud, and he entered it. Those standing on the ground heard a voice coming from the cloud, saying, ***"Behold, this is the shining star of this*** *great generation* ***who has come to restore*** *the image* ***of this corrupt generation and lead the way beyond the flesh to the immortal realm above. Follow in his footsteps, for he will release the Christ from the bondage of the flesh Jesus, for I bore him from the cursed wood and established him in the dwelling places of his father.***

"Again, there it is!" Denton exclaimed. "Classically Gnostic, but clearly portrayed as almost a scene reminiscent of the New Testament Gospel accounts of Jesus' baptism or upon the mount of transfiguration when the voices bellowed out from the heavens, *This is My beloved Son, in whom I am well pleased*, as Matthew recorded in each instance." Denton sat at the edge of his seat, with a twinkle in his eyes. "But in this case, the voice is speaking of Judas, as this shining star who should be followed. Why?"

He let the question hang like a good preacher. Sebastian looked puzzled. Silas refused to answer.

"Of course, because of what you referenced earlier, Silas."

Silas eyes glanced at him in understanding and frowned.

Denton said, reminding him: "'*But you will exceed all of them,*' Jesus said. '*For you will sacrifice the man that clothes me.*"

"Sacrifice the man that clothes me?" Sebastian said, joining the conversation. "Is that referring to Judas handing Jesus over to the religious authorities in the Garden of Gethsemane?"

"Indeed."

"But then, according to what Jesus says here, that wouldn't make what he did an act of *betrayal* at all, would it? But more like an act of obedience."

Denton laughed and slapped him on the back. "Precisely, mate! His so-called betrayal was indeed an act of obedience. Heroic, even. For Jesus, the kernel of Christ-the-spirit needed to be released from the shell of Jesus-the-flesh, as the voice from heaven declared. So his death was not at all the sacrifice that the Church officials made it out to be. Instead, it was a *liberation*."

Silas continued to stew in his seat, considering the ramifications of what had been revealed through the AI algorithm restorations of the Gospel of Judas.

"Ahh," Sebastian said. "So Judas is a hero for liberating Jesus from the material realm of mortal flesh, paving his return to the spiritual realm."

"Exactly! Which actually makes him the *best* disciple, Jesus' most intimate friend for releasing him from the darkness and chaos of the world. And as the Gospel of Judas ends, he's faithful until the end, after all the twelve have fled and Judas remained. '*He received some money and handed him over to them,*' as the Gospel says. So, you see, fellas, Jesus was saved not *in the flesh* upon the cross, but *from the flesh*. Just as we all are upon death. Death truly is a liberation!"

Denton was looking wistfully into the ceiling, a smile played across his face. Silas wanted to smack it right off, to see this man who had been so passionate about the faith give in to this Gnostic heresy.

"But I don't understand," Sebastian said. "Why was he needing salvation, from the flesh as you say? The Church has taught his flesh is what offered salvation."

"Yes, but as Gnostic Christianity taught, life in the material world is not the real life. This is the corrupt material mortal realm, distinct from the heavenly eternal realm of enlightenment above. And salvation comes at death, precisely when the body gives up its last breath, enabling the soul to escape its entrapment to this dark, desperate, chaotic material prison so that it can return to its true heavenly home."

"But why is that version of Jesus' story more hopeful than the Church's version?" Silas interrupted, sitting up straight and proclaiming his question loudly so that both heads snapped toward him. He didn't let them answer.

"I'll answer it for you. It ain't more hopeful. It's pathetic! In the *real* Gospels, we find a message meant for the whole world—not the super elite few that Gnosticism claims. This message loudly and boldly proclaims a God who created the world on purpose and with purpose and said that it was *good*. All of it, material and immaterial. Which is the exact opposite of the Gnostic myth. And our problem isn't that we are ignorant of the divinity within ourselves, but that we are badly bent and in desperate need of rescue. But the good news is that God didn't just abandon us by sitting up in some lofty realm in outer space to leave us to our own devices, as Gnosticism teaches. Instead, God became one of us. Not the pseudo-human deity who wore the human body like a spacesuit as the Gnostics taught. But a real, live human being, Jesus of Nazareth, who lived this life and understands this life. And because he did, because he does, he died for us. For me, for you two, for the whole world. Not to escape it, but to save it! But more than that: to restore it, to re-create it, to put it back together again to the way that he intended it to be at the beginning. Which the resurrection proves. Jesus came back to life in a real, physical body. He ate fish with his friends and showed them the scars left behind on his hands and feet and side. Which means that Jesus didn't want liberation from the flesh; he was happy to live in a body! And he will be plenty happy to give all of his children brand-spanking new ones someday when he returns to Earth to make all things new. The only logical end for redemption with Gnosticism and the Gospel of Judas is suicide. Which is far from hopeful."

After his little speech, Silas stood, took a deep breath through his nose, and smiled broadly. "Frankly, I don't care what the hell this Gospel says or what you two believe. I'll take the Jesus story given to us by Matthew, Mark, Luke, and John above this pathetic one any day of the week. You can keep your story. I've got mine. And it's fabulous."

Then he walked out of the room, leaving Denton and Sebastian speechless.

CHAPTER 15

Silas paced his room, from the bubbling fountain to the bamboo table to his bed and back again, wearing a triangle pattern into the shaggy, beige rug resting atop the pinewood floorboards. He was grinning wide with satisfaction after his little sermon. He was also breathing hard because the revelations of the Gospel of Judas had shaken him. And the sermonette was his way of reassuring himself that his faith was still genuine, that the story of the New Testament Gospels was real.

He was rewinding the conversations with Denton, and the revelations of the AI algorithm's rendered images through his mind, becoming increasingly agitated at what they suggested. That Jesus was not who the Gospels say he was. That Judas was more than the Gospels say he was. That what Jesus and Judas concocted together was what Gnostic Christianity had taught. And far different than the Church had understood. Which had massive implications for the faith. Because if Jesus' death didn't matter, then humanity was still screwed. What hope did we have in saving ourselves through greater enlightenment? History was clear on the subject, especially recent history: zip, zero, zilch.

He kept pacing, running all that had happened the past few

days through his mind, the broader events beyond the translation work. The terrorism and the apostle relics. The compound and the lemmings dressed in white and weird, white-eyeball berries. Schmidt and all his talk about Borg and Project 13 and the Order.

What was really going on? How did it all connect? Because it seemed more significant than just an ancient manuscript.

What he needed was to get in their rooms, because he suspected their real intentions were hidden away inside. But given their dwellings required the two-factor authentication of their ID badge and palm print, it would be impossible to break inside.

He continued his course, then stopped short at the balcony door on his way to his bed. He glanced outside at the horizon, appreciating the beauty of another flair of burnt oranges and reds pulsing on the horizon before giving way to the deep indigo of night quickly creeping westward.

Unless...

He had an idea.

He opened the door and walked to the frosted-glass barrier between him and his brother's balcony. He stopped and stood still, holding his breath even as he searched for signs of life on the other side.

Nothing but the low hum of the Roman countryside and the hush of the gentle breeze trying to breathe life into the naked trees below.

He shuffled to the railing and craned his head around the end of the barrier that flared outward toward, trying to get a glimpse of the other side. It was of no use. Aeon designed each of the living quarters to prevent prying eyes from violating the privacy of its citizens.

But unbeknownst to Aeon, a barrier had never stopped Silas before. It wouldn't stop him now. He knew he needed to get inside those rooms to see if there was anything that could tell him what the heck was going on here. And what both Denton's and

Sebastian's motivations and larger designs were for the Gospel of Judas.

Because he knew Denton and he definitely knew his brother. Which meant there was more to the story than either were letting on.

He brought out his mobile phone and sent a text to Celeste telling her he planned to enter Sebastian's and Denton's rooms, and to have Zoe Corbino, the SEPIO tech guru, on standby to assist with any technical logistics he might require. A few seconds later, she texted back, *All hands on deck. Ready to help.* He stuffed the phone back inside his pocket and got to work.

The barrier was too high for him to jump and grab the top, and there was no furniture to aide his cause. So he hoisted himself up onto the chest-high railing, its brushed steel holding steady. Without looking down, he faced the flared part of the frosted-glass wall and held firm with both hands, feet positioned one behind the other. The wall was still too high to look over, so he slowly raised his feet onto his tip-toes for a better look. Sebastian's room appeared dark.

Perfect.

Without looking down, Silas took a deep breath and leaned around the flare of the wall to grab the mirror flare on the other side, lifting his right leg as he eased himself forward. After taking hold of it and gripping it firmly, in one motion he swung his right leg around to the railing on the other side, praying that he didn't miss.

He didn't. He gripped the flared glass on both ends with purpose, legs spread eagle with feet firmly planted on both sides, face reflecting softly off the polished, frosted glass between the rooms.

Suddenly, he felt trapped. Like one of those dumbass robbers featured on the '90s show *COPS,* who got stuck in the chimney or basement window trying to ransack unsuspecting suburbanites. And there was Silas, hugging both sides of a glass barrier for dear life, increasingly unsure how he was going to get out of the mess

He told himself not to look down, but he did. The harvested earth five stories below suddenly felt threatening. His heart rate jumped, a jolt of electricity ran down his spine, and his palms started feeling slick with cold sweat.

Not now.

He never knew that acute, severe anxiety ran in his family. His mother's side, apparently. It wasn't until after his experience in Iraq and the accompanying PTSD fallout that nearly wrecked his life that the debilitating demon started chasing his hide. His therapist said it was probably triggered by the death of his buddy, Colton, on a mission in Iraq when their convoy was hit by a roadside bomb, and half of his body ended up on Silas. Episodes were usually triggered by high-stress situations.

Like straddling a glass-wall barrier five stories off the ground.

He closed his eyes and slipped into his coping mechanism, counting backward from 1000: *999, 998, 997, 996...*

He had used it as a game-time ritual in Iraq, but then commandeered it through therapy sessions to help with attacks. He continued breathing in and out. In and out. In and out. His eyes were clenched closed and muscles taut like bungee cords wrapped against that blasted wall.

876, 875, 874, 873...

He kept at his ritual until there was a release, like an old train engine sighing in exhaustion after releasing the pent-up steam. His head stopped swimming, vision stopped undulating, ears stopped ringing, palms stopped sweating.

He sighed in relief as he blinked his eyes open. He saw his reflection in the polished glass and felt his face grow warm and red with shame. He sighed, then clenched his jaw and narrowed his eyes with resolve.

In one motion, he tightened both arms and pushed himself up. He inched his hands toward the middle, then swung his left leg around so that he was sitting on top of the thick barrier, and then jumped down to Sebastian's balcony below.

That was easy.

There was a cough. Silas froze. He glanced inside Sebastian's suite, but it was dark and empty.

He made no movement. A gentle breeze brought welcomed relief as he waited, his skin reacting with goose pimples to the coolness colliding with his sweat. Along with it came the distinct smell of burning tobacco.

The cough returned, louder and hacking, a story or two below.

Silas closed his eyes and sighed. One of the compound lemmings out for a night-time smoke. He eased himself upright, then padded toward the door and carefully slid it open. He slipped inside, but left it open in case he needed a quick escape.

The air was cool, unusually so. It was also dry, as if every drop of humidity had been sucked out of the room. The room was a mirror image of his own: in a corner, the same bubbling fountain sounded forth its soothing melody; off to the right stood a bamboo table set for two; near the center next to the dinner table was a king-size bed, perfectly made to Sebastian's standards; and across from the bed sat a desk made of brushed metal with a laptop, screen propped open. Silas wondered what he would find as he padded toward the desk.

He sat down in front of the laptop and clicked the trackpad to bring it to life. As expected, there was a password lock on the screen. He brought his phone back out and sent a text to Celeste: *Inside Sebastian's room. A laptop. Locked with a password. Assist?*

He leaned back and waited for a reply, mesmerized by the fountain and enjoying the spicy scent of tobacco wafting inside the room. He wondered if that would be a problem later, given that Sebastian was angrily against smoking and would have a conniption if the smell lingered. A return text interrupted his thought: *Zoe here. Set phone to hotspot mode, then let me do my magic.*

Silas smiled and obliged. He set the phone on the desk, and within seconds, the laptop was brought to life. How Silas didn't know or care. Then a status bar appeared at the top of the screen. Looked like the entire contents of Sebastian's computer were being downloaded.

Good girl. Get it all and sort it later.

It looked like the process would take fifteen to twenty minutes, plenty of time for him prowl around his brother's room.

Silas started with the desk drawers. He pulled them out one by one and searched inside. Nothing but some scraps of unused paper and a pen with the Aeon Foundation logo.

He moved on, searching the drawers of a wide, low-sitting dresser. Like the desk, he pulled each out, one by one. He felt slightly guilty going through his brother's things.

Until he found something buried in the back beneath a stack of jeans in the middle drawer.

He fished it out. It was a dark-brown book, heavy and large, filling the entire grip of his opened hand. Along the edge sat several brightly-colored tabs marking pages. He brought it to the desk and turned on a lamp. There was no dust jacket, and the spine was bare, so he opened it up to the title page. Inside he read *The Nag Hammadi Scriptures.*

Silas recoiled away from the book and furrowed his brow in confusion. He knew the book well, but what interest did a physicist and computer scientist have in them?

Found around the same time as the famous Dead Sea Scrolls cache containing fragments and entire books of the Hebrew Scriptures, the Nag Hammadi Scriptures as they had become known were a collection of thirteen bound books containing some fifty-two tractates buried near the Egyptian city of Nag Hammadi. Carbon dating placed them somewhere in the second half of the fourth century. They covered a range of source material from early Christianity, Neoplatonism, and Gnostic thought. It was the latter that especially catapulted the collection to infamy, for the so-called Gnostic "gospels" portrayed Jesus and early Christian teaching in tantalizingly alternative ways to the official, dominant story told by the Church, leading a wide range of people outside the faith to spin yarns of religious conspiracies that suppressed the true, unauthorized version of the faith from getting out. The Gospel of Judas was later added to the collection.

Confused, Silas started flipping to the sections marked using the multi-colored tabs. One was set at *The Gospel of Truth* another at *The Secret Book of John*, as well as *The Gospel of Philip*. In the back, the previous translation of *The Gospel of Judas* was also marked. He went back to one of the tabs marking a specific passage, from *The Gospel of Philip*, and began to read: *There were three structures for sacrifice in Jerusalem. One opened to the west and was called the holy place...*

"Wait a minute..."

He quickly turned to another tab, from *The Secret Book of John*, and scanned the passage: *I am the abundance of light, I am the remembrance of Fullness. I am the light dwelling in light, I am the remembrance of Forethought...*

He slammed the book closed and sat stiffly at the edge of the seat.

"Holy cow..."

That's why those passages in the algorithm's translation had such a familiar ring to them. They were swiped from Gnostic Gospels!

His mind was reeling from the revelation. The repaired and restored sections of the lacunae of the Gospel of Judas were actually plagiarized from Nag Hammadi codices! But how? He saw the algorithm render the images himself.

Unless...

Silas closed his eyes, smiled to himself, chuckled, and shook his head. "Sebastian, gotta give you credit. You had me fooled."

Anger started rising as he considered what his brother had done, how he had pulled the wool over his eyes by faking the missing sections of the manuscript pages using the Gnostic Gospels. He must have programmed the text into the AI algorithm somehow. He was a genius, he had to give him that.

He sat back and folded his arms. That meant the whole project was a fraud. He was an unwitting participant who almost gave his professional imprimatur to one of the greatest hoaxes of Christian research! Right up there with the thoroughly debunked so-called Gospel of Jesus' Wife touted a year ago.

And his own brother was part of it.

His eyes narrowed as he stewed in the implications. He slammed his fist into the palm of his hand. How could he be so stupid! He had had his doubts, but he had bought the lie. Hook, line, and sinker. His faith had even trembled a bit in the face of the revelations. Just think how it would have affected other less-grounded believers.

And he was ready to authentic the blasted thing! Playing a part in it would have ruined him.

He stood and huffed and started pacing the room. Then he stopped, spinning toward the book.

But maybe that was the plan all along. To get a third party, a credentialed, bonafide religious academic, with expertise in early Christianity and in the Coptic language, no less, to vouchsafe the restored missing sections and ambiguous words and sentences. To verify the authenticity of the restoration on the lost Gospel and revelation of Jesus to Judas.

All to cast doubt on the New Testament versions of Jesus' story that the Gospel of Judas contradicted.

"My God..."

A sound from Sebastian's computer drew him back to the task at hand. He walked over to the desk and hunched over the laptop. The download was complete. A text from Zoe on his mobile indicated as much. He texted back and thanked her, then wrote he had found something interesting and he would reconnect with SEPIO after he was finished with Denton's room.

Silas took the hefty, brown book and stuffed it securely back in its hiding place in the middle dresser drawer. Knowing how particular his brother was, he inspected its contents to make sure they were in their same neat-and-tidy arrangement as before. Satisfied, he closed it and examined the desk for the same reason. It was just as he left it. He made one more passing inspection around the room, then walked through the balcony door and closed it behind him

One down, one to go.

CHAPTER 16

The burnt tobacco was stronger now. Whoever it was down below was clearly enjoying a cigar or two. Silas peered over the railing hoping the smoker wasn't standing directly beneath him. That would sure put a dent in his plans. Thankfully, he saw no one.

Another cough startled Silas, and he quickly walked to the barrier dividing Sebastian's and Denton's rooms. He hoisted himself up onto the steel railing as before and began the process of crossing over. He made quick work of the burgling gymnastics, this time refusing to give his brain enough of a chance to put the brakes on his operation.

Within minutes, he had pushed himself up onto the wall and carefully lowered himself onto the floor beneath so as not to draw attention to himself from the smoker below. He padded to the glass balcony door, eased it open, and left it that way again, just in case.

The room looked and felt exactly like Sebastian's: the same feng-shui interior design complemented by chilly, dehumidified, climate-controlled air; same bamboo table and bed and brushed-metal desk arrangement. Although, the room was notably messier than his brothers: the sheets were askew, clothes were draped over the desk chair, Denton's dinner had yet to be cleared from his table.

Silas knew Denton could return any hour or any minute, so he got to work surveying the room. No laptop could be found. He rummaged through his dresser drawers, but came up empty. He put his hands on his hips and sighed, staring around the room. One difference was an armoire near the entrance. He walked to it and opened both doors.

On the bottom was a large, black safe of solid steel, big enough to fit a laptop or set of document folders inside. It was one of the newer digital models that allowed the owner to set their own passcode. The door was slightly ajar, and a message in digital red letters was revolving across the input screen: *Enter Passcode.*

Silas smiled. *Score.* Denton must have closed it in haste, neither checking to make sure it had locked securely nor entering the crucial passcode that made it 'safe' in the first place.

Don't mind if I do.

He opened it. Inside he could see Denton's passport and some local change. There was also a journal, but no laptop.

Golden.

He took out the journal, a jet-black Moleskine, and sat down at the edge of the unmade bed. He peeled off the black banding holding it shut and opened it. The pages were filled with barely legible handwriting in pencil. He took out his phone and began taking pictures as he flipped the pages. Maybe Zoe could use her gadgets to make out what he had written. A few times he had caught clear references to the Gospel of Judas, but it all seemed to be his analysis and interpretation of the original. Although...

In the last half, the penmanship became more legible. It looked like a translation of the Codex Tchacos from the original Coptic. He continued flipping the pages and taking pictures while reading Denton's translation. Every so often he would see a set of brackets, with a word or sentence or two. At several points, there were significant gaps and breaks, probably the large missing sections from the manuscript. But then the translation would pick up again, along with the brackets with words or short phrases and sentences.

"Now, hold on..."

He came to something familiar: *They said, "Master, you are [created from] the son of our god."*

Silas furrowed his brow. He remembered Denton making a big deal about the "created from" algorithm restoration from the small lacunae. How it proved Jesus wasn't "not made" as the Nicene Creed and Church insisted, but instead created from. Interesting.

He picked the journal back up and continued reading his translation. He came to another familiar sentence that had been rendered by the algorithm, with more brackets: *"Truly [I tell you], your [last days will] become [a beacon of hope for all who would follow in your footsteps, sacrificing flesh for spirit, this mortal realm of corruption for the immortal realm above]."*

Again Denton had made a big deal about Jesus urging his followers to take after Judas. The other page carried yet another word-for-word rendering of what had been shone on the workstation in the research room: "[Behold, this is the shining star of this] great generation [who has come to restore the] image [of this corrupt generation and lead the way beyond the flesh to the immortal realm above. Follow in his footsteps, for he will release the Christ from the bondage of the flesh Jesus, {for I bore him from the cursed wood and established him in the dwelling places of his father}]." He noticed braces were embedded this time inside the brackets. What did that mean?

He rested the journal on his lap and considered what he was reading. It was hard to tell how recent the entries were in the journal: whether it was penciled in before or after the algorithm rendered its image restoration of the Tchacos Codex. Perhaps he recorded what it rendered. Or...

Maybe he wrote it beforehand!

Silas considered what he found in Sebastian's room. Could the two have translated the newly rendered portions beforehand, and then somehow fed it into the algorithm to spit out the restored images? He furrowed his brow. It was possible, especially what he had seen in Sebastian's room.

He continued reading through the journal until he came to the end. He hadn't noticed anything noteworthy, but he kept snapping pictures with his phone in case he missed something. He opened the envelope on the back flap included in all Moleskines to search for anything of value. A small, folded piece of paper was wedged inside. He pulled it out. Scrawled down the left side in pencil were the names of several cities: *Amalfi and Naples; Compostela and Salerno; Ephesus; Mylapore*; *Toulouse*.

Silas furrowed his brow in confusion, not understanding what the list entailed.

"Wait a minute..."

Chicago was next on the list. Then *Rome, Italy* with several notations in three letter initials: *BHA, BHA; SMC; SMM*.

"Chicago?"

His pulse began to pick up steam as he considered the implication of the city being on this folded piece of paper. Just three days ago the Jude Thaddeus relic had been stolen through terrorism. And here it was, in a journal belonging to Eli Denton.

He glanced over the list again, then set it down on his lap as he stared in contemplation. He ran the cities through his head, searching his memory for a connection. Nothing.

He sighed in frustration. They seemed random, but there had to be a connection. He returned to the piece of paper and glanced over the four initials. Well, three; one was a duplicate set, or so it seemed. Again, he came up short.

And he was running out of time.

Silas took out his phone and snapped a picture of the list. He would have to return to it later, maybe get Zoe and Celeste to help. He slipped the piece of paper back inside the notebook, and then set the notebook back inside the safe. He closed the door, leaving it slightly ajar just as he had found it. He turned around and eyed the room, looking for anything else that caught his eye.

Something did. He walked over to Denton's bed again, kneeling down beside a bed skirt that was turned upright near the headboard. Like it had been lifted one too many times. He leaned down and lifted the corner, then strained to look underneath the bed.

Too dark.

He knew his time was running out, but he clicked on a lamp at the nightstand and leaned back down. He saw a dark, box-shaped object had been pushed far underneath. He smiled and reached for it, pulling it out.

It looked old. Very old. The object was indeed a wooden box, dark and polished to a shiny sheen. On the sides were intricate carvings, depicting scenes of some sort. He lifted it and set it on top of the bed for a better look. Add heavy to the list of characteristics. And something seemed to be rattling around inside, clanging even.

Silas waited to open it, instead of using the light to inspect the outside. He pulled out his phone again and snapped pictures of each side. The carvings reminded him of medieval reliefs above the porticos of cathedrals. On one side, one man was addressing a grouping of men. He counted them; there were twelve. One of them was depicted with horns, a forked tongue, and an arrow-tipped tail. On another side, the same devilish figure was depicted as wagging a finger at a woman hunched over the feet of another man, her hair long and grasped in one hand. Another side showed a table of men, the same horned and forked-tongue man commanding the center. A man was standing to his left at one side of the table and handing him something. The final side showed the devilish man conferring with four other men, whispering into one of their ears and holding a sack of some sort.

Then there was the lid itself: on it was etched a garden scene, the devil-man embracing one man and leaning in with lips puckered. Behind him were armed guards, behind the other man were eleven men.

Silas sat back on his haunches, considering the scenes before him. If he wasn't mistaken, they were eerily similar to ones found in the Christian Gospels.

Ones depicting Judas Iscariot.

He shook his head; it made no sense. Why these particular scenes etched in this wooden box?

Only one way to find out. He took a breath and moved his hands to remove the lid. He wiggled his fingers as they hovered over it, but before he lifted it off, he drew his hand back in shock.

For etched into the handle of the lid was a familiar image of two intersecting lines, with the ends bent at four angles.

"My God..."

It was the emblem of Nous, the ancient threat to the Church stretching back millennia. Whatever the box contained was somehow connected to this cultic group.

Silas reached for the lid, hesitated, but grasped the handle and pulled it. He was greeted by some sort of insert that divided the top portion from another larger one beneath. In it was a leather pouch, tied at the top by a thin, leather binding. It looked ancient and fragile, like shriveled skin that could fall apart at the touch. He knew better than to handle something like this, but he unwound the string anyway. He slowly opened the mouth of the pouch. He could see something glinting inside. He poured the contents in his hand.

Out came several coins. Pieces of silver, by the looks of it.

Silas whistled. "Now this is interesting..." They seemed to be Roman coins, and imperial ones by the looks of the impression of an emperor on one side, though he couldn't immediately place it. He counted them, fifteen in all.

He furrowed his brow, then carefully slipped the ancient

coins back into their leather pouch and set them on the bed. Two notches on either end of the divider allowed for its release. He reached for them, but noticed something in the pale-yellow light. A scene was etched into the surface of the dark, old wood. He turned the box slightly and brought it into the light for a better look. There was a large tree positioned on top of what appeared to be a cliff, with boughs stretching upward and over the embankment. On the end of one of those boughs was a figure hanging from rope, dangling over the side. At the edge of the cliff were several figures, looking on with curiosity or, perhaps, disdain. He counted them. Eleven.

The dangling figure made twelve.

Immediately, the passage from Matthew regarding Judas' death came to mind:

> *When Judas, his betrayer, saw that Jesus was condemned, he repented and brought back the thirty pieces of silver to the chief priests and the elders. He said, "I have sinned by betraying innocent blood." ... Throwing down the pieces of silver in the temple, he departed; and he went and hanged himself.*

A feeling of unease washed over him as he stared at the etching, his stomach beginning to churn with anticipation. He took a deep breath, then carefully removed the divider. He was met by a faded, crimson cloth with a woven pattern of black and gold threads. It was a good quality cloth, rough and ancient-looking, but ceremonial in feel and smelling like a lambswool sweater. It wrapped around the inside of the box and was folded so that it was clearly cradling something inside.

He carefully peeled back the top fold. Underneath was another layer, the other side of the wraparound. He took a breath and removed that one too. He was stunned by what he saw inside.

They were bones. Pale gray-white and stripped of all flesh. They were carefully, reverently arranged, one on top of the other. Resting on top of the collection was a skull, and beside it was an odd, tubular-shaped set of bones bent at an angry angle. As if it had been snapped backward. He failed human anatomy in undergrad, but if he were to place it, it was the spine, some part of it anyway.

Now he understood why the room was so cool and dry. It was being climate controlled for this treasure trove.

Silas sat staring at the box, unsure what to make of it. *What the hell is Denton doing with a box of bones? And whose—*

He gasped, the realization hitting him in the face like a frying pan.

"No way... Can't be!"

Muffled laughter outside the suite's door caught his attention. Then two voices. They were in conversation, and distinct.

Denton and Sebastian.

Time's up. Time to go.

CHAPTER 17

Silas quickly snapped a picture of the coin purse and bones, then put the lid back on the box and slid it under the bed. He clicked off the lamp and hustled over to the balcony using long strides. He carefully eased the door closed so as not to make a sound, then hoisted himself back up onto Denton's balcony. A light flickered on as he swung his left leg over to Sebastian's side of the wall. There he was again: both arms, both legs spread eagle.

Muffled laughter filtered through the glass of Denton's suite. Silas took a deep breath and pushed himself up onto the frosted barrier, refusing to wait for another attack to settle in and praying that neither his brother nor his buddy would come out onto the balcony before he could get over the wall.

He moved his hands quickly toward the center and pushed himself upward, then swung his right leg up onto the barrier.

The side of his foot caught glass, nearly sending him stumbling over the side. He tightened every muscle in his body to keep himself from falling, then eased the leg over the side.

The muffled voices grew more distinct and closer. They were making for the balcony.

Silas quickly jumped down. The door slid open on the other side.

His boots caught the floor, but his center of gravity was off. He wobbled backwards, but was able to twist around toward the barrier before falling down.

Dammit...

He caught the glass wall with his palms and held his breath. Then he waited.

The conversation stopped as the two stepped out.

"Hello?" Denton said cautiously.

A thick veil of silence stood between both balconies. Neither side moved nor spoke.

Silas still held his breath as he leaned against the wall, his arms still holding firmly at the right angles he used to cushion his fall. Beads of sweat began working their way down both sides of his temple.

There was a cough below, the smoker from before. Then another hack, leading to an episode. A low voice said something, words in German and slurring together. Then a door slid open and closed shut.

"Some of these people are truly uncouth and uncivilized." It was Sebastian, sounding his typical self.

"Tell me about it, mate."

They sounded like they moved to the railing, and that they were satisfied the man below was the culprit.

Silas wanted to sigh and heave heavy breaths of thankful air. Instead, he let his breath slip out of both his nose and mouth as he eased himself down to the ground on both knees, then he filled his lungs in quiet content as he waited.

"Yummy," someone said. "Nothing beats Dom Perignon."

Sebastian. *Called that right.*

"Indeed. I thought the circumstances called for it."

"Agreed." Silas heard the faint sound of sipping, one short

and one long. Then Sebastian said, “Do you think he has any clue?”

Silas snapped his head up, eyes wide, mouth opened in shock.

What the...

“I don’t believe so. At least all that has gone into our project. I imagine he questions the purity of our academic pursuits, knowing my bias against the faith. And yours, for that matter.”

“Sure,” Sebastian said.

“But he seems absolutely gobsmacked by the implications of the Gospel. And I have you to thank for that.”

Silas eased himself back so that he was sitting on the back of his feet while kneeling. He closed his eyes. It was true, then: not only was there a broad conspiracy that involved fooling him to fool the Church, all to destroy the faith. His brother was in on it!

Sebastian said, “What can I say? I’m a genius.”

“That you are.”

“But it wasn’t all me. Don’t sell yourself short. You were the one Borg came calling upon when they wanted to re-examine the Gospel of Judas manuscript. And you were the one who concocted the original plan. I was just a willing participant of your ruse.”

There was that name again. *Borg*. And it was clear Denton knew the man, or at least was known by the man Borg. It also struck Silas that Sebastian used his name in such a familiar manner. Which didn’t make sense at all since his brother had as much interest in ancient manuscripts bearing religious significance as Silas was of quantum physics or the nuances of Moore’s law. Yet there he was, a “willing participant,” as he had said.

Silas kept to his haunches, still and unmoving, waiting for what might be revealed.

The slider door opened back into the suite. “When is the ceremony? I’m sure Borg is eager to commence the final phase.” It was Sebastian, referring to some unknown plot. Silas again noted the familiarity with which he mentioned the mystery man's name.

Denton and Sebastian walked inside. The door closed. Silas stood and walked to the edge of the balcony, straining to hear the reply around the wall. It was no use; all he heard was a muffled, indiscernible response.

He cursed in frustration, then hustled back toward his own balcony. After negotiating the wall once again, he slipped back inside his suite. He opened his laptop and attached his phone using a USB cable to download the images he had recorded.

As they transferred, Silas dialed Radcliffe. Time to bring the big guns up to speed.

"Good to hear from you, my boy," Radcliffe answered. "Celeste and Gapinski landed an hour ago and have just arrived at one of the SEPIO safe houses in Rome. Here—" Silas could here Radcliffe fidgeting, then the line went quiet. Several seconds later he came back on the line: "I've just patched in Celeste and Gapinski."

"Howdy, partner," Gapinski bellowed.

"Any news from your front, professor?" Celeste asked.

"You could say that," Silas said. He launched into a review of his burgling activities: Sebastian had a book of the Gnostic Gospels, clearly bookmarked and annotated; a few of those annotations seemed to coincide with passages that had been supposedly rendered into restored, original Coptic text; those renderings had then influenced Silas's translation and authentication of the Gospel of Judas manuscript; he surmised Sebastian had programmed the passages into the AI algorithm to fill in the blanks. It was all a lie, and he had bought it.

He paused his travelogue, his pulse quickening, eyes narrowing at the thought. He shook his head. He would deal with Sebastian soon enough.

"Aside from my brother," Silas continued explaining, "the more troubling revelations were what I found inside Denton's room." He mentioned the journal, with the Gospel of Judas translation and new language added to fill in the blanks of the lacunae from Codex Tchacos. "Which seems to suggest the two were working together to create some sort of new buzz surrounding the Gospel of Judas."

"And completely undermine the New Testament and the Church's accounts of Jesus and the faith," Radcliffe added.

Silas agreed.

"But to what end?" Celeste wondered aloud. "Undermining Christianity and the historical Jesus has been something of a sport of late, particularly amongst the religious-conspiracy crowd."

"Good point," Radcliffe said. "The Gnostic Gospels have been giving them plenty of fodder for the past half century, fueling one religious conspiracy after another. Yet, the Gospels still stand. And so does the Church."

Silas said, "But the Gospel of Judas is a slightly different animal from the other Gnostic Gospels. Unlike the others, like the Gospel of Thomas, for instance, that merely offer supposed teachings and aphorisms of Jesus, there is something of a narrative flow to the Gospel of Judas. Not all that dissimilar from the New Testament Gospels themselves, actually."

Celeste said, "And offering an entirely different story about Jesus and salvation than they do."

"Exactly. And where the Matthew, Mark, Luke, and John accounts are all in agreement that Jesus saves through his death and resurrection, the Gospel of Judas teaches that Jesus saves through his revelation. Through pulling man out of darkened ignorance and into the light of enlightenment."

"Right," Radcliffe said. "And Judas is the one who leads the charge. The one who transcends the Twelve apostles and truly knows and understands Jesus and his mission."

"A true thirteenth apostle," Celeste added.

"Well, that's a whole different ball of wax entirely, isn't it?" Gapinski said.

"Sure is," Silas said.

Radcliffe said, "At least we've uncovered the true roots of the poisonous tree that bore the poisonous fruit. We could have had a real disaster on our hands if the Church's eyewitness accounts of Jesus suddenly had a credible counterstory. So bravo, my boy. Bravo."

"Thanks. By the way, Zoe uploaded Sebastian's hard drive earlier. Do you know if she's found anything useful?"

"Not that I'm aware."

"Have her call me the minute she finds anything."

"Will do," Celeste said. "Anything else?"

Silas nodded. "Oh, yeah. There was a single sheet of paper tucked into the back of the journal. On it was a list of cities and a set of initials."

"Interesting," Radcliffe said.

"How many?" Gapinski asked.

"Eight cities, four initials..."

His head snapped back with realization.

"Eight cities, four initials?" Celeste asked.

"That's the magic number twelve," Gapinski noted.

"What cities? What are their names?" Radcliffe asked.

Before he listed them, he realized one of the initials felt much more familiar than he had realized before. Too familiar.

SMC.

Santa Maria in Cappella. Where Saint Peter's bone relics had been stolen!

"Holy cow..."

"You're making me nervous over here, bro," Gapinski said.

"What is it?" Celeste asked.

"I'm pretty sure these are the locations of the apostle relics!"

Silas listed off the cities. Radcliffe confirmed he was right;

every single one held a relic of the holy apostles, all bearing witness to their memory of the reality and grace of Jesus Christ.

Celeste said, "You mentioned a set of initials, or something or other?"

"Yes. SMC, which I believe refers to Santa Maria in Cappella. And then BHA, which is listed twice."

"That would be the Basilica of the Holy Apostles," Radcliffe interjected. "Which had held the relics of Saint James and Saint Philip. Both stolen."

"The final one is SMM."

"SMM?" Gapinski asked.

"The church of Santa Maria Maggiore," Radcliffe answered. "A Papal major basilica and the largest Catholic Marian church in Rome. Also the home of the final apostle relic."

"Matthias," Silas said.

"Exactly."

"Ahh, yes," Gapinski said. "The dude who replaced the scoundrel Judas."

"'*And they cast their lots, and the lot fell on Matthias. And he was numbered with the eleven apostles,*'" Celeste said, quoting from the book of Acts.

"Impressive," he said.

"There it is," Radcliffe said, "Proof of an organized effort to steal the apostle relics."

Celeste said, "And now we know Nous' next target."

"Finally, we're not the loser dog chasing our tail!" Gapinski said.

"But toward what end?" Radcliffe asked.

Silas grunted and grew silent, considering the final discovery from Denton's room.

"What is it, Silas?" Radcliffe asked. "What aren't you telling us?"

He hesitated, still working out how the box of bones fit into the scenario. But growing increasingly concerned that it was the most significant piece of the puzzle.

He shifted in the chair, then said, "There was one more thing I found. The oddest of it all, underneath Denton's bed."

Gapinski chuckled. "Whatcha find? A dead body or something?"

"You could say that. It was a wooden box, and inside was a pile of carefully arranged bones."

"Egads!"

"I'd say. And they were nestled inside what appeared to me an ancient ceremonial cloth. Similar to those I had seen unearthed in Israel during an archaeological dig in graduate school."

"Who the hell was inside that box?"

Silas hesitated, then said, "That's where it gets weird. On the outside were five relief carvings, four on the sides and one on the lid. And they all seemed to depict scenes involving..."

The absurdity of it all suddenly struck Silas. The idea that the bones of Judas Iscariot were hiding in a medieval wooden box underneath Eli Denton's bed was absurd!

"Scenes involving what, Silas?" Radcliffe asked.

"Well ... Judas."

"Judas?"

"As in, Judas Iscariot?" Celeste said, her voice laced with skepticism.

"I know it sounds absurd," he acknowledged, "but on top of the bones was a wooden divider with another etching. This time it was clearly a man hanging from a noose off a cliff. Here, I'm sending you the images now."

"That does sound like the scoundrel," Gapinski said.

"Let me get this right," Celeste said. "There was a wooden box depicting what appeared to be Judas Iscariot on the side, with bones ceremoniously arranged and packaged inside?"

"Yes. And sitting on the divider was a coin purse with fifteen pieces of silver."

"Fifteen?" Gapinski said.

Celeste said, "But the Bible said Judas threw the sack of thirty pieces of silver at the chief priests and elders, and they used it to buy a plot of land to bury him with it."

"Maybe they got a discount?" Gapinski added.

"That's actually not a bad thought," Silas said. "Burial plots in potter's fields were reserved for the poor and probably wouldn't have cost the entire thirty pieces of silver. Maybe the fifteen pieces of silver were what was left over, and he was buried with the blood money."

"Doesn't the book of Acts say the field where he was buried was called *Field of Blood*?"

"You're right. Probably a parallel to the blood money paid for the plot. And maybe the money buried with him."

"As fascinating as this all is," Radcliffe interrupted again, "how does it connect?"

"I haven't gotten to the best part."

"What's better than a box full of Judas Iscariot's bones?" Gapinski asked.

"What's better is that on the handle of the lid was clearly etched two intersecting lines, bent at odd angles at the ends."

There was silence on the other end for a beat.

"Nous!" Radcliffe and Celeste said in unison.

"Always something," Gapinski growled.

"Silas," Radcliffe said. "I've been doing some more digging in my library, searching my sources from the early Church. And I found in one of Eusebius' ten volumes on Church history a reference to a pseudo-Judas cult that venerated the betrayer with ties to the troublesome Cain sect I mentioned earlier."

"Interesting..."

"It wasn't clear if they were separate from the Cain cult or part of them. At any rate, the early Christian historian makes reference to the Gospel of Judas, implying it to be a sacred text of the Gnostic cult as Irenaeus did. And curiously he made reference to an object of veneration, though apparently, it was of an unknown nature."

"Not anymore."

"Right. Perhaps these bones, ceremoniously wrapped and guarded as they were, served as a totem for these Gnostic worshipers of the thirteenth apostle, a source of strength for perpetuating their heresy as much as the Gospel of Judas did for preserving it through the centuries. Silas, I fear for what your friend and brother are wrapped up in. What you have stumbled into. Particularly if Nous is at the center of the conspiracy, that scourge of the Christian faith!"

"What I've been *bamboozled* into, more like it," Silas mumbled.

Celeste asked, "So what's the play here?"

Silas stood, resolve flooding him. "Time to pay my baby brother a little visit and get some answers."

CHAPTER 18

Silas texted the location of the Aeon Foundation compound to Celeste and Gapinski, who were leaving the SEPIO safe house to rendezvous with him there. Before ending the call, he asked that Zoe call him the minute she found something from Sebastian's downloaded drive. Radcliffe promised he would.

He pocketed his phone and went into the hallway with determination. As he reached to open the door, he heard muffled voices in the hall. He waited, pressing his ear against the door to listen.

Denton and Sebastian.

They had stopped. Then a door closed loudly, the echo and thud close by. Sounded like Sebastian went back to his room.

Time to get some answers.

He opened his door and went to his brother's suite. Except for the stale, cool air and harsh, white LED lighting bouncing off the concrete walls, the hallway was empty. He clenched his jaw and knocked three times. He folded his arms and stepped back a step, looking down the hall as he waited. No one came or went. Denton would be the next stop after he was finished with his brother.

"Come on..."

He pounded the door five times with his fist. "Sebastian? I know you're in there. Open—"

The door flung open as he went to pound again.

"What the hell do you want at this hour?"

Sebastian was holding a glass of red wine, wearing a bathrobe and a look of irritation.

"What, did I interrupt your beauty sleep?" Silas said as he pushed past his brother.

"As a matter of fact—"

"Cut the crap. I know you were with Denton."

"Excuse me?" Sebastian closed the door. "Were you spying on me?"

Silas said nothing. He looked around the room. Good, nothing had been disturbed. Everything seemed just as he had left it. Even the smoke smell had cleared.

He spun around to face his brother. "We need to talk."

Sebastian rolled his eyes and huffed. "What about?" He brushed passed Silas and sat down on his bed. He took a mouthful of wine and waited.

Silas said nothing. The bubbling fountain filled the silence that grew between them as he studied his brother. Uncle Sam had hammered and honed his interrogation techniques while he served in the Middle East. He became especially adept at using a prime tool in the tool chest. Silence. The seconds ticked by, turning into a minute, then nearly two.

Sebastian took a mouthful of the red liquid, then cocked his head and said, "Well? Aren't you going to—"

"How did you and Eli meet?" he interrupted.

He swallowed. "I'm pretty sure we already went over this a few days ago."

"Well, something has come up, and I want to go over it again."

He huffed again. "OK...As I said before, we met at Yale."

"And you stayed in touch all these years?"

"Yep."

"How did you meet?"

"I believe we met through mutual friends."

"What mutual friends?"

"We were all part of the same organization."

"What organization?"

Sebastian hesitated. He took another sip of wine. Then he sighed. "If you must know, it was the Yale Humanist Community."

So there's the shared connection. A shared atheism. But what brought them together for the Gospel of Judas, for Project 13?

"So fast forward, then to now. How did you come to be part of Project 13?"

"Let's just say, a shared interest in alternative Christian teachings."

Silas scoffed at that line. "Spoken like a true Dan Brown fan."

Sebastian grinned and drained his wine. He stood and went to the bar. "You know good and well, *professor* of religious studies and Church history, that the official version of the teachings and life of Jesus is not the *only* version of the teachings and life of Jesus."

"Oh come on!"

He drained the bottle into his glass. "There are plenty of gospel accounts that have surfaced in recent years that tell quite a different tale than the official one by the Church. Including the Gospel of Judas, which I find quite compelling."

Silas folded his arms and frowned. "Compelling. Really?"

Sebastian took a drink and smiled as he swallowed. "You find it odd that I would be attracted to the Jesus of the Gospel of Judas?"

He opened his mouth to speak, but then thought against it. "Why? Why do you find him more compelling than the Jesus found in the New Testament Gospels?"

"For starters, there's none of this business about dying and rising from the dead. But the most profound insight from this version of Jesus' story, and really all the other discarded gospels, is that the mystery of the divine universe is within us, just waiting to burst forth! Enlightenment is what we need, Silas, not some butchered god on a cross. All we need to do is live out of that knowledge of the divine in order to irradiate human ignorance and lead us to a level of awareness of oneself and divine harmony. Surely *that's* what humanity needs. The gods know you sure do," he sneered.

Heat flashed up his neck at the insult. Silas went to offer a comeback, but his phone interrupted.

"Saved by the bell..." Sebastian mumbled.

It rang again. Then again.

"Well, aren't you going to answer it?"

Silas took the phone out of his pocket and swiped it to life, not taking his eyes off his brother. Through gritted teeth, he said, "Yeah?"

"It's Zoe Corbino. From SEPIO."

He smiled. "What have you got for me?"

She took a breath. "Something that I think proves a massive conspiracy that you're at the center of."

He put the phone on speaker. "I'm all ears. We both are, my brother and I." Sebastian furrowed his brow with a look of curiosity.

"I was able to decrypt the downloaded contents off your brother's hard drive."

"You did what!" He roared standing up. His wine sloshed over the sides onto his hand and down onto the rug. He cursed and looked at Silas, his face a twisted mix of anger and disdain and hurt.

"As I was saying...I cracked your brother's computer and found the algorithm he wrote that you all used to restore the codex pages. I must say, I'm impressed. That's damn fine code work."

Sebastian's face transformed from anger to smug satisfaction.

"It's also pretty legit."

"See. Told you so."

"Except for the part that isn't."

His face fell, his eyes darted toward the door and face looked away from Silas out to the balcony.

"Explain," Silas said.

"The program did indeed restore a good portion of the manuscript pages where the text was ambiguous. The AI was even able to fill in some of the blanks based on the scanned fragmentary pieces that had broken off and collected in the original container."

"OK. But what about the rest?"

"That's where it gets interesting. I had to do a multi-layer backtrace through the algorithmic under layers of the code to—"

"Skip the code-talk, Zoe. Just give it to me straight."

She sighed. "I found hidden in the code pre-programmed Coptic text where the gaps had been in the original manuscript pages."

"Really...?" Silas looked at his brother, his face draped with shock. Not so much in surprise at what he had done, but from the confirmation of his suspicions.

"In other words, he programmed the algorithm to not only restore the ambiguous parts of the image, but also insert the pre-programmed Coptic imaging into the missing sections to make it look like the AI had correctly restored the manuscript."

The bookmarked and highlighted portions from the Gnostic Gospels. "So Project 13 is a massive hoax, then?"

"Well, good portions of it is, yes."

Silas smiled. "Thanks, Zoe. I owe you." He ended the call and took a step toward his brother, who was sitting against the headboard of the bed and inched under the covers.

He raised his arms in surrender and made a face. He laughed nervously, "You caught me!"

"I found your little stash of Gnostic Gospels and wondered what they were for. Now I know."

"I can't believe you robbed me blind," he mumbled, turning away.

"Stop being so dramatic. I knew something was going on. So, yes, I pulled a Watergate. I'm glad I did. You could have permanently damaged my reputation as an academic. Not to mention the Church and the biblical witness of the Gospels!"

Sebastian scoffed. "Now who's being dramatic! You heard that Zoe woman. Much of it was legitimate."

Silas scoffed. "That's being generous."

"My AI algorithm *did* restore parts of the Gospel of Judas, there's no denying that! And you and your Church have to face the facts there are more witnesses to the story about Jesus of Nazareth than those in power care to admit! And the Gospel of Judas is a mighty contender for an alternative perspective, no matter the little nudge I gave it."

"Little nudge?" Silas mumbled.

"Well, yes. Denton marked a few passages from the Nag Hammadi codex book you discovered—*while rummaging around in my room*, might I add." He feigned disgust. "Anyway, I just programmed some of the passages he marked and a few other lines he gave me into the more sizable gaps. But the AI worked the rest of the magic, I swear!"

Silas moved his hand across his close-cropped hair and shook his head. It was true, then. But hearing his brother give confirmation to his suspicions made the anger rise again. His right hand started to shake a little. He grabbed it with his left to stay it.

"OK, putting aside the fact there are good, historical, theological reasons why the Church has every right to take Matthew, Mark, Luke, and John at their word well above and beyond that of Judas, or the other Gnostic Gospels for that matter. The fact of the matter is your changes distort the Gospel of Judas entirely, not to mention change the meaning of the Christian faith!"

Sebastian rolled his eyes and huffed. "I would never have let it get that far. Sure, I was thrilled with what Galileo turned out. But the rest was meant as a joke, nothing more."

Silas twisted up his face. "A joke? You think compromising my faith, undermining the faith of billions, is a *joke*?"

Sebastian fell silent. Silas felt like he was boiling beneath the surface and waiting to explode. He regulated his breathing as silence engulfed the room.

"'*The secret account of the revelation,*'" Sebastian finally said, "'*that Jesus spoke in conversation with Judas Iscariot.*'" He quoted the first sentence of the Gospel of Judas. "Let's set aside my little indiscretion and focus on the facts of what is in Judas's account. Why can't there be a secret set of revelation, given by Jesus himself and unknown to the Church until now?"

"Because there's nothing secret about the Christian faith! As Luke said in his Gospels, he set out to share the details of Jesus's story '*which have been fulfilled among us, just as those who from the beginning were eyewitnesses.*' He wrote a historical account—"

"From his *perspective*..."

Silas sighed. "A historical account of what others had themselves witnessed. With their own eyes. Then there's the apostle John: '*This is the disciple who is testifying to these things and has written them, and we know that his testimony is true. But there are also many other things that Jesus did; if every one of them were written down, I suppose that the world itself could not contain the books that would be written.*'"

"Ha! There it is! Why can't the Gospel of Judas be another book that contains the '*many other things that Jesus did*'?"

"Because not only is it anti-Jewish, which the Gospels from the New Testament were steeped in Jewish history and theology. The Gospel of Judas suggests the Twelve apostles got it wrong, and what they passed along was also wrong. That they didn't really understand who Jesus was or what he did. Which also flies in the face of the apostle Paul, who said: '*For I handed on to you as of first importance what I in turn had received: that Christ died for our sins in accordance with the scriptures, and that he was buried, and that he was raised on the third day in accordance with the scriptures, and that he appeared to Cephas, then to the twelve.*'"

He took a breath and sat on the edge of the bed on the other side of Sebastian, facing the wall and feeling like he was slipping back into the role that had created so much distance between the two in the past. He sighed. "I don't mean to preach."

Sebastian scoffed and rolled his eyes.

"The point is that what the apostles passed along through their eyewitness accounts, Paul then passed along and bore witness. Don't you see? If the witness of the apostles is wrong, then not only is that it for Paul, but then the whole Christian faith is over with."

"Yeah, well, soon it will all be over with, anyhow."

Silas whipped around to face his brother. "What do you mean?"

Sebastian looked guilty. It was meant as a throwaway comment, but clearly, he let something slip. He said nothing.

He stood again, with more insistence behind his words: "What do you mean? What else is going down?"

He looked at Silas, then away. "All I know is, Denton was very interested in taking out the memory of the apostles and replacing it with an alternative view."

His mind snapped to the list in the journal, the one corresponding to the apostle relics.

"The apostle relics."

Sebastian shrugged. "I know nothing."

Silas doubted that. But it didn't matter. He got what he needed. Now, he would get the rest.

He got up from the bed and walked toward the door, without saying a word to his brother.

"Where are you going?"

"To pay our mutual friend a visit. It's over. He's got some explaining to do."

He opened the door and went to leave. "Too late" he heard behind him.

He spun around and went back inside. "What do you mean?"

"I mean you're too late. He's already gone."

Silas left his brother and went back into the bunker-like hallway. He pounded on Denton's door. "Denton? Denton, open up!" He pounded twice more, then waited. Nothing.

No matter.

He eased back against the hallway wall, then lunged for the door, kicking it as hard as he could. The jamb splintered and the door popped inward, banging loudly against the beige wall inside.

The room was empty.

He hustled over to the safe. It was cleared. So was underneath the bed.

Denton had taken the box containing the remains of the supposed thirteenth apostle.

And Silas knew where he was going.

"HE'S GONE," Silas said into the phone as he walked down the hallway with purpose. "Denton and the Judas bones."

He pressed his palm against the security reader on the door to the research room. Radcliffe huffed on the other end. "Any idea where he might have fled?"

The palm-reading device flashed green, and the door clicked open. He walked inside. "Well, he isn't in the—" He gasped and cursed.

"What is it?"

"It's gone...." He walked over to the light boxes that held the Gospel of Judas folio pages. They were empty. "Every one of the manuscript pages from the Judas Gospel is missing. Denton isn't here, either."

"Hold on, I've got Celeste and Gapinski at the ready."

Celeste said, "Radcliffe says there is a development?"

"You could say that. Denton has left. And he's taken the Judas bones and Gospel with him."

"Basilica di Santa Maria Maggiore?"

"Has to be." He pushed through the security doors to Area 4. He entered the elevator and punched the button for level 1. "My brother mentioned I was too late, that he had left."

"Too late? For what?"

Silas shook his head. "Not sure. But I don't like the sense I'm getting."

The elevator cleared floor two and began descending to the first floor, its glass windows revealing an empty floor. Not surprising since it was the dead of night. He got out and made his way toward the entrance, glancing out the large courtyard glass doors, confirming that every dormitory light was evaporated.

But then a sight stopped him cold.

He squinted his eyes and edged toward the double doors that led into the courtyard. Raindrops streaked the glass as he peered through, but the light inside the floor escaped through the prism of water to reveal a spectacular sight.

"Holy cow..."

He ran to the doors, they opened. He stopped at the edge of the path he had walked a few days ago and put a hand on his hip in amazement.

The courtyard was totally bare. Barren, even. The vegetation he had witnessed during his evening stroll and that had been picked over was pulled down to the bone-dry ground.

The fruit trees that had been picked over were gone. No trunks, no root systems poking out of the ground. Just gone.

Even the bushes of the mystery berries that commanded the center were shorn down to nothing.

"Silas? Are you there?"

He glanced down at the phone in his hand resting at his side. He couldn't understand what he was witnessing, couldn't make sense of what had happened.

Silas brought the mobile up to his ear. "Yeah, Celeste, I'm here."

"Is everything alright?"

"I'm fine..." He shook his head. "Sorry, I'm at the center of the compound, standing in what used to be a massive farm in an interior courtyard. Now it's just a pile of dirt. It's as if the whole place has just been abandoned. Or, like they were cleaning up..."

"Gear up, partner. Time to roll." It was Gapinski.

He was right. It was.

Celeste said, "There is only one relic left. Which presumably means—"

"That's where Denton is with his pile of bones," Silas interrupted as he walked back into the main floor. He had an unsettled suspicion that the man had unholy plans for it and the rest of the apostle relics, including the supposed bones of Judas. Especially since Nous was involved.

"Do you need a ride?" Gapinski asked.

"No, I'm set. Change of plans. Don't come to me anymore. I'll meet you at the basilica in thirty." He ended the call and pulled out the card the taxi man had given him the last time he needed a ride into Rome. It was still wet from rain, and the ink had bled a little, but he could make out the number. He dialed it. The man was more than willing to help Silas part with his remaining cash.

CHAPTER 19

Thunder rumbled overhead as the taxi eased up to the curb in front of a piazza commanded by an obelisk erected in 1587 by Pope Sixtus V as a beacon for pilgrims in front of Silas's destination: the Basilica of Santa Maria Maggiore, one of four papal basilicas in Rome. It was also home of the manger relic, pieces of wood believed to have been part of Christ's infant barnyard bassinet. However, a different set of relics is what brought Silas to the basilica: the relics of Matthias, the apostle who replaced the disgraced Judas after his downfall. If Denton was anywhere, with Judas' bones and Gospel, it had to be here. Whatever reason that could be.

He got out and paid the cabby the promised wad of American dollars. The man thanked him repeatedly, then drove away. The piazza was empty, bathed in yellow light from lamps in the church square. As the man drove off, Silas looked toward the imposing structure of pale limestone, it's twin domes lit in white underneath the thick, sullen swirl of clouds above. Two windows of the apse on the church's north front that held the high altar shown faint with yellow light, as well. Something was going on inside.

Denton.

A flicker of lightning rippled through the canopy. Beads of rain began dropping heavily on Silas's head as he waited for the arrival of the two SEPIO operatives he had fallen in with just a few months prior. He chuckled to himself as he waited, having vowed to Radcliffe he would never go on mission again for the Order. A life of comfort and tenure, as the Order Master had put it, was all he wanted. That, and engaging his students with the big questions of life and writing papers on obscure doctrines. Both seemed so small in the face of the impending destruction of the Church's apostolic memory bearing witness to Jesus' life and teachings, death and resurrection.

His breath caught heavy in his chest as he thought about the impending mission. His pulse started racing, his head started feeling light. He leaned against the obelisk and closed his eyes, then started his pre-mission ritual to center his nerves.

999, 998, 997, 996....

He breathed in deeply through his nose, then slowly out through his mouth

988, 987, 986, 985....

The screech of brakes caught his attention. He snapped open his eyes and shuffled behind the tall, Egyptian-like structure, unsure of who had arrived. A black sedan sat underneath a row of large trees with its lights off on a central street leading to the piazza. He strained to focus, but when two figures emerged, one lithe and feminine, the other burly and masculine, he smiled. Celeste and Gapinski.

Celeste led the way toward Silas, her long, brown hair braided and swaying as she walked. She wore a warm smile and nice-fitting, black clothes—both causing Silas to catch his breath.

"My man!" Gapinski said, the large man walking to him with arms wide open.

He smirked and opened up his arms as well. The two embraced in a bear hug.

"I didn't think I'd see your ugly mug again on one of our missions."

Silas chuckled. "Sorry to disappoint."

"Not that I'm complaining or nothing. You rocked it last time!"

He smiled and looked at Celeste, then dipped his head awkwardly. She tilted her head to the side and smiled back, placing a lock of hair that had fallen in front of her face back behind her ear.

"Professor Grey," she said.

"Celeste Bourne." He started to reach in for an embrace, then stopped short. He continued when she did the same. They giggled at their awkward start, then hugged hello.

"Alright, you two," Gapinski said. "Chop, chop. We've got some Nous ass to kick." He started walking, crossing the piazza toward the basilica. Silas and Celeste followed. They continued around the north side of the basilica down an empty street that ran parallel to the magnificent building.

"So what's the plan, chief?" Gapinski said glancing back at Celeste.

She took a deep breath and shrugged. "Not sure. You were here before we were, Silas. Did you see anything? Do you know what Denton might be up to?"

He shook his head. "No, on both counts. All I know is that he left the compound. The bones believed to be those of Judas and his Gospel are missing. And the last relic on the list in his room is Matthias'. Which makes the Basilica of Mary Major the final target. They're darker now, but I saw light earlier in those windows. My money is that Denton is inside. Doing Lord knows what."

Celeste nodded. "Right. I'd say let's let ourselves in and have a look. The Order was able to secure keys to the front door, so we're set there."

Gapinski said, "Then let's do this."

They came up around the side toward the front when

Gapinski stopped short, motioning them to press against the structure.

"Humvee," he whispered, indicating the presence of military security.

Gapinski motioned for them to inch forward. He led the charge alongside the building, coming toward the corner for a better look.

No one was visible.

They eased forward. Then Gapinski held up his hand suddenly to halt.

He looked back with a look of worry, then hustled forward to behind the black and green military vehicle. When Silas came around, he saw him stooping down.

There was a man, tied and laying underneath the rear bumper.

Gapinski stood. "Out cold."

Celeste said, "Now we know the man means business."

"I could have told you that," Silas retorted.

"Here, you're gonna need this." Gapinski shoved cold, hard steel into Silas's chest. "And this."

A Beretta M9, his weapon of choice. And a flashlight.

Silas took an uneasy breath, but he took the weapon and nodded. He withdrew the magazine, inspected it, then shoved it back into place and nodded.

Gapinski nodded back, withdrawing his own weapon and looking to Celeste for direction.

She looked at them both, weapon in hand. "Right. Shall we get to it?"

A set of waist-high metal barriers and a white tent guarded the entrance. Probably used as the visitor's queue for Christian pilgrims and tourists. They easily climbed over the barrier and quickly padded up the top of the stairs to five sets of iron gates that barred entrance.

Celeste walked to the middle doors and pulled out a set of

keys. She went to insert one into the lock, but the gate pushed open.

She looked at Gapinski and Silas. "Looks like we're late to the party."

Gapinski huffed. "How could they start without us?"

Silas put out a hand and hushed them. "Quiet a minute." He paused, then said. "Listen. Do you hear that?"

The other two cocked their heads toward the entrance.

"Sounds like some sort of chanting," Celeste said squinting her eyes in concentration.

Silas nodded. "Which means we've got company. Lots of it, not just Denton."

"Always something," Gapinski growled.

Massive, bronze doors, solid and sturdy, stood closed on the set of five main entrances into the basilica. Except for the middle set. It had been hastily pried open and left ajar.

"Over here," Celeste said. She was fiddling with the set of keys again at a small door on a wall off from the main set of entrance doors. "I studied the floor plan before arriving. This will take us through a set of rooms of the baptistery and into the nave."

"Score one for SEPIO!" Gapinski said, slapping Celeste on the back.

She gave a short smile, then twisted open the lock and opened the door. The three quickly entered into a small alcove that led into a larger room of mosaics and gilded ceilings and walls. Denton echoed toward them in muffled tones through a heavy, dark wooden door. Silas couldn't understand what he was saying, or why he was carrying on so. It sounded like the ravings of a madman.

Gapinski grasped the burnished-bronze door handle, looking at Silas and Celeste. They both nodded. He returned their acknowledgment, then held his breath and slowly turned the handle. So far so good. He eased the solid door open, swinging it toward them. Thankfully, it gave not a peep.

With the door open, the three slipped into the darkened space adjacent to the cavernous nave that pointed toward the high Papal altar at the front, the source of Denton's ravings.

And then Silas saw it, the sight causing him to gasp audibly. Celeste nearly joined him. Gapinski did. The three of them padded toward the entrance of the baptistry for a better look, keeping to the left of the opening for cover.

Arrayed from front to back was a crowd of men and women wearing bleached-white frocks, from top to bottom. Had to be a hundred or so, with the same kind of garments Silas had spied earlier at the compound.

"You weren't kidding when you talked about these people being all Heaven's Gate-like," Gapinski mumbled.

The scene reminded him of the old *1984* Apple commercial, where a bunch of people in similar drab clothing were staring forward at a screen, entranced and sedated, as a talking head droned on about reaching a new state of enlightenment. It was most unsettling.

"... coming enlightenment has dawned," a man boomed from somewhere toward the front. "The barriers toward its full manifestation are increasingly being dismantled as science and reason overtake the naive fairytale stories of those *Christians*. And today we will purge the world of that remnant witness, eliminating it through the fires of Hell!"

The crowd crowed with approval, its cackling call echoing off the vaulted ceilings of marble and gold.

Silas looked to Celeste, then Gapinski. *What was he talking about?*

The three eased out of their hiding spot, inching out of the doorway and toward one of the twenty-eight Corinthian columns arrayed along the nave. They were at the very rear of the gathered crowd, ensuring their secrecy and offering them the perfect view of what was transpiring.

Rain rapped against the windows above as dim, yellow light

shown through the expansive, sacred space from an array of candelabras from the high altar, glistening off the gold-lined ceiling and spreading across the nave below. Standing at the high altar was a familiar face.

Denton.

Silas narrowed his eyes and clenched his jaw. He furrowed his brow and leaned forward around the column.

The man was preparing something between the four massive Corinthian columns of crimson granite spirally entwined with gilded, bronze palm fronds supporting the massive, golden-leafed canopy above.

What was he doing?

Denton was arranging several items. On top of them, he arranged what looked to be wood. He paused, then continued his arrangement, adding more wood on top. Almost like a pyre. Then he started speaking.

"He called his disciples and chose twelve of them, whom he also named apostles," Denton intoned, his voice strong and steady, "Simon, whom he named Peter, and his brother Andrew, and James, and John, and Philip, and Bartholomew, and Matthew, and Thomas, and James son of Alphaeus, and Simon, who was called the Zealot, and Judas son of James, and—" He paused as if gathering his breath. "And Judas Iscariot, who became a traitor."

He scoffed loudly. Others joined in.

"Traitor. Traitor? Is this how Jesus actually described his most trusted, faithful, *loyal* disciple?" Many answered his rhetorical question: "No!"

"Listen to these words from Jesus, written by the apostle himself."

Silas could see Denton holding one of the folio pages from the Gospel of Judas. He started reading:

Jesus answered and said, "You will be the thirteenth,

and you will be cursed by the other generations,
but eventually you will rule over them.

Denton put down the manuscript, saying, "Judas is truly the thirteenth apostle. The one who transcended the twelve, who stood outside of the twelve as the one, true divine-man, full of the enlightenment and transcendence that Jesus imparted to him. And what did Jesus say of the twelve?" He picked up another manuscript page and read:

I tell you again, my name has been written on the twelve of the generations of the stars through the generations of people. They have planted trees in my name, without fruit, in a shameful way.

"Without fruit. Shameful way. That is the verdict Jesus handed down to not only those who desecrated the good name of Judas, but have led the world astray with their dogma and doctrine—the Church!"

Silas clenched his jaw. The orange light and shadow, combined with the ravings made Denton look like a pagan priest. He shook his head. What happened to his old friend?

"And now..." Denton bent down and picked something up, "... we will alight this pyre to the gods as a token of our devotion, irradiating these relics of false memory from the face of the earth!"

Silas's eyes widened. Instinctively, he moved forward toward the altar to do something about the desecration.

Celeste grabbed his arm. "No, wait. See how this plays out first."

"But the relics—"

"We're not going to let that happen. Promise."

He held her gaze, her indigo eyes commanding, penetrating. He nodded and settled back behind the column.

Denton continued, his voice loud and purposeful: "Three days before Jesus was handed over to the ruling authorities of this corrupt world, Jesus spoke to Judas secret revelations unveiling the mysteries of the universe before his eyes, bestowing upon him the gift of enlightenment. Insights that we have beheld and will gaze upon in full measure this night.

"'But you will exceed all of them,' Jesus said, 'For you will sacrifice the man who bears me. Already your horn has been lifted up, and your anger has flared up, and your star has burned brightly, and your heart has grown strong. I tell you the truth, your last days will become something to be grieved by the ruler, since he will be overthrown. And then the image of the great generation of Adam will be magnified."

He paused and raised his arm, fist clenched. Then he shouted, "'Look,' Jesus continues in the Gospel of Judas, 'you have been informed of everything. Lift up your eyes and behold the cloud and the light that is within it and the stars that are circling it. And the star that leads the way is your star.'"

As one the group raised their hands, fists clenched, as well.

Are they holding something?

"Today is the day of salvation, joining Jesus in shedding the cloak of corruptible flesh to find release from the prison of misery and chaos of this condemned world, joining our beloved thirteenth apostle who blazed the trail before us, who lifted up his eyes and beheld the cloud of light, and then entered it with purposeful abandon."

Then Denton turned his wrist and opened his hand, palm upright. The men and women in white did the same.

Silas noticed something resting in each of their hands. He squinted to get a better focus on the hand closest to him. It took Silas a minute for it to register, but then he realized what it was. Balls of white, each bearing a single black dot.

The creepy doll-eye berries! They must have harvested them before going en masse to the basilica.

His mind jumped to how Zoe described the effects of their cardiogenic toxins: having an immediate sedative effect on cardiac muscle tissue, they can eventually lead to cardiac arrest.

And death.

All at once it hit him what was going on.

"This is a mass suicide, Jim Jones style!" he exclaimed to Celeste. Denton had somehow bought the Gnostic lie that salvation lay in release from our mortal bodies. And then convinced a hundred more to follow him, literally killing their flesh to liberate their inner soul!

"Not going to happen on our watch," Celeste said.

"Follow my lead," Silas said.

He stepped forward and raised his Beretta high into the air. Then he fired four times toward the golden ceiling, yelling wildly, then fired off three more rounds. The sudden burst of gunfire sent the crowd into a panic, crouching and running for cover and away from the mayhem.

Exactly as Silas wanted.

The three stepped forward and ran toward the high altar to confront Denton.

Gapinski turned around and fired off five more shots high toward the ceiling, more incentive to keep running. He smiled with delight as the place quickly cleared. "Nothing like a few gunshots to get the party started, my pappy used to say."

"Not another step, Grey," Denton shouted, his eyes wild and possessed. He was holding a long stick of wood, ablaze with fire.

Silas noticed that part of the altar was smashed, and resting on it was an array of bone fragments and wooden pieces, in the shape of a funeral pyre. And on top, the skull and bones he had discovered earlier in Denton's room.

The bones of Judas Iscariot.

"I see you found the final apostle relic," Silas said. "The last piece in your diabolic scheme to rid the world of the apostolic memory of the true story of Jesus."

Denton grinned and shrugged. "Not rid the world entirely. But certainly, help it along a bit. Christians have been venerating these bones and their memory for generations. Time to put that silliness to an end."

Silas stepped forward. He lowered his head, narrowed his eyes, clenched a fist and flexed his fingers around the grip of his Beretta. "Not gonna happen, Denton."

His grin faded. "Watch me."

A gun blast sounded from over Silas's shoulder. The stick of flaming wood held by Denton suddenly split into pieces. He recoiled in shock and panic.

Some of the flaming pieces landed on the pyre. It quickly caught fire, incentivized by fuel, no doubt.

"Always something," Gapinski growled lowering his weapon.

Silas cursed. Denton took off, leaving the relics to burn.

The three ran up onto the altar to save them.

"You go after Denton," Celeste instructed Silas. "We've got this."

"Are you sure?" he asked, searching for something to put out the fire.

"Dude, listen to the woman," Gapinski said. "Like she said, we've got this."

He looked from Gapinski to Celeste to the burning pile of wood and bones desecrating the sacred altar, then back to Celeste. He took a breath, nodded, and took off toward Denton.

Time to end this.

CHAPTER 20

The flames were rising higher as Silas took off in Denton's direction, threatening to destroy the Papal altar and all twelve of the apostle relics. He caught sight of the man darting into a chamber between a set of columns off the nave. He called after him, but it was no use.

Silas slowed his pace and flexed his hands around the grip of his Beretta, holding it low toward the ground, but having it ready just in case. He stopped at the corner, then eased around the marble wall of white and gold, the candlelight from the front altar barely giving relief from the night's darkness.

In one move, he came around the corner, arms outstretched and weapon ready. A bronze gate guarded the chapel, but its door was slowly swinging closed from having just been thrown open. He inched forward, scanning the chamber, but it was empty, except for a large altar commanding the center of the room. On top stood a massive, golden urn supported by four golden angels. Shadows danced off the colorful frescos and white marble statues carved into the wall behind the object. The ceiling was vaulted high with a central dome, covered with frescos and gold gilding.

He inched forward, weapon outstretched. "Denton?" he called.

Something caught his attention to the left. He swung his weapon toward it and nearly fired.

It was a statue embedded in the wall, the shadows playing tricks on his mind believing it to be a person ready to pounce. He took a breath and brought one hand to wipe his forehead free of sweat.

There was a sound ahead, coming from somewhere near the altar. He stepped forward toward the imposing structure and noticed a knee-high, marble railing. The darkness had clouded his vision from seeing a stairwell leading down beneath it to a crypt. He peered over the edge, training his weapon down. A small, wooden door stood open beneath.

He padded slowly down the marble stairs to the bottom. A small table with a linen runner sat to the right, along with a few votive candles, the flames of the penitent having gone out hours ago. He said a prayer himself. For protection, for resolution. One way or another.

He clicked on his flashlight and held it out with one hand underneath his outstretched hand wielding his Beretta. He used the barrel of the torch to open the door slowly, its sure beam casting a blanket of white on pale sandstone that looked markedly older than the marble and limestone above. The floor was hard, compact dirt, not the exquisite mosaic of brown-and-white marble tiles in the nave. He walked further into the narrow space, hunching over with the low ceiling. He felt claustrophobic knowing how many tons of basilica stood up above.

Silas licked his lips and swallowed, then took a breath and reached toward his head with the side of his arm to wipe his brow.

Steady, Grey. Steady.

He pressed forward, trying not to be mesmerized by the ancient history that greeted him with every step. Walls of red brick covered an arch that clearly looked to be from the early centuries of the Roman empire. Sketches of people and events in rusty red and faint bluish-green were etched into another wall, seeming to depict a calendar of sorts. In another section he could see pottery and what looked to be coins embedded into the sediment near the base of the path, having been abandoned long ago. It was a treasure trove that he imagined was off limits to most guests. The inner archaeologist was screaming for him to stop. But footfalls ahead snapped him back to the task at hand.

Denton.

Silas eased around a corner, fearing the man was lying in wait. He held his breath and pushed around, but no one was there.

Where was he?

His light caught an expanse up ahead, what looked to be a chamber that stretched higher. He smiled, thankful for the relief from the tight conditions. But he imagined Denton might have been, as well. Caution was in order.

He flexed his fingers around the grip of his weapon and padded forward with purpose, not giving his old friend a chance to surprise him. Inching toward the opening, he twisted toward the left trying to clear the space with his light before entering. He did the same to the right, pleased Denton wasn't around. When he entered, the sight caught his breath. He felt as if he were entering into sacred, hallowed ground.

Arrayed around the room were multiple levels of alcoves, from floor to ceiling, carved into the limestone walls deep beneath the basilica and streets of Rome. They were a foot or more high and probably five to six feet long. Just long enough and high enough to fit a body inside. Every one of the alcoves was holding the holy remains of God's holy people.

"Catacombs..." Silas whispered.

Had to stretch back into the earliest days of the Church. For a few centuries before the Roman empire had officially sanctioned Christianity and allowed Christians to practice openly, the first martyrs and persecuted believers were buried in these underground chambers, or *coemeterium*, which derives from the Greek and means "dormitory," stressing the Christian belief that burial was merely a temporary residency for the dead while the believer waited for the final, bodily resurrection. Eventually, Christians worshiped in these chambers for fear of imperial retribution.

He lowered his weapon to his side, keeping the flashlight trained ahead. He swept the room, clearing it of any sign of Denton. An exit to another passageway stood ahead, and another entryway stood off to the right. Looked to be a chapel, complete with a small altar and kneeling bench.

Denton must have continued on ahead. He wasn't going anywhere, so Silas stepped forward to the bones for a closer look. He caught himself grinning, overcome by the weight of the moment being in the presence of the earliest witnesses to the Jesus movement. The remains had been mostly untouched, kept safe in the dry conditions deep beneath the earth, preserving their own memory of the faith for centuries. He walked around the perimeter, eyeing the remains, overcome by the great cloud of witnesses that had attested to the once-for-all faith of Christ.

He walked closer to the chapel, wondering what remnants of early worshipers he might find inside—

The light of his flashlight caught sight of a long, pale object swinging toward his face. Silas went to bend out of the way, but it caught him in the shoulder, sending him stumbling against the wall.

Instinctively, he held fast to his weapon, but sent his flashlight across the floor to reach for anything to keep him upright. His right hand slipped into one of the alcoves, sending a pile of bones scattering out and over onto Silas as he fell to the ground.

Denton!

The white object came at him again, a bone from one of the faithful. He raised his arm holding his Beretta to shield himself from the blow. It connected squarely with his wrist, sending his weapon skittering across the floor.

Denton raised the bone over his head to strike again, his eyes wide and teeth gritted with fury. He swung down, but Silas rolled to the side to miss the blow.

He managed to grab hold of his weapon and twist around. He pinched off three shots, shooting wildly without any clear aim or direction. All went wide, exploding off the earthen walls of the *coemeterium*.

A dark shadow moved to his right. He hesitated, not wanting to actually hit the guy. It was all Denton needed to land a solid kick into the arm, which sent the weapon a yard away. Then he slammed his foot into Silas's stomach.

Silas bent forward and coughed, his breath leaving him. He struggled to regain himself as Denton climbed over him for the weapon.

He grabbed Denton's foot, and with a yell, he yanked and twisted it so that he flipped the man on his back. Silas lunged for his friend, but he kicked him off in the chest. Silas fell backward.

Denton stood, frantically searching for the weapons, the light from the flashlight making the search deceptive. "You just couldn't leave it well enough alone, could you?" the man yelled as Silas recovered. "Always like Silas to ruin it for everyone."

His eyes were bulging. He was hunched slightly, with arms held out and fingers extended like he was guarding someone's basketball shot. He was twisting this-way-and-that.

Silas let the comment go. He ran for the man and spun him around, drawing his arm back and hitting him squarely in the nose. He heard a crunch.

Denton recoiled and put his hands up to his nose, a few seconds later blood started pouring down.

"You broke my nose you sonofa—"

He didn't finish the sentence, but instead lunged back at Silas, face bloody and eyes full of wrath. He went to offer Silas's face a right uppercut, but paused mid-punch.

Silas took the bait and tried to weave out of the way, but was met with a stiff hook from the left, squarely in his left eye. Pain blossomed inside of his head, and it immediately began to swell. He faltered, but charged at Denton in equal fury.

They were two former military men who were evenly matched, and angry as hell. Years of frustration from their frayed friendship was spilling out in sight of the Christian remains.

Silas connected his head with Denton's gut. He drove him backward, the length of the *coemeterium.*

But then his foot caught on something, the force of his stride causing his foot to slide out from under him and lose his balance.

He went down hard, smacking his chin on the ground. Denton fell on top of him in a pile. And the two realized all at once what Silas had stepped on.

His Beretta M9, which was sliding to a halt a few yards away.

Denton clambered over Silas's feet to retrieve the weapon, then scrambled to stand. He chambered a round and took aim at Silas, who was slowly raising his hands in defeat and turning around to face his friend.

It was over, just like that.

CHAPTER 21

"Whoa, mate. Look what I got here!" Breathing hard, Denton's face was still wearing the same crazed look. He wiped his bloody nose on his sleeve, then spit a mouthful of blood and smiled. "You always could pack a punch."

Silas knelt, breathing hard himself and doubled-over on the ground. He couldn't catch his breath.

Denton laughed. "My, how the mighty have fallen. But good show up top. Didn't see that coming. Nice and easy, mate. Don't do anything stupid."

He backed up as Silas slowly stood. "Check, mate," Silas growled.

The man merely smiled, sizing Silas up.

"Now what?" Silas said.

"You tell me. This was your party."

Silas began running scenarios through his mind, ways to get out of the mess he had made. He didn't see any good ones to follow. So he did the next best thing. Tried to get Denton talking.

"I found your little stash."

Denton furrowed his brow in confusion. "My, my stash?"

"The bones. Under your bed, presumably of Judas. And then the list of apostle relics."

The man took a step and smiled, his nostrils flaring slightly. "You went through my room?"

Silas said nothing.

"Makes better sense why you showed up with your two pals."

"Yeah, and Sebastian filled me on all the rest of the details. How you leveraged him and his own issues with Christianity to con me into helping you authenticate the restored Gospel and throw doubt on the true Jesus story. So that part of your project is over. And my two pals upstairs put out your little bonfire, saving the apostle relics—and their memory of Jesus' story. So you lost, my friend."

Denton clenched his jaw and tightened the grip of the Beretta, clearly not pleased.

"But what I can't understand is," Silas said, "*why*. Why go through all the trouble? Stealing the relics, the charade with the Gospel of Judas manuscript. What was the point?"

"The point?" Denton said, taking another step forward.

Good, almost there.

"Yeah, the point. You used to be so firm in your faith. At least when you left Iraq. You were going to save the world, that's what you said. You wanted everyone to experience what you had experienced with your faith, and teach what you had learned from the Bible."

Denton scoffed. "But don't you see? You asked what changed. Enlightenment, that's what."

"What do you mean?"

"At university, after Iraq, I was indeed ready to take my place amongst the faithful saints and preach the gospel and argue for my faith and do all of the things a good Christian does. But then I began to actually investigate my faith and take stock in what the Church teaches. What was most striking is that the Bible isn't simply error-free. There are mistakes and differences in the original texts of the New Testament. In fact, there are more variances amongst our manuscripts than there are words in the New Testament!"

Silas shook his head. "But that's nothing new. And none of those variations have any bearing on the core beliefs of the Church, have any impact on the essence of Jesus' story and faith in his death and resurrection. A supermajority are inconsequential errors in grammar or punctuation."

"But others are plenty profound," Denton corrected. "Take the last section of the Gospel of Mark, the bit about Jesus' resurrection, which appears to have been added to the text years later. Or what about the Church's teaching on the Trinity? The First Letter of John is the only place where this cornerstone belief is spelled out in the entire Bible—"

"That's not entirely true," Silas responded. "At Jesus' baptism, you have the clear picture of the Father, Son, and Spirit. And then Jesus instructs us to baptize using the same three-fold name."

Denton waved his hand in dismissal. "My point is that for someone like me who believed the Bible was the inspired Word of God, I began to have this sneaking suspicion that the evidence for belief is there if you look closely at the Bible, at the resurrection for instance. Sure enough, you'll find the evidence for it. Which gave me one horrifying conclusion."

He paused, taking a breath and tilting his head back as if he were reliving the pain of the memory.

"There was no real historical record," he continued. "It was all just myth, told by illiterate country bumpkins, which hadn't been written in any meaningful or coherent way for decades. And then the so-called Gospels weren't four, but a ton more! The ones bound in our Bibles were just the ones chosen by those in power because they fit their evidence for belief."

"That's bull. The oral practices of the culture during that time created a strong, sturdy oral tradition that faithfully passed along the eyewitness accounts of the apostles. And within decades they were written down, anyway, and then widely passed around in the Church among the believers."

"But it wasn't just that." He stopped again, searching for words for the memory of his experience charting the loss of faith. "I had a rather painful episode, several years after Iraq. It was odd, really, because I half expected to go through a thing or two after what we witnessed, all of the chaos and death. But it wasn't until midway through my problem that I had a mental breakdown. The roadside bombs. The famine in full swing throughout much of the country. Starving infants, mass death."

"Understand that," Silas said. "I had my own struggles. But unlike you, they drove me deeper into the Bible and my faith, helping me to make sense of this broken world."

"Well, jolly for you," Denton said. "Because I began to lose my faith. Though, it wasn't for lack of trying. I just couldn't believe there was any sort of God or divine being or whatever in charge of this mess ... all of the chaos and corruption, the death and destruction. It was such an emotionally charged season of my life. I came to believe that not only was there no evidence of Jesus being divine, and what evidence there was in the Bible was simply concocted. There wasn't a God paying attention to us in the first place. And on the other side, I felt the last particles of my faith leave. Almost like the fizz of champagne escaping upward, their bubbles just...evaporating into the air. There was no God, nor should there be any. And that was that."

Silas's face fell. "I had no idea. Why didn't you call me? I could have helped you work through it all."

"Call you? You made it pretty clear with your petty jealousies of my work and my success that you weren't interested."

That stung. It was biting, but true. Silas felt a wave of shame wash over him. And regret. How could he have been so blinded to his friend's spiritual needs by his own self-centered ego? He wanted to wretch from the realization.

"So now you can understand the motivation for my little project," he said, taking a step forward. "Eliminate the apostolic memory markers of the supposed eyewitnesses and discredit the faith that failed me time and time again."

Silas smiled. There we go. Just a little closer.

He said, "And you were the mastermind behind it all? The apostle relics theft, the Gospel of Judas restoration?"

Denton chuckled. "Regrettably, I can't take credit for the main plot. I was just a loyal foot soldier in an army stretching back millennia."

Silas thought about the Judas cult Radcliffe mentioned. About Nous and its war against the Church.

He continued, "So what, you tracked me down and showed up at the cathedral, pretending to just happen to run into me, using the explosion and relic theft to rope me into your conspiracy? I bet you even staged getting beat up behind the post office while I was tracking down the two Nous agents. Am I right?"

Denton smirked and said nothing, inching forward with Beretta outstretched.

The truth of the matter stung. His friend had played him from the beginning. He swallowed, then smirked himself.

Bingo.

In one motion Silas shoved the man's arm upward with his left arm, then grabbed the Beretta with his right and twisted it around so that he was holding the gun, pointing it at Denton's face. It was a maneuver he had trained for often a decade ago. Which came in handy today.

Silas grinned, flexing his fingers on the grip and widening his stance.

Denton's mouth hung open, then he was chuckling. "Nice trick! Her Majesty's military didn't teach us that."

"What can I say? America's the best of the best."

Denton held up both hands in surrender, then smiled. He took a step back and put them in his pockets.

"Whoa, whoa, whoa. Hands where I can see them."

Denton frowned. His shoulders slumped, and he sighed, but then straightened himself. "All is not lost. There's still one more matter to take care of."

Silas tightened his grip. *What was he talking about?*

"No, there isn't. It's over, Denton. Take your hands out of your pockets and let's go. We'll sort this up top with the authorities."

Denton threw his head back and laughed, then grinned widely, maniacally. "Not for a long shot, mate."

Suddenly, one arm shot out of his pocket, fist clenched. Silas startled and nearly fired a shot into his friend. Years of training made him hold the shot and hold his ground.

He looked at the hand. "I'm warning you...."

Denton held his grin and held his arm out toward Silas as if he was handing him something. Then the man's hand flung open, revealing a handful of the white berries resting in his cupped hand.

Silas's face fell, his gut tightened.

No...

He shook his head, holding Denton's gaze. "Don't do it, Eli."

Denton took a step backward, his face set as flint. Eyes unblinking, jaw set and unmoving

"I will shoot you if I have to. I will not let you go like this. Don't make me—"

In one motion, Denton fell to his knees.

Silas, taut with anticipation, popped off a shot that was aiming for the man's shoulder, meant to stop him.

But he missed, the bullet shattering a skull of the faithful behind where Denton had been standing.

The man was on his knees, chewing and swallowing, his

mouth stained purple from the poisonous juices of the white berries.

“No...” Silas yelled. He rushed over to his friend who was sloughing toward the ground. He caught him before he fell over and smacked his head. He held him in his lap, his mind racing with a solution.

Denton continued swallowing. He licked his lips and sighed in satisfaction. His breath smelled sour, a putrid mixture of the toxic fruit and impending death. He grinned, his teeth a swirl of brilliant white and crimson.

“Eli, what have you done?” Silas moaned.

“What Judas himself did. Liberate me from the trappings of this dark world and corrupted flesh.”

Silas shook his head as he watched the color slowly drain from the man’s face. Perspiration started beading up to the surface of his skin.

“Liberation... But that's what neither you nor the Gospel of Judas gets about the Christian faith. God created a good world, he created us good. Sure, creation groans and labors with birth pangs, as Paul wrote. But he reveals that creation will be delivered from the bondage of corruption, and into the same, glorious liberty that the sons of God will: fully restored humanity.”

“Rubbish,” Denton groaned, his face wincing with pain as the toxins started taking over. A tremble shook him. “And besides, you Christians yourselves speak of the same kind of other-worldly liberation, singing songs about some glad morning when you’ll fly away from this life, like a bird liberated from his cage.”

Silas smirked. "You're right. Such talk is heresy. Totally, not biblical. Because the real hope of the Christian faith is what Paul continues to say. That while we groan within ourselves just as creation does at all the chaos and corruption, we eagerly await the adoption, the redemption of our body. Our physicality still matters. Our bodies and souls combined matter because our bodies will be made new."

"Not mine..." Denton said softly, trailing off and staring into the distance.

Silas furrowed his brow and cocked his head. Were the toxins talking? No, it seemed deeper.

"What do you mean?"

Denton sighed and managed to say: "I've got cancer. I'm dying."

Silas was stunned. He shook his head. His friend was dying of cancer? Is that what this was about?

"Eli, it's not over! You can fight this—"

"No, I can't. You don't fight stage-four colon cancer. It's already won. Over my lungs, my liver, several of my lymph nodes."

He couldn't believe what he was hearing, this man whom he had fought alongside, whom he had respected and looked up to. Who had provoked ungodly envy.

"But...you look fine. I don't understand."

"That's mostly from a cocktail of injections I've been taking to stave off the inevitable. All to give me enough wits in the last few weeks to embark on this final endeavor. Connecting with your brother. Finding you and conniving you into helping me blind-side the Church." He looked at Silas. "Which I nearly pulled off, no thanks to you."

Silas chucked. "You're welcome."

Denton managed a smile, then grimaced, his eyes closing and face twisting into pain.

Emotion started overcoming Silas. How foolish he had been, letting go of this dear friend and wasting the relationship that had been forged through the fires of adversity. And faith. He could have been there for him in his struggles, he could have shown him a different way to believe, one that made sense of all of his questions. He could have reasoned with him, showing him how and why Christianity made sense, why it still mattered.

Suddenly, Denton heaved chestfuls of air in rapid succession, as if he thought the world was emptying of oxygen. Then he clenched his chest.

Silas panicked. "Denton, it's alright. I'm going to get you out of here and get you help." He reached for his flashlight and started easing himself upright.

"No, Silas. No! It's over. Leave me here." He clenched his chest again and arched his back, writhing in pain. No scream left him, he was holding his breath.

"I'm so sorry, Eli. For everything. For how I treated you. For not being there when your faith was fraying. But there's still hope. God will—"

"Stop!" Denton screamed. He breathed rapidly, heaving more lungfuls of air. "No death-bed conversion, Silas. I've made my choice. There's no going back. Besides, death is like an on-off switch," he continued. "Flip, you're done."

Silas stared at his friend. *What a hopeless way to think about death. What a hopeless way to face death. On, then off. Nothing more.*

This was why the ending to the Church's central creed, the Nicene Creed, is so important: *We look for the resurrection of the dead, and the life of the world to come.*

Silas looked away from Denton and scanned the room, his eyes beginning to well with tears. This was what the many remains that surrounded them believed, the goodness of the body and the hope of the resurrection in the life to come, with Jesus Christ as the first fruits of what they would experience. That's what the real Gospels themselves bore witness to. What the apostles bore witness to and the grace their bones still testified to.

He opened his mouth to say something along those lines, but then closed it again. What more was there to say? He wiped his eyes with his hand, then looked down at his friend.

Denton's mouth was open, eyes staring blankly at the floor.

Silas held his breath, waiting for his eyes to blink, straining to sense any rise and fall of his chest.

Neither came.

He eased his friend to the dirt floor, then checked for a pulse.

He closed his eyes and bowed his head, then took a deep breath and sighed.

Lord Jesus Christ, have mercy on Eli, a sinner. To you, I commend his spirit.

CHAPTER 22

WASHINGTON, DC. THE NEXT DAY.

A steady hum permeated the dimly-lit, modest chapel of Indiana limestone, filling the sacred space with a sense of sacred significance. Little flames danced on four long candles near the solid white limestone altar in front of an intricate limestone facade of miniature statues of the four Gospel writers, behind oak altar rails with kneeling cushions patterned in red and gold. Beautiful stained-glass windows depicting biblical scenes in crimson red and leafy green, gold yellow and indigo blue hung void of their awe-inspiring light, the sun having set several hours ago.

Silas continued meditating, eyes closed, legs outstretched, and arms folded sitting on a polished-oak pew in the third row of the Bethlehem Chapel a floor beneath the National Cathedral, America's church and headquarters of the Order of Thaddeus.

After Denton passed, he had carried his body back through the underground passage and up to the surface of the basilica. By that time, the police had arrived, and he was an emotional wreck. Gapinski was kind enough to take over while Celeste comforted him in his loss. Once the gendarmerie had finished taking his statement, Radcliffe wondered if Silas might make a stop at SEPIO headquarters in DC before returning back to Princeton to debrief on the events of the past few days. He had hesitated, but agreed. After the all-day, nine-hour flight in the Order-issued jet, Silas had crashed early in the same austere guest room deep beneath the Cathedral he had stayed in that fateful day a few months ago when his life took an unexpected turn working with the Order to secure the memory of the faith. He woke during the late evening and came down to the chapel to meditate on what he experienced—and pray about his own future contending for the faith.

What is my place in all of this fighting-for-the-faith business?

He shook his head because the idea of 'fighting for the faith' made him want to puke. He had seen up-close-and-personal what happens when religious zealots are incited to fight for their faith. It was one of the reasons he had sworn off anything that smacked of *military* for a life of tweed jackets and tenured teaching. He had one aim: inspire a new generation that Christianity still made sense in a world with superconducting supercolliders and semiconductors, the human genome and human suffering. Yet he saw the skeptical looks on his students' faces, wrestled with their questions of faith and doubt, tried to give them the proof they needed that the Christian faith was still relevant, still reliable.

Then there were those within the Church itself who were trying to reimagine it for a new day, compromising and watering it down for the sake of *progress*. Jesus had warned against such people. So had Paul the apostle. This was the very reason Jude Thaddeus had written his letter urging Christians to contend for the faith. And that wasn't even counting everyone outside the Church who was actively trying to dismantle and discount, suppress and strip the Church.

Like Nous. And Denton, for that matter. Even his own brother.

Yet Silas knew that if the Church had survived the persecutions of Nero and Diocletian; the heresies of Valentinus and Arius,

Marcion and Pelagius; the alternative, anti-Christian worldviews of the Enlightenment and Communism, it would undoubtedly survive whatever else the twenty-first-century world could throw at it.

Including Nous.

And yet...he wondered whether it was indeed time to take a more active role in contending for and preserving the faith, in fighting for and defending what the Church had always believed.

But was he the one to do it?

After another minute of silent contemplation, he opened his eyes and grabbed the well-worn, red lectionary that would guide his prayer and contemplation. He carefully turned its browned pages until he reached the lectionary for the evening. He breathed in deeply through his mouth, then slowly exhaled through his nose to center himself.

"Worship the Lord in the splendor of his holiness," he said quietly, "tremble before him, all the earth. Let us confess our sins against God and our neighbor."

He closed his eyes and ran through his list of sins, both of omission and commission. Top of mind were his sins against Eli: his envious heart, not loving him as his neighbor, failing him and his faith. He continued by reciting the prayer of confession, then recited the next several phrases from memory: "O God, make speed to save us; Lord, make haste to help us. Glory to the Father, and to the Son, and to the Holy Spirit," he said, crossing himself, "as it was in the beginning, is now, and will be forever. Amen."

He paused and closed his eyes again, wondering if the help he had been searching for from the Holy Trinity would ever reach him. Then he continued with the *Lumen Hilare*, the earliest known hymn of the Church still in use today:

O gracious Light,
pure brightness of the everliving Father in heaven,
O Jesus Christ, holy and blessed!

Now as we come to the setting of the sun, and our eyes
behold the vesper light,
we sing your praises, O God: Father, Son, and Holy
Spirit.
You are worthy at all times to be praised by happy
voices,
O Son of God, O Giver of life, and to be glorified
through all the worlds.

"Amen," he mumbled, crossing himself again. He turned in the prayer book toward the back, searching for the evening Psalter, Psalm 23. Finding it, he stiffened and scooted to the edge of his seat in reverence. Then he read aloud: "The Lord is my shepherd; I shall not want."

Exactly what I need to hear. He continued reading:

The Lord is my shepherd, I shall not want.
He makes me lie down in green pastures;
he leads me beside still waters; he restores my soul.
He leads me in right paths for his name's sake.
Even though I walk through the darkest valley, I fear
no evil;
for you are with me;
your rod and your staff—they comfort me.
You prepare a table before me in the presence of my
enemies;
you anoint my head with oil; my cup overflows.
Surely goodness and mercy shall follow me all the days
of my life,
and I shall dwell in the house of the Lord my whole
life long.

"Glory to the Father, and to the Son, and to the Holy Spirit," he said again, crossing himself as he had done before, "as it was in the beginning, is now, and will be forever. Amen."

A sound caught his attention. A footfall coming from the back. He glanced over his shoulder to see the source.

"Mind if I join you?" Radcliffe was walking down the aisle, his black cassock swishing slightly with each step.

"Please," Silas said, moving down the row to give him room.

Radcliffe sat silently, a slight smile hanging on his face as he stared forward. Silas joined him, wondering what he was thinking.

"I was told I might find you here."

Silas said nothing.

"When you failed to turn up for dinner, I had worried you fled back to your nest at Princeton. But Celeste said you crashed early, but that I might find you here later in the evening. I'm glad I did."

Silas glanced at the man. "Why is that?"

"Because I had hoped you would give me another chance to convince you to join our cause." The slight smile had transformed into a boyish grin. The first time Radcliffe had made such an advance, in the Chapel of the Shroud in Turin, Italy, Silas had flatly denied his invitation. He wasn't sure he was any more open to such overtures.

"You are persistent, I'll give you that."

He chuckled softly, low and almost Santa-like. "My persistence is only outmatched by my discernment. And I discern in you the rare qualities of academic acumen and physical pluck that would do the Church a world of good."

Silas couldn't help but be flattered. But he said nothing, staring off toward the altar in silence.

Radcliffe turned in the pew toward him. "This is the second time Nous has struck in as many or more months. Their brazenness is something the Church has not encountered in centuries. The barbarians are at the gates, my boy, and I'm afraid the ramparts are in disrepair, and we are horribly outmatched and undermanned."

Silas said nothing.

"Every day, SEPIO operatives continue to feed us information regarding the latest Nous designs on exterminating the Church of Jesus Christ."

Radcliffe was certainly one for the dramatics.

"Perhaps that's a bit dramatic. Even I don't think the Church is that fragile, like a tealight candle at the mercy of a tornado. But the growing number of Nones who neither identify as Christian nor identify as religious and marked increase in rampant secularism is certainly grounds for concern. As are these latest, renewed attacks on the Church."

This time Silas pivoted toward Radcliffe to engage. "But see, that's my point. Isn't it best I stay put, devoting my life to shaping one mind at a time, influencing one life at a time? Rather than these sweeping gestures of grandeur on the battlefield? Frankly, I'm not at all ready to give up on teaching, and neither ready nor interested to jump back into the kind of work I left behind in Iraq and Afghanistan. Besides, in my experience, the battle is won on the field of hearts and minds, one person at a time."

Radcliffe smiled, seeming to concede and give up the fight. "Well, why don't you have a think about it? Have a pray about it? Let the Holy Spirit sort it out. And let's finish our evening prayer service, shall we?"

Silas smiled. "Fair enough." He opened the red prayer book back up and held it between the two of them, turning to the Apostle's Creed. The two stood, arm-in-arm as brothers and fellow co-workers of Christ to recite what billions of believers throughout the ages had recited. The final line was especially striking, in light of yesterday: *I believe in...the resurrection of the body, and the life everlasting.*

In unison, they said: "Amen."

The two continued standing and closed their eyes, then prayed the Lord's Prayer.

"By the way," Radcliffe said when they finished, "I was sorry to hear about your friend Eli Denton."

Silas's face fell. "Yes, well, he chose his path long ago. I only which I had chosen to stick around long enough to walk with him on it."

Radcliffe reached around his shoulder and squeezed it in a comforting embrace. Afterward, he gestured toward the red book and asked, "Would you mind affording an old man the honors of closing our time of prayer?"

Silas nodded and handed it to him.

Radcliffe took it and held it with both hands, then closed his eyes. After five decades of ministry, he certainly didn't need the help.

"Almighty God, Father of all mercies, we, your unworthy servants, give you humble thanks for all your goodness and loving-kindness to us and to all whom you have made.

"We bless you for our creation, preservation, and all the blessings of this life; but above all for your immeasurable love in the redemption of the world by our Lord Jesus Christ; for the means of grace, and for the hope of glory.

"And, we pray, give us such an awareness of your mercies, that with truly thankful hearts, we may show forth your praise, not only with our lips, but in our lives, by giving up ourselves to your service, and by walking before you in holiness and righteousness all our days; through Jesus Christ our Lord, to whom, with you and the Holy Spirit, be honor and glory throughout all ages. Amen."

Silas echoed in agreement. "Amen."

"And now, O God and Father of all, whom the whole heavens adore," he intoned as he closed the time of worship, his voice rising toward the heavens and filling the sacred, limestone space. "Let the whole earth also worship you, all nations obey you, all tongues confess and bless you, and men and women everywhere love you and serve you in peace; through Jesus Christ our Lord. Amen."

Amen, Silas prayed silently, desiring nothing more than to be the answer to this prayer.

What he couldn't tell Radcliffe was that he secretly wondered how best to realize it. Stay at Princeton or join the Order to contend and fight for the once-for-all faith entrusted to God's holy people. For people like Eli Denton. For his brother.

Only time would tell.

AUTHOR'S NOTE

THE HISTORY BEHIND THE STORY...

This is the second story in my series of a fictional religious order I created, called the Order of Thaddeus, inspired by Jude 3: "I found it necessary to write to you exhorting you to contend earnestly for the faith which was once for all delivered to the saints." Jude is also known as Jude Thaddeus, or simply Thaddeus to some Christians.

I'm an avid reader of James Rollins and Steve Berry who themselves have created fictional organizations to thwart evil schemes of nefarious groups bent on wreaking havoc. So I thought: why not create a similar world in which the Church is threatened by an ancient order hellbent on its destruction and the demise of the Christian faith? One that mirrors similar threats to "the faith which was once for all delivered to the saints," a faith that needs to be intentionally contended for?

Thus was born this series, combining my personal love for action-adventure thrillers and Dan Brown-style religious conspiracy stories, along with my academic background in Bible, theology, Church history, and the vintage Christian faith. I chose the Washington National Cathedral as the worldwide headquarters of the Order and SEPIO (another fictionally-crafted organization) because of my acquaintance with the sacred space while living in the DC area and working on Capitol Hill. Of course, there really isn't a secret special-ops group and religious order headquartered underground. That we know of...

First and foremost my aim with this series is to entertain, spinning propulsive stories that take readers on an action-packed adventure, delighting and thrilling along the way. However, these stories also offer a dose of inspiration and information for the journey of faith, leveraging research into Church history, biblical studies, and theology. They're definitely not sermons, but you'll gain a few insights on your adventure!

Now, onto the history behind this particular tale, which deals with the theme of Jesus' story and the apostolic witness—and why that story is more compelling and believable than alternative ones told from the beginning of Christianity and down through the ages—even just recently.

Over 15 years ago, the Western reading world alighted with a tantalizing tale told by Dan Brown in his *New York Times* best-selling book *The DaVinci Code*. The yarn he spun suggested the story about Jesus wasn't the one that happened. That the *real* story was suppressed by powerful forces within the Church who wanted an alternative one to rule the day, one where Jesus was divine, performed miracles, made atonement for the sins of the world on the cross and was resurrected back from the dead and ascended into heaven. Consequently, as the theory goes, minority voices within the faith were not only suppressed, but *oppressed*, hunted and hacked down by so-called heresy hunters who were hellbent on preserving the officially sanctioned narrative of the powerful, dominant group within the church.

The premise of this book is that there were Dan Browns spinning similar stories well before Dan Brown. As you read, they were called Gnostics, and they wrote a number of books—the so-called gnostic gospels—that told alternative stories to the one told by the Christian Church. One of those surfaced a few decades ago: *The Gospel of Judas*.

At its heart, this gnostic gospel turns the entire narrative of the New Testament Gospels on its head, presenting Judas not as the great betrayer, but the great hero who had been ordered by Jesus himself to carry out his deed of handing Jesus over to the religious authorities. Not since another gnostic gospel, the *Gospel of Thomas* had there been such a challenge to accepted belief surrounding the person and work of Jesus. Of course, the religious conspiracy theorists insisted it was proof that the Church had suppressed and oppressed alternative stories told about Jesus' life by minority voices, requiring a complete rethinking of traditional Christian orthodoxy. Which is what Dan Brown himself had argued in his novel and several others have since argued with the renewed attention given to the gnostic gospels.

It was one of the most significant finds from early Christian literature discovered in our lifetime—right up there with the Dead Sea Scrolls and Nag Hammadi gnostic texts of the early twentieth century. Here is a little overview of *The Gospel of Judas*:

- It offers "The secret account of the revelation that Jesus spoke in conversation with Judas Iscariot during a week three days before he celebrated Passover."
- The secret of Jesus' true person and work is given to Judas. He alone understands Jesus, and the disciples do not. In fact, they follow a different, false god from the one of Jesus: the God of the Old Testament, which is typical of Gnosticism.
- Not only is Judas the true disciple who knows and understands Jesus, he is the true disciple who does what Jesus wants. The vision referenced where the disciples were portrayed as priests perform holy duties and actions in unholy ways underscores this. The other eleven disciples are portrayed as violating the religious laws while invoking Jesus' name; their deeds of defilement don't match their confession of Jesus.

- The eleven, then, not only don't truly know Jesus, they also don't truly follow him. What's more: they've lead everyone else astray! Which means the historic orthodox faith is a false representation of the real revelation of Jesus—an important feature of Gnosticism.
- Judas is portrayed as the 'thirteenth spirit' who leads humanity into a true understanding of Jesus and a true understanding of themselves. (Ironically, I had already named the book *The Thirteenth Apostle* before I discovered this nugget! Needless to say, I was happy for the serendipity.)
- There is a lengthy section where Jesus teaches Judas about cosmology, the origins of the universe, earth, and humanity. Of particular interest is what it says about us: that a certain elite group of people have *gnosis*, knowledge of their true inner divine-selves, and will live on; others don't and not only live in ignorance but will die, simply fading away into oblivion.
- Jesus tells Judas "you will exceed all of them," so that he becomes the thirteenth apostle standing above and outside the other Twelve, having achieved *gnosis*.
- In the end, while the other disciples abandoned Jesus, Judas reminded his true, faithful disciple by handing him over to be killed. This wasn't an act of betrayal, but instead an act of obedience. Typical to Gnosticism, Jesus needed to escape the trappings of the physical body to return to the eternal spiritual realm. Judas made that happen, making him the best disciple and Jesus' most intimate friend.
- Ultimately, Judas does Jesus a favor, showing how salvation not only comes through Jesus' revelation of our true humanity, solving the problem of ignorance. But showing how salvation comes at death when the

soul can escape back to the eternal spiritual realm, our true home.

The Gospel of Judas had been known by experts on early Christianity because of a reference made by Irenaeus, bishop of Lyon, in his famous *Against Heresies* tract combating false teaching in early Christianity. Radcliffe references this fascinating revelation:

> Others again declare that Cain derived his being from the Power above. They declare that Judas the traitor was thoroughly acquainted with these things, and that he alone, knowing the truth as no others did, accomplished the mystery of the betrayal; by him all things, both earthly and heavenly, were thus thrown into confusion. They produce a fictitious history of this kind, which they style the *Gospel of Judas*.

Up until the twentieth-century, scholars wondered about this cryptic reference, whether it was a genuine text or not. And if so, what did it contain, and what was Irenaeus's concern with it? Those questions were answered in 2006 when the so-called Codex Tchacos was unveiled by National Geographic containing it and three other known gnostic texts. The history behind this fascinating early Christian document coming to light recounted in the book is accurate.

The third-century codex had originally been found in 1978 during an excavation along the banks of the Nile River 120 miles south of Cairo. Inside a cave were some baskets of Roman flasks, a number of human remains, and two limestone boxes. Inside one of those boxes were four different manuscripts: a mathematical treatise, a fragment copy of the Old Testament Book of Exodus, some fragments of Paul's letters from the New Testament, and a codex containing the Gospel of Judas and three other Coptic gnostic texts previously known from the Nag Hammadi discovery from the 1940s. Remarkably, they had laid undisturbed and preserved in the dry desert chamber for over sixteen hundred years.

Eventually, the manuscripts wound up in the hands of Frieda Nussberger Tchacos, a wealthy dealer in ancient art. She eventually persuaded National Geographic and a small team of scholars to translate and verify the manuscript's authenticity. Once they showcased the find and translation through a special television production and in print editions, the gnostic gospel made international waves—mostly because of the alternative story it told about Christianity's most infamous, nefarious character: Judas Iscariot.

The Maecenas Foundation for Ancient Art is the current guardian of the codex, safeguarding it and providing for its publication. The Aeon Foundation is a fictional creation I used to serve as a bridge between *The Gospel of Judas* and Eli Denton's exploits. Not much by way of restoration and translation work has been undertaken since the initial effort. And there are indeed small gaps and large missing pieces to the manuscript folio pieces, which gave me an idea:

What if it was possible to retrieve the information contained in those missing pieces—much of which had broken off from the main manuscript pages through time and mishandling? And what if someone was able to undercut the apostolic witness to the story of Jesus contained in the New Testament Gospels using the revelation within those pieces?

That's where Silas's brother, Sebastian, came into play. The artificial intelligence algorithm he created to analyze the fragments and restore the distorted images of the original Coptic text is mostly accurate. There is some pretty fascinating technology that does indeed infer an image from the damaged pictorial data using the surrounding information to generate a near-accurate image that's fully restored. The little demonstration Sebastian offered his brother as proof—the one with the old school English telephone box with the curved roof and restored TELE text from pixilated nothingness—was taken directly from a scholarly journal article showcasing the technology. I just fictionalized it a bit to serve my story, but the underlying premise is genuine.

All of the text from the original Gospel of Judas is also genuine, as quoted from *The Gospel of Judas* published by National Geographic. The sections where Sebastian "restored" the original Coptic that we later learn were actually programmed into the AI algorithm are a combination of actual gnostic texts from *The Nag Hammadi Scriptures* (New York: Harper Collins, 2007), a volume that includes the gnostic gospels discovered in Nag Hammadi and some others, as well as some of the biblical text manipulated to appear as though the Gospel writers plagiarized from *The Gospel of Judas*. Everything in italics is original to *The Gospel of Judas*, and the bold text is what was added from these sources.

Now a word about the other angle of this story: the apostles and their supposed relics.

Like Silas, growing up I had serious reservations about venerating such objects of the faith, believing such acts to be if not outright idolatry, then at least borderline. But then I read the perspective of the famed New Testament scholar, N. T. Wright in his book *Pilgrimage Today*:

> the cult of relics can be explained...in terms of the grace of God at work in the actual physical life of a person. Even after their death (so the argument runs) their body can be regarded as a place where special grace and the presence of God were truly made known. (4–5)

He goes on to connect that logic to that of secondary relics, like places where saints have lived, and the special feeling and experience of God's presence he himself has felt in such places. As he explains, "The only answer I have to this day is that when God is known, sought and wrestled within a place, a memory of that remains, which those who know and love God can pick up" (5). Why couldn't the same be true of apostolic relics?

As Wright suggests, there's a sense in which the relics of the Christian faith can be explained in terms of God's grace working in and through the physical life of the person, even after death, their bodies becoming regarded as a special place where God's love and presence are made known, to both the faithful and those seeking faith. If this former Anglican bishop could accept such practices, one every bit committed to the historic Christian faith and gospel of Jesus Christ, then perhaps there is a place for these religious artifacts within the life of the Church—and the life of the Christian.

Now, does that mean if we didn't have such religious artifacts, like the apostle relics, or if some diabolical ex-Christian with an ax to grind against the faith destroyed them the Christian faith would be in trouble? Not at all! The enduring witness of the apostles preserved for us in the Gospels of Matthew, Mark, Luke, and John are more than sufficient to recount the good-news story of Jesus—life, death, and resurrection. And there is more than enough historical and manuscript evidence to verify their original story, which can and should form the foundation of our own faith in Christ. However, there may be something to what Wright and others who appreciate the relics of Jesus' earliest disciples claim: God's grace, love, and presence can be made known, to both the faithful and those seeking faith, through the fragments of their remains, offering a tangible, experiential place to remember the story of Jesus through their witness.

Regardless if you or I place much stock in such things, at minimum the idea that the memory and witness of these apostles, preserved in their Gospels, is important. And what this story is conveying is that the witness of the apostles is being constantly challenged. People are seeking to destroy the memory of this witness—whether by actually destroying the fragments of their remains or undermining the story told in the Gospels. We must be on guard, preserving and protecting that memory. Because in contrast to Gnosticism and *The Gospel of Judas*, the story told in the Bible generally and Gospels specifically is radically different:

- Its message is meant for everyone in the world—not the super elite few that Gnosticism claims.
- God created the world on purpose and with purpose and said that it was good. All of it, material and immaterial. Which is the exact opposite of the gnostic myth.
- Our problem isn't that we are ignorant of the divinity within ourselves, but that we are badly bent and in desperate need of rescue.
- The good news is that God didn't just abandon us by sitting up in some lofty realm in outer space to leave us to our own devices, as Gnosticism teaches.
- Instead, God became one of us. Not the pseudo-human deity who wore the human body like a spacesuit as the gnostics taught. But a real, live human being, Jesus of Nazareth, who lived this life and understands this life.
- Not only did he live with us and for us, he died in our place. For you, for the whole world. Not to escape it, but to save it! But more than that: to restore it, to put it back together again to the way that he intended it to be at the beginning of creation.
- Which the resurrection proves. Jesus came back to life in a real, physical body. He ate fish with his friends and showed them the scars left behind on his hands

> and feet and side. Which means that Jesus didn't want liberation from the flesh; he was happy to come back to live in a body! And he will be plenty happy to give all of his children brand-spanking new ones someday when he returns to Earth to make all things new.

Perhaps N. T. Wright said it best at the conclusion of *Judas and the Gospel of Jesus*, his scholarly analysis of the gnostic gospel. After reiterating the above summation of what the Bible teaches, he writes, "This is the real gospel. It has to do with the real Jesus, the real world, and above all the real God. As the advertisements say, accept no substitutes" (146).

Especially, the tale told by *The Gospel of Judas* and religious conspiracy writers like Dan Brown and, as Radcliffe says, his counterparts: the Dan Browns with PhDs who sow doubt about the story of Jesus and what really happened. The Gospels of Mathew, Mark, Luke, and John are the only ones that tell the historic, truthful old, old story of Jesus and his love. Accept no substitutes.

Research is a vital part of my writing process for creating compelling stories that entertain, inform, and inspire. Here are a few of the resources I used to research the Gospel of Judas:

- Kasser, Rodolphe, Marvin Meyer, and Gregor Wurst. *The Gospel of Judas*. Washington, DC: National Geographic, 2006. www.bouma.us/judas1
- Ehrman, Bart D. *The Lost Gospel of Judas Iscariot*. New York: Oxford University Press, 2006. www.bouma.us/judas2
- Wright, N. T. *Judas and the Gospel of Jesus*. Grand Rapids: Baker Books, 2006. www.bouma.us/judas3

- You can view a PDF of the original Gospel of Judas text I used as the basis of this story for yourself, here: www.bouma.us/judas4

ABOUT THE AUTHOR

J. A. Bouma is an emerging author of vintage faith fiction. As a former congressional staffer and pastor, and bestselling author of over thirty religious fiction and nonfiction books, he blends a love for ideas and adventure, exploration and discovery, thrill and thought. With graduate degrees in Bible and theology, he writes within the tension of faith and doubt, spirituality and theology, Church and culture, belief and practice, modern and vintage forms of Church, and the gritty drama that is our collective pilgrim story.

He also offers nonfiction resources on the Christian faith under Jeremy Bouma. His books and courses help people rediscover and retrieve the vintage Christian faith by connecting that faith in relevant ways to our 21st century world.

Jeremy lives in Grand Rapids, Michigan, with his wife, son, and daughter, and their rambunctious boxer-pug-terrier Zoe.

www.jabouma.com
jeremy@jabouma.com

facebook.com/jaboumabooks
twitter.com/bouma
amazon.com/author/jabouma

THANK YOU!

A big thanks for joining Silas Grey and the rest of SEPIO on their adventure saving the world!

Enjoy the story? Here's what you can do next:

If you loved the book and have a moment to spare, **a short review is much appreciated.** Nothing fancy, just your honest take. Spreading the word is probably the #1 way you can help independent authors like me and help others enjoy the story.

And if you're ready for another adventure...check out the first story in the series: *Holy Shroud*. A "Bonus Sneak Peak" has been provided for your reading pleasure. When you're ready, just go to this link to join the adventure: www.bouma.us/holy-shroud

GET YOUR FREE THRILLER

Building a relationship with my readers is one of my all-time favorite joys of writing! Once in a while I like to send out a newsletter with giveaways, free stories, pre-release content, updates on new books, and other interesting bits on my stories.

Join my insider's group for updates, giveaways, and your free novel—a full-length action-adventure story in my *Order of Thaddeus* thriller series. Just tell me where to send it.

Follow this link to subscribe:
www.jabouma.com/free

ALSO BY J. A. BOUMA

J. A. Bouma is an emerging author of vintage faith fiction. You may also like these books that explore the tension of faith and doubt, spirituality and theology, Church and culture, belief and practice, modern and vintage forms of Church, and the gritty drama that is our collective pilgrim story.

***Order of Thaddeus* Action-Adventure Thriller Series**

Holy Shroud • Book 1

The Thirteenth Apostle • Book 2

Hidden Covenant • Book 3

American God • Book 4

BONUS SNEAK PEAK

HOLY SHROUD (BOOK 1)

PROLOGUE

PARIS, FRANCE. 1314.

It was the spicy scent of something burning that first needled Jacque de Molay's consciousness to awaken. Crackling pine logs and burning hay connected the synapses in his brain to the impression of a distant childhood memory, when times were simpler, happier, less threatened.

It was the putrid smell of burning flesh that snapped him back to reality.

Jacques' eyes flittered open, a darkened picture fading in and out of focus. The right side of his head made him regret his decision.

What...Where am I?

A wave of nausea crashed against his stomach, forcing his eyes shut. He caught his breath, suppressing the urge to retch. It wasn't working. He tried to sit as his mouth watered and the gag reflex began working overtime, but he was bound. Both arms, both legs. He strained weakly against the cords, the tide rising within. There was nothing he could do. He strained again, trying to pivot his body and head as much as he could, but it was no use. His mouth exploded in sour bile, and half-digested potatoes, carrots, and venison awash in fermentation.

Jacques gulped for air and spat to clear his mouth, then

weakly sank back against the table, the memory of the events from so long ago beginning to surface in his aching head—reminding him of what had led to this fateful day.

The Brotherhood had been celebrating the birthday of one of their members the night before. Ian, the youngest of the brothers and his godson, had turned twenty-five. Which meant he was now a full member of the religious order. Smoked venison from the day's hunt, and tart mead brewed from the early spring, were plentiful. As was enough song, dance, and laughter to last a lifetime of memories.

Jacques was in high spirits and beaming with pride. He raised his glass, brimming full with the finest wine from the choicest grapes from Burgundy, ready to toast the young man's milestone, when it happened. So suddenly, so unexpectedly.

A series of *thumping* sounds beating rhythmically, like a war drum from the outer wall, first caught his attention. At first, he mistook them for the sounds of celebration. But shouts of disturbance rising from the outer courtyard of the mighty fortress of the Brotherhood quickly dispelled those impressions, twisting his gut with fear. A large crashing sound was immediately followed by more shouts and then screaming. The unmistakable sounds of thousand-pound horses and a raging fire removed any confusion.

They were under attack.

Jacques hurried to a large window in the gathering hall of the second floor. Flames were consuming the gatehouse. Mounted horse units and infantry bearing the seal of King Phillip IV of France were flooding the courtyard, their navy-blue banners bearing gold fleur-de-lis, demanding entrance into the main compound. He caught sight of women and children running, seeking shelter from the onslaught, before he rallied his men for the fight ahead.

Rumors had swirled for months among the fellow Brotherhood chapters across Europe and the Holy Lands that the king was moving against them, having become panicked over their outsized wealth, power, and influence. Reports told of mounted units of fury and fire raiding secret compounds in outer regions. Arrests were made. Brothers were tortured. "Confessions" were extracted, though for what reason was beginning to come to light.

An ancient holy relic bearing the power of faith and life was being sought.

They knew the day would come. They had prepared for it. Signed up for it, even. The holy relic had been entrusted to their care, and they would die protecting it. Some did that day almost seven years ago. Many more through the years undergoing "ecclesial procedures." Also known as the Inquisitorial hearings.

Now it appeared his day had come at last.

A face emerged from the soft light and hard shadows sending a jolt of adrenaline to Jacques's stomach, threatening another round of retching.

It was the face of an ancient threat, the dreaded ibis Bird-Man. Thoth, the Egyptian god of knowledge. The man who wore the ancient face was bare-chested and tanned to a burnished bronze, his upper shoulders ringed by an intricate weave of gold and turquoise beads at the base of his neck. A long beak of onyx black, silent and probing, peered down at Jacques from behind a mask of gold, flanked by ribbons of indigo.

It can't be true...

Jacques swallowed hard, his head throbbing in protest. He strained forward against the thick cords of rope holding his well-muscled body, tilting his head for a better look at his surroundings. He was in the center of a large rectangular barn made of stone and vaulted by solid oak beams, punctuated with the sour smell of manure. Stacks of hay were shoved to the periphery. The stalls had been emptied of their four-legged creatures, and in their place were his brothers, strapped to tables like his own. Shadows danced around the vast interior, mirroring the ghastly beings hovering over his brothers.

Like the one staring him in the face.

A bloodcurdling cry sent his skin crawling with static shock, snapping Jacques's head toward the large entrance drenched in dancing yellows and oranges and reds. The view through the maw of darkness sent his stomach to the dirty ground beneath. Within minutes the screams faded, and Jacques's brother was resting in the arms of his Savior.

"That," said Bird-Man, "was a trial run for the main attraction." He leaned in, a large grin of white gleaming behind the gold mask. "The lad who I've been told is your godson, Ian."

Jacques went pale, and bowels went weak, at the mention of his precious son. He eased himself upright, straining to see into the nightmare of darkness beyond, seeking a glimpse of the young man.

He could make out a tall, slender figure tied to a pole, hands bound behind him. He was older than the last time Jacques had seen him. Straw-colored hair hung to the man's broad shoulders. His face was unmistakable with its high, angular cheekbones. A gift from his late mother.

"Noooo!" Jacques screamed, spittle flying out of his mouth. Another wave of vomit threatened to arise as he strained uselessly against the thick cords bound to his wrists and ankles. He screamed until his lungs gave out, his voice fading into hoarse nothingness, face darkening crimson as he raged and strained forward. He paused and heaved large breaths, then screamed and strained again, mind swimming with delirium.

"Molay," Bird-Man intoned silkily. "I had no idea you were such a sentimental man."

The figure masked in gold and indigo pressed a glove-encased hand on Jacques's chest, shoving him back against the table with purpose, stilling him. He turned back and stared into Bird-Man's beady, little eyes. Then launched a well-aimed glob of spittle into Evil Incarnate.

Bird-Man recoiled. Pale goop dripped off the golden mask

onto the dirt floor. A smile curled coolly upward as he slowly wiped what remained of the insult away. Then he leaned down over Jacques's face, holding his gaze.

"What a beautiful lad," he said. "A real shame he has to die. Unless, that is, you co-operate."

"What is the meaning of this?" Jacques roared uselessly.

The masked figure leaned in closer, his beak nearly touching Jacques's chest. "I think you know exactly the meaning of this."

He did. Jacques sank back against the wooden table, then turned his head, panic welling within as he stared at a shadow on a distant wall.

His Brotherhood had been commissioned to keep the holy relic safe stretching back a hundred years. Since the sacking of Constantinople, they had pledged their treasure and lives to keep it from falling into the hands of the wicked once again. Given their unique position within the political and religious climate, the Brotherhood was strategically positioned to act as the relic's guardians. Their heavily guarded fortresses would ensure the secrecy and safety of the Church's most important object of veneration.

For decades rumors had swirled that the Brotherhood was in possession of an object of great religious prestige and power, capable of turning the hardest of hearts and doubters into true believers. During their initiation ceremony, members were given a momentary glimpse of this most sacred object: the supreme vision of God attainable on earth. The Image of Christ himself.

Even more, rumors circulated throughout Europe of an idol before which they prostrated themselves at their headquarters at the Villeneuve du Temple, a massive fortress complex of stone and iron in Paris. The holy object was said to be like an old piece of skin, as though embalmed, and like polished cloth, pale and discolored with a divine image etched in its fibers.

Several groups and individuals had attempted to seize its likeness over the centuries. One, in particular, had attempted for generations to destroy it, with ancient roots stretching back to the early Church. At times they had sought a syncretic version of the faith, resulting in aberrant variations deemed heretical by the Church. Ultimately, it sought the Church's extinction.

And the face representing that ancient evil was now hovering over Jacques de Molay, Grand Master of the Poor Fellow-Soldiers of Christ and of the Temple of Solomon. Also known as the Order of Solomon's Temple.

The Knights Templar.

Suddenly Jacques's face exploded leftward in pain. A geyser of blood burst from his nose.

"Where is it?" Bird-Man roared.

Jacques sputtered and coughed as blood poured down the front of his face, the metallic taste of copper threatening another retching episode.

"My patience is thinning, Molay," Bird-Man said silkily. "We know the Order assumed guardianship of the Church's most prized relic a century ago. We've been tracking its movement for decades, biding our time until we had full confirmation, until the moment presented itself. Fortunately, one of your own was willing to offer us the necessary information."

Shock pinged Jacques's gut. The right side of Bird-Man's mouth curled upward.

"Oh, yes. Squawked like a chicken, telling us quite a tale about a long span of cloth with the faint image of a man in death's pose."

Jacques strained toward Bird-Man with all his might, coming within an inch of his face. He roared and snapped his jaw at the abomination, but it was useless. He collapsed onto the table, weakened and breathing heavily.

So the secret is out. The one the Church has been guarding for nearly thirteen centuries.

"And you'll be as cooperative, won't you? Because if you aren't—"

Bird-Man took Jacques's head in both hands and shoved it up off the table so that he was looking once more at his helpless godson outside. Bird-Man nodded, as if signaling to someone far off into the dark of night.

A few seconds later, a faint light flickered to life in the distance beyond the open barn door. It bobbed and weaved in the blackness, growing with each second. Then the tiny flame roared to life near the ground beneath someone else's bound, erect body just beyond Ian. Long, undulating, breathy cries of agony joined the snapping flames as the fire started at the base of the pole and worked its way upward, crescendoing into a dirge of death.

"Do you see that, Jacques?" Bird-Man whispered, steadying the Grand Master's head and eyelids. "There are eleven more left, just like him. Including your precious godson. All waiting to die for your secret. Is it worth sacrificing these lives to protect your pathetic relic?" Bird-Man shoved him against the rough wooden surface, the cries of agony dying down to nothing as the victim passed on from this life to the next. "Now tell me. Where is the Holy Shroud?"

I cannot. I will not. The Shroud must be protected at all cost.

"I will spare the young man's life and yours and the rest of your brothers if you tell me the location of the Holy Image. Last I knew, it was safely tucked inside the parish within your compound. Now it's missing!" Bird-Man slammed Jacques's head against the table, the sounds of agony outside drowning out Jacques's own pain.

Lord, Jesus Christ, I will not abandon you. I will not forsake your Image.

"What was that?" Bird-Man asked in irritation. "Do you have something to say?"

Jacques swallowed, trying to clear his dry, raw throat. But it was no use. He winced instead, and whispered, "I have nothing to say."

Bird-Man stood next to Jacques's table, head cocked. "Nothing to say? Really?" Then he paused, nodding off to the side again. "So be it."

Suddenly, a burst of flames illuminated the darkness. Jacques leaned forward.

Ian!

"Noooo!" he screamed.

He strained against his bindings, twisting them this way and that, fighting like hell to rescue the young man he'd vowed to protect.

Flames licked Ian's feet before moving up his legs. He arched his body as the flames rose higher, as if to escape the maw of fiery death awaiting him. As the inferno began stretching higher, his long, blond hair flittered away, like dandelion seeds carried along by a mid-summer afternoon breeze.

Punctuating the screams of pain and agony was a final cry in Latin: "In nomine Patris et Filii et Spiritus Sancti."

In the name of the Father, the Son, the Holy Spirit.

Then it ceased. No more screams. No more cries.

Jacques sank into the wooden boards, his body spent of all energy and emotion, delirious from the agony of losing the one person who was like family.

The next hour was something out of a nightmare. Bird-Man grabbed the same scythe he used against the young captive and thrust it probingly, deliberately underneath Jacques's right bottom rib. He moved it to and fro, as if the secret to his question about the Shroud's whereabouts were hidden deep within Jacques' chest cavity.

But nothing fell out. No secret. No confession.

Jacques gasped for breath, but he was undeterred. As Grand Master, it was his sworn duty to maintain the secret in order to preserve the memory of the central element of the faith: the resurrection of his Lord and Savior, Jesus Christ.

Even at the expense of his brothers.

And his own godson.

This went on for another hour. Blood was seeping through the cracks of the table, pooling beneath. Bird-Man had another of his brothers lit on fire, and then another to wear down Jacques's resolve. It didn't work.

Exhausted mentally, emotionally, and physically, the Grand Master finally offered: "You could burn the countryside down, but I will never betray the memory of our Lord's resurrection. Neither will the other brothers. And they'd torch me themselves if they discovered I'd told you the secrets of the Shroud's location."

Bird-Man stopped. Splattered blood shone crimson on the golden mask. He threw the scythe to the ground and smeared his hands clean on his bare chest.

"So be it, Jacques. I have to admit, I admire you for your strength and resolve. But it's fruitless. Eventually, we'll find it. Eventually, we'll destroy it. It may take a decade. Centuries, even. But Jacques..." His beak slid over Jacques' face as he whispered his final growl: "When we do, we will blot out the memory of your faith's central belief forever. It will wilt under the weight of our might—our *resolve*—until there is nothing left of it."

He stood and motioned to another of his associates. "Take him to meet his godson and the rest of his Brotherhood. And his dead god."

Jacques's head was swimming with pain and confusion. "What...where are you taking me? Ian...Ian!"

A burly man began dragging the table holding Jacques through the barn doors and into the deathly dark night still lit by the waning embers of his brothers. The man lifted Jacques's table on end, propping him up with two strong beams from behind, next to Ian's charred remains.

"One last chance, Molay. Just say the word. The location where you've hidden away the Holy Shroud."

Jacques, barely conscious, raised his head. He took three deep, wheezing breaths before replying: "Abba, I pray for their forgiveness. For they know not what they are doing." He slumped forward against his bindings, his life slipping away as blood oozed out from the wound in his chest.

Bird-Man's eyes narrowed. He nodded and walked away.

The fire quickly consumed the hay and branches before hungrily moving up the wooden table. The pain was more than Jacques could have imagined, but he had neither the energy nor the breath to protest. The flames ate away his feet and legs before quickly moving upward toward his outstretched arms *in crucifixio*.

Lord Jesus Christ, Son of God, receive my spirit, he silently prayed to the risen God to whom he was bearing witness, in order to protect the memory that sat at the heart of his faith for over fifty generations.

CHAPTER 1

PRINCETON, NEW JERSEY. PRESENT DAY.

Silas Grey was going to be late for class, again. But for good reason. He was waiting for the results of a scientific test that would rock the religious and non-religious worlds to their core.

Why teach class when he held the fate of faith and doubt in his hands?

He stood and grabbed his favorite cream-colored ceramic mug stained brown from a decade of use, emblazoned with a crimson Harvard University logo, his rival alma mater. He shuffled over to Mr. Coffee for a refill, took a swig, and grimaced as he swallowed the leftover brew gone stale, tasting of burnt toast. It would have to do.

He paced the inside of his Princeton University office, one once held by the venerable Protestant Fundamentalist J. Gresham Machen. Which was ironic, because Silas was a former Catholic turned Protestant. At another level it wasn't: like Machen, Silas relished the opportunity to inspire a new generation to rediscover religious faith in the face of a modern world that rejected it as a delusion, the ravings of madmen, an opiate for the naive masses. And he did it in a way that would make ol' Machen turn over in his grave: through relics.

His "History of Religious Relics" class was the most popular elective in the Department of Religion. Indiana Jones probably had something to do with that. As did Dan Brown, having popularized relics after wrapping them in the garb of religious conspiracies. Silas also guessed the experiential nature of religious objects of veneration also made the topic inviting.

Gone were the days when any of the religious faiths could justify themselves purely on tradition alone. Personal experiences, not dogmatic beliefs, ruled the day. And the relics from every religion offered interested students—from the committed Christian to the spiritual-but-not-religious type—the chance to explore their spiritual questions through objects rooted in historical experience.

As an academic, Silas had spent the majority of his research probing these objects and plumbing the depths of their history. As a Christian, he was interested in connecting historical objects of Christianity to his faith in a way that enhanced and propelled it forward.

Which was remarkable, considering Protestants dismissed such things as fanciful spiritualism at best and gross idolatry at worst. Perhaps it was the inner Catholic convert rearing its head. Or maybe it was an extension of his own longing for more tangible ways to experience the God he had been searching for his whole life. Maybe still, it came from his interest in helping his students find faith.

Regardless, his research had led him down interesting paths, including becoming one of the foremost experts on the single greatest, most well-known of Christian relics: The Shroud of Turin.

Which was the topic of the day's lecture. The one he was running late for.

Silas flopped back down in his well-worn burgundy leather chair, one of the few things he took from his late father's estate. He checked his watch, then huffed. *Where are those blasted results?*

He went to drain his mug when a football-sized furball bounded up onto his lap, nearly sending the remaining brew onto his checkered dress shirt.

"Barnabas!"

He swung the mug upward just as his feline friend nuzzled against his chest and curled up in his lap.

"Make yourself at home, why don't you?" he mumbled. But then he set the mug down, took a breath, and smiled. He scratched his faithful friend's ears, thankful for the interruption to his worrying. "There you go. That's a good boy."

Silas had picked up the beautiful slate-gray Persian while serving with the Rangers during the early days of Operation Iraqi Freedom. The skin-and-bones feline had wandered into camp looking for a handout. He had always been a dog lover, but the pathetic sight and the cat's single clipped ear, which told all the story he needed, tugged on his heart. He knew he was breaking protocol, the U.S. Central Command having created an order called GO-1A just before 9/11, which outlawed companion animals. But he was nearly done with his tour, and it seemed like the right thing to do. And when things went south that fateful day on the road to Mosul, Barnabas lived up to his name: son of comfort. Now he was fat and happy, offering continued comfort when times got stressful.

Like today.

Silas drained his mug as Barnabas stood and stretched. Barnabas bounded off Silas's lap and trotted out of his office. He glanced at his watch again, then his hand instinctively moved toward his middle desk drawer, where a bottle of little, blue pills nested. Just one of his friends and a glass of water would make the anxiety go away.

No. Not yet.

Instead, he called out, "Anything?"

"They'll get here when they get here," Miles called back, Silas's teaching assistant for the past three years.

Silas sighed and leaned back in his chair, bringing a hand up to a knot that was needling his right temple. “Well, did you call him to check on the sample?”

“Three times!”

Silas grimaced with a mixture of pain and pleasure as he worked on the knot with his knuckle. “And you're sure he said he actually ran the sample? That he’d get word today?”

Miles appeared in the doorway, folded his arms, and leaned against the wooden door frame. “These things take time—”

“I know, I know, I know," Silas said cutting him off. He closed his eyes as he continued to massage his temple. "But today is D-Day. I can't wait any longer! I've got deadlines for that journal paper. And I need time to sift through the data beforehand—”

“Professor!” Miles said, cutting him off in return. “Dr. Avery is your friend. He won't let you down. If he said you'd get the results today, you'll get the results today.”

Silas leaned back and took a breath. He nodded, then ran his hands across his crew-cut black hair, a hold-over from his days with the Army Rangers. "Fine." He took another deep calming breath and startled. "Gosh, I'm gonna be late!"

He grabbed his coffee mug and walked over to Mr. Coffee for another refill. He poured himself the rest of the brew and took a swig. He grimaced again but took it back to his desk. It was going to be one of those days. Mr. Coffee portended it.

“By the way,” Miles said loudly from his outer office adjacent to Silas's. “This came for you.” He came back in and handed Silas an expensive-looking, cream-colored envelope. “Dr. Silas Grey” was scrawled in black ink across its face, written by a black fountain pen by the looks of it.

Silas smiled. He knew that handwriting well, having received plenty of notes on that paper stock and written by that well-used nib.

“It came by courier this morning,” Miles said walking back out.

"Courier? From Henry?"

"Don't know," Miles shouted. "I'm not in the habit of opening your mail."

Dr. Henry Gregory was a long-time family friend. A friend of his father from West Point. After serving in Vietnam together, the two had become war buddies, but the relationship was deeper than that. They were like brothers, inseparable even though they pursued different paths: one military, one academic. When Thomas Grey died in 2001, Henry had driven down from Boston to DC to comfort Silas during his junior year of college at Georgetown University. He became something of a second father, eventually taking on the role of an academic mentor when Silas studied under him during his doctoral work at Harvard, studying historical theology and church history.

Henry had taken an early interest in Silas's academic career, bringing him in as his teaching aide and research assistant. Like Silas, he was also a Catholic-turned-Protestant. And as one of the foremost experts on the emerging field of relicology, the study and research of historical religious relics, he taught Silas everything he knew about early Christian religious artifacts and their significance for the Church. Which led Silas to his own relic passion project, the Shroud of Turin, the cloth believed to be the burial garment of Jesus Christ of Nazareth—and the most significant Christian religious artifact.

Silas caressed the thick envelope, then began tracing over the black curves of his name with his index finger. He frowned, wondering how his dear friend was getting along. A year ago, Henry had suffered a stroke. He had survived, thank God, and the damage was minimal. But he'd had a harder time getting around physically. Thankfully, his mind was still sharp; his wit was even sharper.

Miles walked back in and set another stack of mail on Silas's desk. "How is he?"

"I don't know. Last I heard he was wheeling around campus

on one of those motorized carts. Poor guy. He was preparing a paper on a recent discovery surrounding the history of the Shroud between AD 1200 and 1300. He was thrilled where the research was going. Couldn't wait to share the details. That was a few weeks ago."

"Well, what did he say in his note?"

"I haven't gotten to it yet."

"You better get to it," Miles said, walking out again. "You've got class in five."

Silas looked at his watch, then tore open the back of the envelope, the scent of musk drifting out. Inside was a single sheet of cream parchment, folded in half with the letters HAG stamped on the front in gold foil cursive lettering. Henry Alfred Gregory.

He opened it and saw two short lines of cursive text, scrawled in black. Silas furrowed his brow. He could feel his pulse quicken, his breathing picking up pace as he read:

We need to talk. ASAP.

It's about our faithful friend. He's in ill health.

-HAG

That was it. Silas turned over the paper. Nothing else. He laid it flat on his desk, then re-read his friend's note.

What on earth?

He fixated on "faithful friend" and "ill health." Faithful friend was a nickname the two had given the Shroud years ago, a sort of code name they had developed for the Holy Image when they were working closely on developing more of the history of the relic. After all, that's who Jesus Christ had been to each of them. It seemed fitting.

But in ill health? What did that mean? The cloak-and-dagger routine was unusual for Henry. Silas surmised it was more code, like "friend." Danger, perhaps. But why? How could the Shroud be in "ill health," in danger? It was under strict Vatican protection. Seemed overly melodramatic for Henry.

Silas folded his arms and leaned back in his chair. Then he picked up his cell phone to dial his mentor. It rang. He got nothing but his voicemail. He smiled. It was good to hear his voice. He hung up without leaving a message.

"He's probably teaching," Silas mumbled.

He checked his watch. Probably right.

He looked at his phone again, then picked it up and dialed his friend once more. It rang again. He looked at his watch again, remembering that Henry only had morning classes. So he should be free. And should be answering his phone.

It went to voicemail again. Silas sighed before leaving a message telling him he had received his note and to call as soon as he could. He was worried about their "friend" and wanted to get the news on his health.

He tossed the cell on a stack of papers and sat back in his chair. He sighed and stared outside, growing increasingly worried about the health of his actual friend.

The door to his room was thrown open, thudding heavily against a bookcase. It was Miles. His eyes were wide. His nose was flared. He looked grim.

Silas widened his eyes and cocked his head. "What's wrong?"

"It's Father Arnold. Line one. You need to take this. It's about Henry."

CHAPTER 2

Silas snatched the headset from his desk phone. "Hello?"

"Yes, Silas, it's Father Arnold. How are you?"

"I'm fine, Father. But Miles said something has happened to Henry. What's the matter? Did he fall again?"

Ever since that blasted stroke, Henry hadn't been the same. At the start of the school year, he had fallen and broken his hip in the shower after slipping and falling out of the tub. He needed surgery, and with no one to care for him afterward, Silas had volunteered. Henry's wife had passed away a few years ago, so managing his care was up to him. He had rejected a nursing home, insisting he was "fit as a fiddle!" His mind sure was, still able to run laps around Silas. His body was not. But Silas had relished the few weeks he took over Christmas break to care for his mentor. It gave him the chance to repay the debt he owed the man who had been a second father to him after his first one had died.

"No, it wasn't a fall..." Father Arnold trailed off.

Silas waited for a few beats, willing him to continue. Finally, he said, "Father, what's going on?"

The man sighed, then said softly: "He's dead, Silas."

All the air left his lungs at once, like he was sucker-punched in the gut. "Dead?" he whispered.

"I'm afraid so."

His mind swam in a cauldron of questions that assaulted and paralyzed his mind in rapid succession: How? Why? What? He couldn't manage to get them out. His mouth literally hung open in disbelief. Emotion tried to climb its way to the surface, but his past wouldn't let it.

"There's more," Arnold said, emotion choking in his own throat.

Again, more silence. This wasn't like Father Arnold. He was usually straightforward, very to-the-point. These short, clipped responses were telling Silas more than what Father himself was.

"Father, what's going on?" Silas asked again.

Father Arnold hesitated. "Henry died...mysteriously."

Mysteriously? Silas squinted his eyes and shook his head, staring at his desk, his right hand raising involuntarily to his forehead. He leaned forward resting his elbow on his desk to consider this massive turn of events.

"What does that mean? Mysteriously?"

"It means his death may not have been an accident." Father Arnold paused again. "By all accounts, it was a natural death. Died in his sleep from a heart attack. Which doesn't make sense, because nothing about the man would have suggested such a health problem was looming over the horizon. After his stroke, he had been fine last I heard."

Arnold was right. Aside from some nerve damage from the stroke, Henry was indeed fit as a fiddle, as Silas' old friend had said.

"OK..." Silas said, not understanding.

"And yet, dead of a heart attack. Pronounced at the scene."

"So what's the problem, then?"

"The problem, Silas, is that three other STURP members

have also passed away from heart attacks in the last twenty hours."

Silas felt his mouth open again. His hand involuntarily moved from his forehead to his temple. Four members of the Shroud of Turin Research Project, the premier research group of the Holy Image, were dead? Of heart attacks? Within twenty hours of each other?

How could that be a coincidence?

"Who, Father?"

"Carson from England. Selvaggi and Boselli from Italy."

"Not Carson," Silas said, stunned. He was one of the few sindonologists who had appreciated Silas's contributions to the international cohort of Shroud experts. "And Sevaggi and Bosseli?"

"I'm afraid so. And you know the latter was from the Vatican." Arnold paused, then whispered, "Which has caused quite the stir, to say the least."

Four international deaths under the same circumstances, with people among the same association. Definitely not a coincidence.

"So what's being done about this? Is the Vatican involved, the gendarmerie perhaps investigating the links?"

"Nothing's being done. Too soon. I've only learned about the deaths a few hours myself. I'm sure there will be an investigation, but on what grounds? The link is circumstantial, at best."

"Circumstantial?" Silas said, voice slightly raised. "Four STURP members die under suspicious circumstances, and nobody cares?"

Father Arnold sighed. "I know you and Henry were close. Like a second father to you, caring for you and your brother Sebastian after 9/11. I didn't mean to rile you up. And I could be wrong. All four were getting on in age so it could be a coincidence. Regardless, it's a shame. Tragic. And yes, mysterious, and I assure you we'll get to the bottom of all of it."

"Because four men dedicated to uncovering and unveiling the secrets of the Shroud..." Silas trailed off, sitting straighter.

He looked at his desk, eyeing the cryptic note Miles had given him. He picked it up and reread it. Then set it back down and turned around in his chair to look out the window. The note seemed to grow in significance in light of this revelation about Henry. These were the last words his friend wrote before he died. And they were addressed to him. Wanting to meet and discuss the health of their faithful friend?

What was going on, old chap?

"Silas? Are you still there?"

Silas closed his eyes and breathed deeply.

"Yes. I'm still here."

"I thought the line went dead. Are you alright? I know this is a lot to take in. Henry dying and all. I know how much he meant to you."

"No. It's not that," Silas said softly. He turned back toward his desk, then picked up the note again. "Well, it is. But it's more than that."

"OK..." Father Arnold said, trailing off. "Silas, do you know something?"

Silas took a breath. "Before you called, my assistant Miles handed me a note. It was from Henry. Sent by courier, which I thought was odd. He wanted me to get his message quickly because he overnighted it yesterday."

"Yesterday?" Arnold interrupting.

"Yesterday."

"But that doesn't make sense. He died yesterday. Well, in the evening, according to the coroner's report. The last of the four, actually."

"Which means he wrote the note in the morning or early afternoon, then hired the messenger to deliver it today."

Silence fell between the two.

Silas continued. "Did he know this was coming? That his life was in danger?" He stopped. "That the others were in danger?"

Father Arnold himself took a beat. "Well, what did the note say?"

Silas unfolded the note again and scanned his friend's last words. "He wanted to meet. Here, listen: 'We need to talk ASAP. It's about our faithful friend. He's in ill health.'"

Father Arnold said nothing.

"Cryptic, right?"

"Indeed. Who do you suppose *our faithful friend* is? Do you have any ideas what he meant by this? And why he would send this to you?"

"I wondered that myself. We did often refer to the Shroud as our faithful friend."

"The Shroud?" Father Arnold said in alarm. "The Holy Shroud of Turin?"

"Right. Though maybe it was a slip of the tongue, and he meant one of our colleagues." Silas paused. "Perhaps talking about another STURP member? Maybe one of those who died in the last day, overseas?"

"Maybe," Father Arnold said softly, as if in thought.

Silas added: "But how could he have known about those other deaths? Or the threat of their deaths?"

"Mysterious, indeed."

"Has any protection been given to the other members?"

"It's in the works. I have been in touch with Vatican officials, as well as coordinating with a friend at the FBI. He hadn't heard about the other deaths overseas. But it made him concerned, for sure."

More silence fell between the two as they considered this added layer to the death of their friend.

"Can you email me a copy of the note. Make a scan of it and forward it along? Maybe my friend at the FBI can help."

"Sure thing, Father."

"I know you're busy and probably have a class to teach soon, so I won't keep you."

Silas looked at his watch. Ten minutes had already eaten into his lecture.

Father Arnold continued, "But I have a favor to ask of you. I need your help. This seems almost pointless now in light of the circumstances. And I hesitate even to ask...but Henry was supposed to give the keynote address to our annual sindonology conference tomorrow." Father Arnold paused, took a breath, and sighed. "Obviously, that's not going to happen."

Silas had forgotten about the annual gathering of the sindonologists, a band of researchers and scientists dedicated to studying the Shroud of Turin. There was usually fascinating tidbits of information and gossip passed around between the researchers, but nothing groundbreaking. Hadn't been for some time. He wasn't going to attend because of his own research and the impending results.

"Sorry, Father, but I wasn't planning on it this year," Silas simply said.

"Can I change your mind? I desperately need you to fill Henry's shoes and give the opening remarks this year."

Silas sat up straighter in his chair. "You want me to give the keynote? At the annual gathering of sindonologists?"

"Now, I know you haven't exactly seen eye-to-eye with many of the members."

"No, I haven't," Silas said. He was the youngest scholar among a cohort of aged, mostly Catholic men, who had given their lives to the Shroud. To them, Silas was a young buck who was trampling on their turf. It didn't help he had gone directly to the Vatican for samples of the Shroud for his latest research project, without their knowledge or blessing. But Silas wasn't going to let a bunch of old fuddy-duddies stand in the way of his research goals. And the recognition that came with them.

"But think of this as an opportunity to show those old farts a thing or two. And I've heard your research has been going swimmingly, so you should have material. Have you gotten your results back yet? Something about the Shroud and nuclear radiation?"

"Right. Not yet." Silas looked at the door, thinking he had heard someone outside. Another courier with his results, perhaps? "Should be here soon. But you know Avery. Said I'd get word when I get word, that I was as impatient as his six-year-old."

Father Arnold chuckled. "Yes, I do. And yes, you are!"

Silas laughed. He also liked the idea of sharing his results with his colleagues. Maybe they would take him more seriously if he had a thing or two to show them.

"Would it be OK if I share some of my latest research? If I get them in time, that is?"

"That would be splendid! A real show, I reckon, for the annual conference."

A knock at his door caught Silas's attention. His heart skipped a beat. The results?

"Come in."

It was Miles. Silas smiled and tilted his head, begging for some news. Miles shook his head, then tapped his watch. It was almost a quarter past two.

Silas nodded. "Sorry, Father, but I really should be going. I'm late for my lecture. On the Shroud, actually."

"Go. Go. And inspire those young minds of the memory of the resurrection contained in the Holy Image. Who knows, maybe you'll even convert one or two."

Silas smiled. "Lord willing."

Father Arnold offered condolences for the death of Silas's friend and mentor, vowing to get to the bottom of his death. He said he would email Silas the details of the conference, then said goodbye.

Silas sat still. He blinked, then sat back.

He closed his eyes and breathed deeply. He tried to feel something for Henry's death. Sorrow. Loss. Even shame for not visiting him more often. But nothing came. No emotion. Nothing. The walls he had built after his father died wouldn't let him.

Dead? He looked back at the note from Henry again. His mouth had gone dry, so he licked his lips and swallowed.

What a bittersweet day. The day I receive word my mentor and second father died is the day I'm getting results to an experiment that could change the course of my career.

Silas stopped, chiding himself. *That could change the course of the Church, proving the resurrection of Jesus Christ was scientifically and historically real.*

"You better get going, Professor," Miles said softly. He offered a weak smile, handing Silas his book bag and laptop.

Silas smiled back and nodded. He stood and grabbed both, stuffing the laptop in his bag.

"By the way, looks like I'm heading to Washington, DC, later."

"DC? Why?"

"Father Arnold needs me to stand in for..." He trailed off, still not able to believe his mentor was dead. He cleared his throat. "For Henry Gregory. He was supposed to headline the annual sindonologist conference there. Obviously, that's not going to happen."

Miles nodded. "I see..."

"But Barnabas—"

Miles waved a hand and cut him off. "Say no more. I'll feed him again while you're away. Two scoops a day, right?"

He smiled. "Right. Thanks, you're a lifesaver."

"However I can help. But you'd best get going! Run along."

"Alright, alright. Get me the minute you get those blasted results," he called back as he jetted off to his awaiting lecture.

CHAPTER 3

A bitter wind and biting rain threatened Silas's face as he hustled across campus. He pulled the collar of his charcoal wool coat tighter against his neck for relief. It was barely working.

"Good afternoon, Dr. Grey. Late again, are we?"

Silas stopped short, nearly colliding with Mathias McIntyre, his department dean.

"Not according to my watch. One minute to spare." Silas held up his wrist and nodded as he continued on toward the burnt-colored stone building wrapped in ivy that housed his lecture hall. While not a lie, it was less-than-honest; the cheap gift hadn't kept the time well in years.

He glanced down at the faded fake gold-plated Seiko watch clinging to his wrist, a high school graduation gift from Dad pockmarked from ten years and three tours of duty with the Rangers across the Middle East. He picked up his pace, the rain having the same idea.

It was days like this he missed his father. Come bitter rain or crisp sunshine, the two ran eight miles well before the rest of the world was ready for their feet to hit the floor. The training kept his military father in tip-top shape. Same for him, both as a quarterback for the Falls Church Jaguars and in preparation for his future life as a grunt. Though the latter didn't happen until later, much to the disappointment of his father.

Silas pushed aside the memory as he hustled into the hundred-seat lecture hall, a time capsule of decades gone by. If those walnut walls could talk, they would tell tales of fascinating lectures on Proust and Freud, logarithms and algorithms, thermodynamics and microeconomics that had shaped the minds of nearly three hundred graduating classes of America's brightest.

Today's lecture was of a different sort entirely.

"Good afternoon, class," Silas bellowed as he hustled down the aisle to the front of the lecture hall. Pockets of students huddled in conversation began to break up and return to their seats. Others quickly finished sending a text and checking Facebook before putting away their digital devices. He had a strict policy against using such things in class; it was a paper-and-pen-only zone.

"Professor Grey!"

He stopped short, nearly running into a clean-cut junior wearing torn blue jeans, a faded red and blue flannel, and Converse shoes. Jordan Peeler, quarterback for the Hoyas, and one of his brighter, more engaged students.

"Yes, Jordan," Silas said taking off his coat.

The young man handed him a well-worn paperback. "Finished it last night."

It took Silas a moment to register, but then he smiled as he took the book and looked at the cover. His copy of C. S. Lewis's *Mere Christianity*, still bearing the dust of Iraq and Afghanistan where he first discovered the Oxford professor.

He stuffed the book in his satchel. "So, what did you think? Especially his argument about Jesus being a liar, lunatic, or Lord?"

"See, I had this idea," Jordan said excitedly, "that there could be another 'L' word." The junior leaned in like he was about to drop a knowledge bomb on his professor. "Legend," he whispered, then smiled.

Silas loved it when his students were eager to best him. Showed they were using their brains and trying. But that argument wasn't new. Pop theologians and genre novelists with a Christian ax to grind had recycled it from dead Germans for years.

"Interesting," he smiled knowingly. "Go on."

Jordan's eyes widened slightly with delight. "The way I see it, maybe Jesus' disciples had created all of these stories to sort of keep his memory alive after he died. You know, like the Roman hero narratives. Jesus' disciples *made* him legendary."

Silas nodded and brought his eyebrows together as if he was contemplating Jordan's fresh insight.

Jordan crossed his arms in satisfaction. "So, what do you think?"

"I think you'll be very interested in today's lecture. But I like your thinking." He slapped Jordan's back and continued on toward the front. "Let's talk more after class, maybe grab coffee or something."

Jordan nodded, then took his seat.

Silas kept smiling as he reached the front. He lived for those kinds of moments, the chance to engage his students with religious ideas and help shape their spiritual journey. Whether they committed to Christianity or not, at least they were forging a path. Unfortunately, such conversations were few and far between. He hoped today's lecture would change that.

"Sorry for the delay," he said as he hoisted his bag onto the A/V cart and brought out his laptop. He opened it and hooked it into the room's projector system, then he brought up his PowerPoint lecture. The class settled down and settled in for the next three hours.

After arranging his notes, he began. "If you were to name the central element to the Christian faith, what would you say that is?"

The multi-faith and non-faith group of students were silent. Some of them shifted in their seats. Others looked around for guidance. One student shot his hand in the air. It was Jordan.

Silas nodded toward him. "Go for it."

"Jesus."

A few classmates giggled.

"Thank you, Captain Obvious! I'd say that's pretty much a given."

More classmates giggled.

"The Bible," a co-ed from the front offered.

"Nope, but good guesses. Think about the central belief of Christianity."

Silas received nothing more. So he brought out a well-worn black-covered book, its sides stained crimson red. He opened it and began searching its pages, turning them gently, reverently.

"Try this on for size. It's from the first letter a man named Paul wrote to a town called Corinth." He cleared his throat, then read:

> *Now if Christ is proclaimed as raised from the dead, how can some of you say there is no resurrection of the dead? If there is no resurrection of the dead, then Christ has not been raised; and if Christ has not been raised, then our proclamation has been in vain and your faith has been in vain.*

He closed his Bible and set it on the lectern. He walked out in front of it and stood before the students, arms crossed.

"Anyone?" Silas questioned, leaning back against the lectern.

Jordan raised his hand again. Silas nodded toward him to answer.

"The...what do the Christians call it. The resurrection?"

"Is that a question?"

"No. The guy in your reading said it. If Jesus didn't come back from the dead, then the Christian faith is bunk."

Silas chuckled. "Bunk. That's probably a good twenty-first-century translation of *your faith has been in vain*. And *the guy*, as you say, was the apostle Paul. A Jew who became a follower of Jesus and a missionary to non-Jews. And you're right."

He returned back behind the lectern and changed slides. "The entire Christian religion hinges on the claim that a dead guy came back to life."

"Like, a zombie?" Jordan blurted out.

The room laughed. So did Silas.

"Good one. No, not like a zombie. Early followers of Jesus didn't claim he was undead. They claimed he was alive. And, as Paul said, if Jesus hasn't been resurrected, then the faith of billions of Christians is empty, completely worthless. And they are to be pitied above all other people."

Jordan's hand shot up in the back again.

Silas saw it and nodded. "Go ahead."

"I don't mean to be rude, but I didn't sign up for no catechism course, Mr. Grey."

Silas smiled. "And I don't mean to be preachy. Obviously, this isn't Christianity 101. And today's lecture isn't about the Christian faith, but a *relic* of the faith that has preserved the memory of this most significant event in Christianity for two millennia."

Silas paused, scanning the room. "Anyone care to guess which relic I'm talking about?"

A few shifted in their seats. Mostly, there was silence, and several quizzical, interested looks.

Silas sighed with disappointment. Apparently, his life-work had done little for the generation behind him. Which made tomorrow's revelations all the more critical.

"I'm speaking of the Holy Image. Or, as it has been commonly known, the Shroud of Turin. Anyone familiar with the Shroud, or at least has heard of it?" A few hands rose in recognition.

That's a start.

"There is a long and sordid history surrounding this most fascinating fourteen-by-four-foot piece of burial linen. It's been known by many names: the Holy Image, the Image of Edessa, the Mandylion, and more commonly the Shroud of Turin, where it keeps its home in Italy."

Silas brought up his first slide. On it was a ghostly, ghastly black-and-white image of a man many have puzzled over for centuries, his front and back sitting side-by-side: underneath his closed eyes was a mustache and beard, and long hair fell beyond his shoulders to the center of his back; his arms were crossed, one hand over the other, and engraved with several white markings; hundreds more of the same white etchings shone brightly on the man's back and chest, crisscrossing each other at jagged right angles; similar white zig-zags marked the crown of his head and seemed to be dripping down his forehead; the same white lacerations marked both sides of his legs.

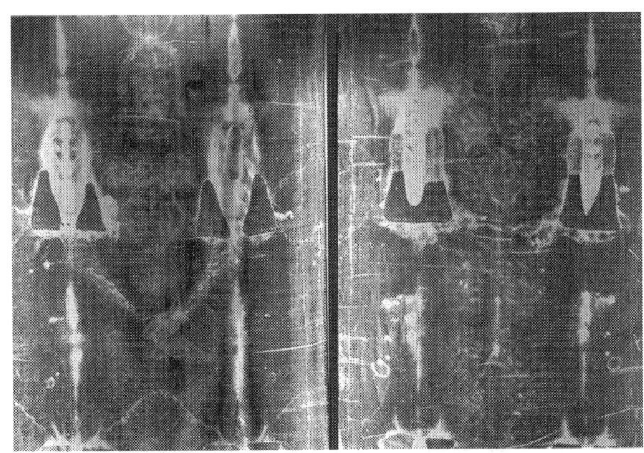

The story this image told was clear: whoever it was, the man had suffered the worst kind of death imaginable.

Several students gasped from seeing the image for the first time. Several others whispered to one another, marveling at the sight. Not a one were dozing off or sloughing. All were at respectful attention, as if the ground on which they were sitting had suddenly become sacred, holy.

Silas let the image hang in the air for a while, marveling at it. He never tired of looking into those eyes, never tired of looking at him. Some insisted it was a medieval forgery, but he believed without a shadow of a doubt that it was the genuine burial cloth of Jesus of Nazareth—who died, was buried, rose again, and was witnessed in bodily form.

Now, if only he could prove that beyond a shadow of a *scientific* doubt.

Silas looked to the back of the room, willing Miles to come bursting through the back doors triumphantly with news of the results.

Suddenly, one door opened. Silas's pulse quickened. Just a student, probably coming back from using the restroom.

He frowned, then stepped back to the lectern, having realized several minutes had ticked by.

"What are your thoughts?"

In unison, the students stared back at the faint image of the man thought to be the resurrected Savior of the world. Jordan was the first to raise his hand.

"Honestly? Sorta creepy. No offense."

Creepy?! The back of Silas's neck started turning red, his ears warmed at the disrespect. "Interesting," was all he could manage. "Anyone else?"

"I can kind of see it," said a woman said near the middle.

"See what?"

"Jesus. What I would imagine him, anyway."

"Speaking of which," Silas said, clicking forward a slide in his PowerPoint, "why don't we get into the main historical, scientific evidence for the Shroud's authenticity?"

Silas looked down at his notes, then back at the class.

"Are you ready?" he asked before launching into the heart of his lecture. In response, the class brought out notebooks to take notes.

Silas smiled. *Good.* "Let's start with the most compelling evidence. The faint imprint you see there is that of a real corpse in rigor mortis. In fact, the image is of a crucified victim!" Silas's voice rang high and loud with this revelation. He couldn't help himself.

"This was the conclusion of multiple criminal pathologists during one of the most pivotal periods of dissecting and testing the Shroud in the '70s. One of those pathologists, a Dr. Vignon, said the anatomical realism was so precise that separation of serum and cellular mass was evident in many of the blood stains. This is an important characteristic of dried blood."

Silas stopped for effect, looking out at his audience. "Did you catch that? That means there is real, actual dried human blood embedded in the cloth."

Many of the students whispered to each other. Just as Silas wanted.

"Not only that, but those same pathologists detected swelling around the eyes, the natural reaction to bruising from a beating. The New Testament claims Jesus was severely beaten before his crucifixion. Rigor mortis is also evident with the enlarged chest and distended feet, classic marks of an actual crucifixion."

He let that revelation settle before continuing. He turned around and looked at the screen of the ghostly-looking figure.

"The man in that burial linen," Silas continued whispering, his lecture hall mic barely picking up his revelations, "was mutilated in exactly the same manner that the New Testament says Jesus of Nazareth was beaten, whipped, and executed by means of crucifixion."

Silas brought up on the screen an enhanced version of the Shroud in blue and white.

"This positive image taken from the negative one left on the

Shroud shows in detail many of the historical markers that connect to the Gospel accounts of Jesus' death. You have the scourging marks from a Roman flagrum on the arms, legs, and back. Lacerations around the head from the crown of thorns. His shoulder appears to be dislocated, probably from carrying his cross beam and falling. According to scientists who examined the Shroud, all of these wounds were inflicted while he was alive. Then, of course, there is the stab wound in the chest and the nail marks in the wrists and feet. All consistent with the eyewitness accounts recorded in the Gospels."

"That's crazy," Jordan said aloud.

Silas grinned. "Dude, I'm just getting started! The image of the man, with all of his facial features and hair and wounds, is absolutely unique. Nothing like it in all the world. Totally inexplicable. And given there are no stains indicating decomposition on the linen itself, we know that whatever body was in the Shroud left before the decomposition process began. Just as the Gospel writers testify."

He stopped again and turned around to marvel at the thing of beauty staring out into his lecture hall.

"But how? How did this happen? How did a dead man come back to life? Not as a zombie, thank you very much." The class laughed. "But as a real, live human being. Fully restored back to life. New life. How did this happen?"

He let the question hang in the air before launching into his closing argument.

Just then, the door to the lecture hall creaked open and thudded heavily against the back wall. A few heads turned. As did Silas's. In stepped Miles.

From what Silas could tell, Miles was breathing heavily, as if he had just run a 5k. His eyes were wide, his mouth open and nostrils flaring as he heaved heavy breaths.

A few more of the seventy heads turned back to see the commotion. Silas's adrenaline spiked, quickening his pulse and breathing. He cocked his head as if to ask a question: *Are the results in? Good news or bad?*

Miles leaned against the door, trying to catch his breath. His mouth narrowed flat and he shook his head. He motioned for Silas to follow him. It didn't look good.

Silas took in a breath and heaved it out. He furrowed his brow and looked out at his class of students before looking down at his lecture notes again.

What happened?

Silas looked back up. Miles had left into the hallway, the door closing with a thud behind him. He still had forty minutes left in his class period. He looked back at the Shroud, the ghostly eyes staring back at him. He had done enough damage for one day. There would be time for more tomorrow. But his presentation awaited. So did those blasted test results.

And from Miles's indication, the tests were not good. Something had happened.

Silas closed his laptop. "Class dismissed."

CONTINUE THE ADVENTURE...

An ancient threat. A sacred relic.
A belief that hangs in the balance.

Ex-Army Ranger and professor Silas Grey is on the verge of proving a central belief of the Church that will rock the religious and non-religious worlds to their core: scientific proof of Jesus Christ's resurrection. But before he can, a series of devastating blows not only threaten Silas and those close to him, but the Christian faith itself.

Coming to his aid is an ancient religious order, the Order of Thaddeus, that has been battling an ancient cultic threat, Nous. Spanning the globe from Washington to Paris to Jerusalem, Silas and the Order combine forces to embark on an urgent mission for the very survival of the Church. Can they save the Church's most important sacred relic before the memory of its central belief is destroyed forever?

Holy Shroud is the first book in the Order of Thaddeus action-adventure thriller series that combines the religious conspiracy suspense of Dan Brown with the historical insight of Steve Berry, and wraps it in the special-ops muscle of James Rollins and inspiration of Ted Dekker.

Explore this innovative new adventure by emerging author J. A. Bouma that straddles thrill and thought,

Get your copy today at this link:

http://www.bouma.us/holy-shroud

Made in the USA
San Bernardino, CA
12 March 2019